KEYMAKER'S DAUGHTER

ANYA STASSIY

ISBN: 978-1-7329053-5-1

I dedicate this book to my daughter.

My little spark, your light will only shine brighter.

Acknowledgement

I would like to thank my parents Svetlana and Vladislav Stassiy for instilling in me the love of reading. I tortured them with requests to read the story of Perseus and the Gorgon Medusa over and over again, a strange, but favorite childhood story of mine. At some point, they grew so tired of my requests that they recorded themselves reading it aloud so I could listen to this myth as much as my heart desired. They continue to be excited, proud, and supportive parents who brag about my writing achievements.

A special thank you, as always, goes to my husband, who was my first beta reader for this novel while working in the hospital during the COVID-19 pandemic. I treasure your support and love every minute.

I'd like to express my gratitude to my friends, and other beta readers, Monica Dolack and Gabriela Drakh. Your enthusiasm, support, and excitement about my writing feeds my inspiration and joy of being an author.

My words can't express how thankful I am for the work of Katya Simonov. I appreciate immensely your attention to detail and the time you devoted to this novel.

Michael Pilgrim, my editor, thank you very much for giving my story the polish it needed.

Dale, from the ebooklaunch.com team, thank you very, very much for another great cover and interior design.

To my kids, thank you for your love.

Chapter 1

Iraklis

Nine days before the alignment of the planets.

"C'mon, get up." Iris, my old friend is next to me, unexpected and not welcomed. My head is hurting, my eyes don't want to open, anticipating the assault of daylight. I am in no mood to know why she is here all of a sudden.

"Go away," I bark, turning toward the wall.

"C'mon, we've got to talk." This time she kicks my bed and the vibration hurts deep inside my head.

"Leave me." I raise my voice.

"I have work for you," Iris insists, walking across the room, each step on the hardwood floor is firm and loud.

"I don't want it." I continue to lay face down. There is nothing she can offer that I will be interested in. I am done with the business of the Divine.

"The keymaker is missing," she continues, ignoring my displeasure and seemingly making a purposefully loud slurping sound drinking something through a straw. I throw my pillow in the direction of the sound, but I know Iris is too fast for me and I have missed.

"I received a message from him just before his disappearance." She pauses, sighs and recites,"'Find Iraklis to protect what is mine. He is bound by the promise. Now it's his time'."

I turn on my back and stare at the ceiling. "That's all?"

"Yes." She puts her phone screen with the message displayed to my face. I rise, squinting my eyes and hold my hand to protect myself from the bright light seeping in from the windows. Iris has opened the blackout blinds to make sure I wake up. She is dressed in bright pink sweatpants, a hoodie and bright neon sneakers. Iris has never been a fashionable dresser, but she always makes a statement with outfits in the brightest colors when she is not performing her duties at Port Security.

"Here. Drink up." She passes me a paper cup covered with a lid.

"Why?" I ask, bothered that she's ordering me around.

"Really? Don't act like a moody teenager. You drunk yourself stupid. Don't you know what is happening?" She pulls the chair across from the bed and sits down.

"Grr," is the only sound I make. I take a sip of bitter hot liquid that is coffee with no milk or sugar and rub my forehead to quell her attack. I have been avoiding TV, radio and any means of communication with the world. I have no interest in its perils.

"The planets will align in nine days. Enzio said the keymaker was worried that Hades might try to unleash the Titans before his disappearance. If he succeeds you know that the world as we know it will end. The keymaker knows Hades needs him. He doesn't want to be found. He broke the tunnel of reflection in his office." She stares me down and then takes another loud sip through the straw in her Styrofoam cup giving me a chance to process her answer.

"Get someone else. I don't want the job." I take another sip of coffee, cringing at the bitter taste, as my mind's pistons and wheels start to turn, igniting the engine of thought. I couldn't care less what happens. I know I can make it in this world or any new one.

"The job is to protect his daughter," Iris says, detaching her mouth from the straw.

"Daughter?"

"Yeah, her name is Aurora," she replies as the light creates a halo effect around her.

"No." I cut her off and go to the bathroom.

Iris is standing by the window when I get back. I hoped she would have left by now. She doesn't turn to me, her fingers play with the light as if it is a string instrument.

"It's interesting how the sun rises every day. It doesn't judge the people that it shines upon, it just does, because without it there would be death." Her fingers pause and she turns toward me, her brow is arched high up.

"Come, your father wants to talk to you."

"Argh." I throw my head back. "I thought he didn't want to be involved in the dealings between Gods and mortals."

"He doesn't. He just wants to talk."

I grow more annoyed by her intrusion. I don't want to be bothered by any of it. I am tired. I step away from her, shaking my head, but she comes close, barely reaching my chest, and tilts her head to the side smiling. I know that smile and I know I will not be able to refuse her anymore.

"Fine."

"Come here, you big, drunk log. Let Iris shine some light into your dim life." She grabs me tight by the waist. "Don't you throw up, you hear me?" She looks up and wags her finger.

"I'm not of weak stomach," I grumble, anticipating a trip that will push and twist my insides.

"To Zeus we go then," she announces. As she speaks these words a bright light beams right over us, summoned by her. We are lifted off the ground and pulled into the glow toward a destination that Iris commands. We are traveling at the speed of light through an illuminated, warm tunnel. I know that our journey is creating a rainbow across the sky, but Iris and I are invisible to any human. Inside the light beam time is slow. I feel no pull of gravity, no headache, or pressure inside my ears although we are covering thousands of miles as the light controlled by Iris carries us over to my father. We will reach our destination in a few seconds.

CHAPTER 2

AURORA

Seven days before the planetary alignment

"Five planets will align…"

I pull my long, tangled hair off my face and put it a bun before I open my eyes, awoken by the news on my TV. I have gotten into the habit of falling asleep on the couch after staying up late with work. I glance at the clock on my laptop screen. Shit! It's eleven o'clock already.

"The five planets are Jupiter, Saturn, Mars, Venus, and Mercury," the news anchor continues and I lower the volume.

I close my laptop, go to my room, brush my hair and redo it into a messy bun. The only mess I allow myself to have. Today is Saturday, the day when my room-mate Jennifer and I agreed we would clean the apartment. She is already vacuuming when I come back to the living room. She always starts cleaning very enthusiastically, but her attention gets preoccupied by things that she finds and soon she feels too tired to continue. I can't stand her whining and would rather continue cleaning by myself.

She is a chaotic person, creating mess all around her and I despise chaos. There is beauty in the order of things. I gravitate to the precision of numbers, the simplicity of straight lines, the logical flow of thought and mathematical formulas. We finish in about an hour, and Jennifer looks over our small apartment with satisfaction.

"You are not so bad of a roommate Aurora."

"I'm a great roommate," I snap.

"You're just strange…" She pauses, pops her hip and rolls her eyes to the ceiling, "You're just not like a regular girl."

"And what is a regular girl?" I narrow my eyes at her. She shrugs her shoulders, goes to the fridge and opens a soda.

"You don't wear makeup, you are like super smart at math, you have no boyfriend…ahhhh," she gasps, then covers her mouth with her hand as her eyes grow big.

"What?"

"Are you gay?" she whispers.

"Jennifer. No. I am not gay." I raise my voice.

"Why are you here then? All the girls leave this town once they graduate and go back to their parents. You are pretty and smart, what are you doing here?" She makes the littlest stump with her foot, seemingly frustrated by her inability to figure me out.

"I just can't decide where I should go." I shuffle back a few steps and shrug my shoulders, avoiding looking at Jennifer. In truth, I wanted to stay in this little college town because I had no home to go back to and I'd rather be hidden here. Anywhere I would go, my last name would be recognized, and I would prefer my father not know where I am. Of course, I thought about changing it, but my mother loved that name and carried it with such pride. I feel it would be a betrayal of her memory. So after graduation, I decided to stay here and earn a living by tutoring and working as a freelancer writing code.

"Mm-hmm." Jennifer nods, her eyes narrowed, she doesn't seem to be satisfied. I know she will keep pestering me with more questions. I might have to look for another apartment, which is unfortunate. The windows of my room face a pond and just beyond it there is a nature reserve where I love to go for hikes.

"Anyway, we're done. See you later," I tell Jennifer who just grunts, already preoccupied by her cellphone. I leave her be and go to my room where I fall face down on my bed and scream into the pillow. I scream because I feel so lost, so alone. My own father despises me. My mother suddenly passed away as I was finishing up high school and it was as if my father could no longer stand the sight of me. His pain and grief were quiet at first, but soon changed into angry outbursts. He said things, mean things, and as soon as I graduated, I decided to go to a small college far away from New York City to forget the pain of losing both my parents, one to an accidental death, another to immeasurable grief.

I've hoped that one day I would be walking on campus and my father would be standing there looking for me among the crowds of students. When he'd see me, everything around us would slow down, and I'd see on his face that he loves me, that he's missed me, that he's regretted all the time that has been lost. He'd open his arms and I'd rush into his embrace, crying tears of joy. We'd then talk for hours catching up. He'd be proud of my accomplishments in school. Then we'd decide that it'd be best for me to transfer to a school in New York so I could start working in the company he'd eventually love for me to manage.

But it hasn't happened. Not only have I not seen him, he's never even attempted a phone call or an email. My sadness has turned to anger and eventually acceptance and now indifference.

I punch the pillow, decide that I've had enough self-pity, sit up, and open my laptop to an online fundraising page where I browse the stories and donate an allowance that I budget for every week.

"What are you doing?" A bubble pops up in the messenger app on my screen. Sunny is my online agent who connects me with clients seeking out services of web site developers or security specialists. I've never met her, but since my social circle is non-existent in this small town, we banter sometimes.

"Spending money," I reply.

"What are you buying?"

"A little bit of hope."

"?"

I smile and type, "I'm donating money to people who need it. And animals. And non-profits."

She sends me a smiley face emoji and a clapping one.

"I have a big job for you. Port Security is searching for programmers. There is a rumor they're struggling with recent hacker attacks."

"No, I'll pass." I type fast, holding my breath as a heat wave spreads from my head down at the mention of my father's company.

"Are you sure? They pay really well, and I don't have much of anything else available for you right now."

"Yes, I'm sure."

"Ok, I'll let you know if anything else comes up. Bye!"

"Thanks! Bye!"

Port Security is the largest security company in the Northeast. My father created it almost thirty years ago. It started with a small store of locks and safes that my father made himself and since then has grown as the word got out that his locks are unbreakable. He has expanded into digital security and is managing many international clients. I shut the laptop and just stare at the wall, wondering why my father's company would all of a sudden be experiencing hacker attacks. Are they really in trouble? What do the hackers want? Is it the usual, personal data, or are they searching for something else? I shake my head, trying to quiet the thoughts. "I don't care. I don't care," I say out loud. There is a loud knock on the door. I stay still, waiting to see if Jennifer will open it since her bedroom door is closest, but when another impatient knock and a ring on the doorbell follow, I sigh and go see who it is.

CHAPTER 3

IRAKLIS

Iris and I land gently in a field of tall grass. My father chose a small town in the middle of America as his home, far away from large cities. Here, everyone minds their own business. I haven't been here in years. The line of trees framing the edge of the field has grown from small twigs into leafy giants. A small two-story house is the only building besides a shed as far as the eye can see. This is the house my father lives in.

Iris and I head toward the house, prompting a multitude of grasshoppers to flee from under our steps. My fingertips glide over the overgrown, tall grass. Its smell releases memories of a carefree childhood and simple living from many, many thousands of years ago. It's intoxicating. I didn't know I've missed it until now.

Iris nods in the opposite direction of the tree lines as the sound of a car reaches my ears. "Olympus Electrician - local, trusted, insured" is written across the side of the white van. The old man has finally opened up a business to keep himself occupied. He parks in front of the farmhouse, gets out of the car, and gives us a wave.

"Hello, son." My father opens his arms wide for the embrace. He is smiling underneath his beard. He hasn't changed. Grey eyes are sharp, bushy eyebrows hanging low, salt and pepper hair slicked back. He is dressed in jeans stained with dirt and oil and a plaid pattern button down shirt that has seen better days.

He has adapted to looking plain and ordinary. He doesn't want people to fear him. That fear is an enemy of anything that is different and unusual. It is what hunts us.

"Father." My long arms can't wrap all the way around him and I give a few slaps on his still wide back. He has gotten just a bit shorter than me over the years, but his strength could still be felt in the body of this celestial. We pull away and my father stares into my eyes, squeezing my arms, giving me a slight shake.

"I'm happy to see you, Iraklis. I wish you'd also come visit me when the world is not in danger." Small wrinkles appear in the corners of his eyes, and he looks over my shoulder.

"Tell me, Iris, did you have to force him to come here?" he asks and his eyes dart back to me.

"Your son isn't the man who can be forced to do anything, although I did have to use some very intricate persuading skills." She glances at me and gives me a wink, then she walks over to my father and they give each other a hug.

"Come, come in. Care for a beer?" he asks, heading into the house.

"Yeah, I'll take one."

"None for me, the light doesn't like my cells to be permeated with alcohol, it will be dangerous to travel inebriated, we might end up somewhere very unpleasant." Iris shakes her head.

My father opens the unlocked porch screen door, the entry door behind it isn't secured by any locks either. There is nothing to steal anyway, the furnishings are sparse. He snaps his fingers and the light turns on. We follow him into the kitchen where he grabs a beer out of the fridge. Iris and I wait for him to start talking, but he stays with his back turned to us, not closing the fridge. We hear a crack, then a fizz, loud gulps, followed by a long burp, which fills the small space. My father then bends and reaches for another beer and finally turns around, passing me the can.

"C'mon," he motions for us to follow him into the back porch, grabbing another can out of the fridge before closing it. He sits down in the rocking chair, staring into the fields where the wind gently strokes the tall grass. Iris sits on the sun lit steps, and I lean against the banister, taking a sip of the cold beer. My father has never been the first to start talking. So I take a deep breath and begin, "Hades and the keymaker, huh?"

My father takes a long sip, leans back and pushes off with his feet lightly to start a slow and squeaky rocking of his chair. "Hades wants what Hades always wants. More souls, more power."

"Why now?" I ask.

"The great alignment of the planets is coming. It will undo Portus' lock. And Hades will unleash the Titans. They will enslave many and murder even more. People will believe again and fear as before, but…" he pauses, squints his eyes, and takes a few gulps of the beer, and when the can is empty, he smashes it with his fist into a thin disc, "…but this time Hades wants the power all to himself, all of it, the skies, the oceans, and the underworld. There will be no place for other Gods in a world ruled by Hades and the Titans."

"I thought the Titans were locked up for good. Why did you make it so that this alignment undoes all that you've done?" Iris speaks up as the last of the sun rays disappear behind the horizon, the shadow falling on her face.

"I didn't do it. The keymaker did." Zeus stops rocking his chair and looks at Iris and I from under his brows, leaning his elbows on his knees, rubbing his large fists, his grey eyes becoming stormy.

Iris glances at me, then back at my father, her brows come together into a deep frown, and she cocks her head to the side, waiting for an explanation.

"I put the Titans into that prison. The keymaker made a lock and a key to keep them in there. He is the one who still has the key and only he can put on a new lock." My father rubs his chin, looking to the ground.

"Why does his daughter need to be guarded then? Why didn't you summon me to guard the keymaker himself?" I ask.

"This is what he has requested, and this is what he said you promised him. He doesn't want her to know about her divine genetics. He pushed her away, so she has no interest in returning to him. He always knew the risk that came with his power. But he doesn't want his daughter to pay the price," my father explains.

"So, he will not destroy the key unless this condition is fulfilled?" Iris asks.

"He will not."

"So why is there a key at all?" Iris asks an obvious question.

"Ah…" My father sighs and rubs his forehead. "I think the keymaker has done it all as a security."

"A security against what?"

"Me. I am Zeus, the vengeful, jealous, lustful, egotistical. I was…all of it and worse. He made sure that if I ever decided to end humanity, there would be something that could be used to overthrow me." His brows come together, his lips pressed into a thin line, a distant storm is raging in his eyes, but he closes them for a moment, and when he opens them up the storm is no more.

"Well, that makes sense." Iris nods.

My father chuckles and gives her a wink. "Son? Are you on board?"

"Yeah…yeah, of course." I run my hand through my hair, slowly pacing the porch.

"Enzio will be made aware of your coming," my father tells us.

"That old bird is still keeping his watchful eye over the business of the Divine?" I joke, and it produces a chuckle and a wag of the finger from my father.

"Don't call him that," Iris scolds me. "He has been a partner and a dear friend of Portus for ages. He once was a glorious falcon who has delivered many messages for Gods, he deserves respect."

"Oh c'mon, it was just a joke, a bad one, I'll admit. I won't do it again." I am not a fan of Enzio, there are no great deeds that he has accomplished, no heroic sacrifices, but he has impressed Iris and my father enough that it's not worth pointing those things out.

We go inside and eat delivery pizza for dinner. Iris takes the mattress in the spare room and I lie down in the hay covered barn. The space is warm, with the moonlight streaming through the wooden plank walls, the hay is prickly, releasing the smell of summer. I hear mice starting their nightly rustling through the dry straw, and their fussing soon puts me to sleep.

###

In the morning, the sunlight shines bright into my eyes, and no matter how much I try to hide and turn away, it finds my face and doesn't stop annoying me until I am wide awake. "Iriiiiiis!" I yell, knowing all too well that she is using her powers to irritate me into waking up. She doesn't answer but the spot of light disappears. I sit up and stretch my sore back. I follow the smell of bacon into the house. My father is standing in front of the oven with the meat crackling on the pan, and Iris is sipping bright orange juice from a cup.

"Morning, sunshine!" she greets me, and my father raises his spatula up in the air. When he turns around, I see that he is wearing an apron with "I am God of the kitchen" written on it.

"Mmmm," I grumble. When my father puts a plate of eggs and bacon with a perfectly toasted piece of white bread in front of me, my mood gets better.

"Not happy until your stomach is full, right?" He puts another plate in front of Iris before he sits down himself.

"We'll leave after breakfast. I'll go visit Aurora with Enzio and bring her back to New York," Iris speaks, biting the crunchy buttered toast.

"Mm-hmm."

"She is a sweet girl…"

"I don't care," I cut her off, and she smiles but says nothing else. Portus' daughter is just a human and clueless. I want to finish this job and then disappear again.

"Protect her, and you will also need to find Hades' invisibility helmet. You have only eight days until the alignment. Hades can't control the Titans without the helmet. It's the concentration of his power. Something tells me that the keymaker has the helmet, and that's why he went into hiding. Coffee is on the counter, OJ in the fridge. Help yourself," my father says.

We finish our breakfast and walk to the sunlit porch. Iris gives my father a hug, and I extend my hand for a handshake, but he pulls me in toward him and throws both of his arms around me, giving me a brief squeeze. "This is serious, Iraklis, don't underestimate Hades. He's desperate, and like an animal who feels its death, he is blinded by the agony of demise. He will not miss this opportunity to rule. Fear him."

"Yes father." I squeeze his upper arm and turn away swiftly, step off the porch and walk toward Iris who is covering her eyes, trying to look at the morning sun.

"I'll see you soon. I hope you'll have good news," he says.

"Where are we going to meet?"

"I'll find you, don't worry." He smiles and raises his arm in the air to wave goodbye.

"We'll be in New York in no time." Iris motions for me to come closer, and when I do, she wraps her arm around me and smiles, "Light is the way, bring us to where I desire, keep us safe from the darkness." As soon as she is done speaking, a warm glow surrounds us, my father and his farm quickly disappear in the glare of the light, only the ticklish sensation in my stomach lets my body know that we are traveling at the speed of light.

New York City greets with the gloom of rain and fog, I have to hold on to Iris tight as our bodies are thrown wildly by the turbulence because the light has trouble penetrating thick clouds. I know this time I will be overtaken by nausea once we land.

We crash on the floor of an apartment, both thrown in the opposite direction by our landing. My stomach churns, and I feel the sour taste of bile in my throat as I try to get up.

"No, no, no. Don't you dare throw up. Bathroom, bathroom is right there," Iris screams, seeing my back arching as I try to contain the contents of my stomach. I make it to the bathroom just in time. When the breakfast my father prepared is flushed, I rinse my mouth with mouthwash and then find Iris by the window.

"When are you going to get used to light turbulence already?" she says with a hint of sarcasm and takes a sip of water.

"Err… Never," I reply.

"Don't you worry, sunshine, light travel is out of business for now due to all this rain. We have to use our feet to get us where we need to be. Get comfortable. We will go to Port Security tomorrow. You can sleep on the couch." She goes to a closet and gets out a pillow and a blanket and throws them to me. "I have to go see Enzio. I'll be back in the evening."

"See you," I reply.

CHAPTER 4

AURORA

"Aurora! Door!" Jennifer yells from her room. The knocking on the door continues, firm and impatient.

"I'm coming. I'm coming." I undo the lock and open the door. "Enzio," I breathe out. The tall thin man is my father's old friend and partner, I've always thought of him as an uncle. He hasn't changed much since I last saw him. As a child, I would stare at his face, and my mother would need to distract me from my fascination with his features. His hooked nose is so prominent it's as if all the power of bone formation in his face went to building it. His chin is a small square, retracted back, hiding within his neck, flat cheeks are tan and always clean shaven, and his quick black eyes are small, sitting close to his nose.

"Hi Aurora! How are you?" He smiles. I've never seen him dressed in anything other than a business suit. He'd wear a shirt with a tie and dress pants, always pressed with crisp lines even when he'd come over to my parents' house for dinner on a weekend. But today he is wearing jeans and a wrinkly casual shirt, and I immediately know that something has ruffled his feathers.

"Fine." I raise my voice in a high pitch as I keep staring at his unusual presence here. I haven't seen him since I left for college, and he hasn't made any attempts to contact me. It seems that everyone has been avoiding me, or wanted to forget that I exist.

"May I come in?" he says after clearing his throat.

"Yeah, yes, of course, come in." I step aside to let him in. Jennifer is singing loudly in her bedroom, I cringe and take Enzio to the kitchen where her screeching voice can be heard less.

"You want tea or coffee?" I offer, feeling nervous in his presence for some reason.

"No, Aurora. I've come to tell you that your father is missing, and I'm here to bring you back to New York," he says, hiding his hands in the pockets of his pants. He always seems to be embarrassed to show his hands, his fingers are twisted with arthritis and he'd often joke that he has claws rather than hands. Enzio rocks on the balls of his feet, looking at me from under his brows.

I sit down on a chair, overcome with bewilderment of my own shock at the news. I didn't think I cared so much about my father or his wellbeing. I have so many questions, so many emotions.

"What do you mean, missing? What do you mean, 'bring me back to New York'?"

"Haven't you seen the news?"

"No, no I haven't, I don't watch much TV." I shake my head and scout the room for the remote. I spot it on the couch, a few strides and I reach it. I press the power button, several times, fast, impatient. The screen finally brings up the image of a weather announcer waving his arms across the map, explaining large areas besieged by rain. The running headline at the bottom, highlighted in red, reads. *The biggest security company is now in danger. Stock holders are panicking. What will happen to Port Security without Mr. Port?* "Shit." I say under my breath and turn off the TV.

"He didn't show up to work two days ago. He left his cell phone on his desk, and his car was found in long-term parking, empty. Police are involved. But there is more, Port Security has been experiencing a lot of hacker attacks, they are sporadic, but intense, we can't figure out what they are after. We think it's all connected. Your father has possibly been kidnapped, and since you are his only daughter you might be at risk. Kidnappers may want to contact you. You need to come with me."

"No, no, it's definitely a no, Enzio. My father didn't care to know where his only daughter has been for the past four years. He, he told me that he wished he wasn't my father. He told me that he wished that I'd go away, disappear, so no one knows where I am." My father's harsh words ring fresh in my ears. My brain has been playing them to me on repeat for years. I remember when he said it to me for the first time. I came home from my friend's house, late. I made every effort to spend little time at home. It was lonely without my mother in the large house, and my father was avoiding me. I snuck into the kitchen to grab a late night snack. The house was dark and quiet. The light from the open fridge made a shadow stir, I thought I'd woke up a monster. When my eyes adjusted, I saw that it was my father, slouched over the table. I froze, the sound of a glass object falling made my father growl in displeasure. He picked up an empty bottle of Scotch, slamming it on the table, and slowly raised his bloodshot, swollen eyes at me. I looked at his tense lips as he started to slur hurtful words at me and it seemed that time slowed, it tortured me, punishing me for something I didn't realize I did wrong.

"And you honestly expect me to now care about his whereabouts, about his company? No, Enzio. It took me a long time to stop caring. You can't come here and expect me to give a damn," I say, almost in one breath. My body is tense and hot, and when I'm finished, I realize that my fists are clenched tight.

"I'm concerned about your safety, Aurora. I will be able to look after you in New York, at least until your father is found. The company is in disarray. Since your father's disappearance we can't access any of our internal programs. I don't want the company to start losing business if clients find out that we can't handle this problem. If we don't resolve it soon, a lot of employees might lose their jobs and Port Security will be no more. I know you wouldn't want that. You know a lot of people that work for your father." He pulls out a chair and sits down. "Your father was mad with grief when your mother died. Yes, he said things, unpleasant things, but this company, this company is his legacy. I know at one time he hoped for you to inherit it, and now you have an opportunity to save it. If you come with me, it will show people that even though he is gone, we've got the next best thing, his daughter. And with a fresh set of eyes you might help our team figure out the security breach and give us access to run the company like nothing has happened. I would feel much better to have someone like you on our team. A person who has a personal connection to the problem will work the hardest to solve it."

Enzio knows how to press my buttons. I grew up running the halls of the Port Security building. I've known a lot of the employees and met their families. I rub my forehead, press my fists over my eyes, and growl, "Fine." Then I raise my index finger, "but when my father is found, I'm gone."

Enzio lifts his hands up in defense and raises up to his feet, "If, he's found, Aurora," he says grimly, "we are just hoping for the best. C'mon, pack up. Just the essentials. I'm sure you'll find everything you need back home. I'll wait in the car."

I am ready in less than half an hour. I hesitate at the ajar door of Jennifer's bedroom. She is wearing her headphones, belting out a tune rather badly, by a new pop band. I throw my small bag behind my shoulders which contains a few changes of clothing, my hairbrush, a few hair ties, a tooth-brush, and my laptop. I decide that it would be best to leave her a note, my month is paid up, and she has a security deposit. I know she won't be too distraught about my leaving.

A black town car waits for me right at the entrance. I linger on the steps of my building. My heart is filled with trepidation. I am going back. I take a deep breath of the warm summer air and close my eyes for a moment. Am I making the right decision? My brain doesn't formulate a clear answer. I open my eyes and squint at the bright sun above me, then back to the building behind me, and finally to the car in front of me. The anxiety and fear fade when Iris steps out of the car, a petite woman who has been working as a driver for my father and Enzio since I can remember.

"Iris, you came too?" I run into her open arms. She hugs me tight, giggling. Her dark hair is smoothed and pulled back. She is wearing her usual white dress shirt and a black suit. I've never seen her in any jewelry or make up, and I've always felt an aura of kindness around her. I would always feel instantly relaxed in her presence.

"Hello, Aurora, look at you, so grown, so beautiful," she sings in her soft Caribbean accent. Iris steps back, lifting my arms to the sides while looking me up and down.

"Thank you, I'm so happy to see you." I hug her again. We shared many conversations in her car when she drove me to and from school. She wiped my tears when my mother died. She drove me to the bus station when I left for college. I made her promise not to tell anyone what bus I took. I told her I wouldn't want her contacting me. Any reminder from the world I used to know would be too painful, and she is a big part of that world.

"I wish I had better news for you, but you coming with us will be great news to a lot of people, pretty girl." She pats my cheek gently and opens the passenger door for me. Just as I am about to get in, a bright flash of green somewhere deep in my brain pierces me with pain, making my surroundings go dark, I yelp in pain, squeeze my eyes tight and press on my temples.

"You still get migraines?" Iris rubs my back and takes the bag out of my hands.

"Yeah, they've been getting worse lately." I shake my head and get in. Enzio is in the passenger seat typing something on his cell.

This bright green blinding light is always accompanied with sharp pain, sometimes the throbbing will last for a few days. The diagnosis is a migraine. I remember the look on my mother's face every time I would get it, it's as if she felt my pain in those moments as well.

"She's in so much pain," I remember her complaining to my father as I listened and peeked out of my bedroom, "I feel so helpless, so guilty." She would twist her slender fingers.

"She's a strong girl. Don't feel guilty, we are all given a burden that only we can carry," he replied and kissed her on the forehead.

My mother later soothed me with her cool touch and a gentle massage of my forehead, she hummed softly to me, and her pretty voice made everything instantly better. She seemed to have been glowing at that moment, sitting on my bed. I wonder if I was just delirious with pain or was it my childish sense of being loved that surrounded my mother in a warm light. The car takes us to a helicopter that has landed on the campus helipad, surrounded by curious students. I climb in, put on the headphones and we take off right away. The pulsating force of my headache is getting worse, I take my medication and soon doze off, soothed by the loud vibrations of the propellers. Two hours later we land in New York City and the company's car takes us directly to Port Security.

Chapter 5

Aurora

It's almost four o'clock in the afternoon, and at this time the offices are always filled with people, the sound of phones ringing, conversations, and keyboards clicking, but today it's rather quiet. "We decided to give non-essential staff a few days off until we could figure some things out," Enzio explains as we walk toward my father's office.

Nothing has changed inside of it since I left: the same dark wood cabinetry and a large desk in the center. The room still has his smell, a familiar, unchanged over the years cologne, a barely there scent of cigar smoke. My mother would look at him sternly when he wouldn't admit that he was smoking, and he then would promise her he'd stop. I guess he hasn't. And then there is another smell that I don't recognize at first, but it is the smell of alcohol. It was rare that my father would drink, yet there was a wet bar now in this office, and something else is different. It takes me a moment to realize that everything in this room is in slight disarray. There is his jacket over the chair, a pile of papers spread over the desk, a few partially filled glasses on the shelves and on the desk. A large floor mirror is covered with a throw and broken pieces of it lay underneath it on the floor. I come and pull it down only to find an empty frame.

"The police said that we can now clean everything up, they haven't found anything of use here. I'll give the detectives on the case a call to let them know you're here," Enzio says and steps out of the office.

I come up closer to my father's desk with Iris right behind, quietly observing me. I find stacks of articles on the planetary alignment which is happening next week and maps of stars and planets. There are scrolls written in a language I don't know and a collection of drawings. I frown, lift them up and show them to Iris. "This is a depiction of Zeus battling the Titans and locking them away in Tartarus. Your father has become a bit obsessed with this over the last few months." She sighs.

"What happened to him?" I ask, looking around.

"We don't know, but he has grown reclusive, agitated, he hasn't been his usual self. He has started going to sleep late and waking up late, and he didn't care, he didn't care about being organized like he used to."

"Did he sleep there?" I point to a blanket and a pillow on the couch.

"Sometimes. When he stayed up too late, he'd send me away. No one could persuade him to take a break, to rest," says Iris. I feel a pang of guilt at hearing this. But I quickly realize I wouldn't have been able to do much, only my mother would have known how to deal with his sudden mania. He would probably just ignore me or would yell and scream that I knew nothing, that I should not put my nose into things that don't concern me. I wonder why my father was suddenly so obsessed with stars and planets. I look up at Iris to ask her just that and catch her looking at me intently, her head tilted to the side, mouth partly open, like she is studying me, seeing me for the first time.

"Do I have something on my face?" I ask her. She startles, shakes her head, and smiles.

"You look so much like your mother, Aurora, the resemblance is uncanny, yet your brain is all your father's," Iris says softly.

"What do you mean, my brain?"

"He is a math genius, he is brilliant, he can see patterns and order in things. He can solve puzzles no one else can, and if there is a lock to be picked, he is the man to do it." She chuckles and I smile at the kind words.

"I am not as smart as him." I shake my head and sigh, sitting on the edge of his desk, taking in the surroundings of his office in slight disbelief that I am here, due to circumstances I could have never predicted.

Enzio returns, walks straight to the window and without turning to us says, "Alright, the detectives will be here in about an hour, they'll ask you standard questions, nothing to worry about. There is an office on the other side that you can have for yourself, Aurora." He finally looks at me and points across to the other side of the floor.

I leave Enzio and Iris and walk over to the mentioned empty office. It's small, dusty and facing the brick windowless wall of the next-door building. It has an ordinary office desk with a computer, keyboard, and a phone. Two armchairs are pushed against the wall under the TV. A pile of magazines with their pages curled up is sprawled on top of the nearby coffee table, waiting to be finally thrown out or kept for future reading.

I sit behind the desk and swivel to the window, and then notice if I sit diagonally to the left of it, I will get a small view of the Hudson. The skies are overcast, pouring rain is flooding the streets, and the thick fog hides the tops of concrete jungle from my view. I feel dizzy looking into the white, thick curtain, and for a moment I feel I am levitating. A bolt of lightning startles me. I turn away, shake my head, and turn to my desk.

A thick layer of dust covers the dark wood, wide desk. I write 'Aurora Port of Port Security' with my finger and then blow on the dust and watch it rise up in the air, erasing what I've written.

I then move the keyboard dead center in front of me, two fingerbreadths away from the edge of the table and align the mouse pad exactly parallel to the right of it about a palm width away. I find a pen box and a writing pad in one of the drawers. The pen box goes to the left on the same line as the computer screen and the writing pad to the right of the mouse pad. Next, I organize the magazines into a straight tower right in the middle of the glass surface of the small coffee table and then center the table between the two armchairs. I look around, satisfied with my creation of order, when the phone on the desk buzzes, and Enzio calls me into my father's office because the detectives have arrived.

###

"That was a waste of everyone's time." I sit back down, sigh heavily, digging my fingers into my scalp when the detectives have left. They have no answers, no leads. They didn't even seem that concerned.

"They are experienced detectives. I know it's frustrating, but we have to trust the process. Now, where would you like to stay?" Enzio says.

"Is there a hotel nearby? I can't imagine going back…" I pause, thinking of what to call the place I used to call home, "…my father's place," I say.

"We have an apartment all ready for you across the street," Iris says.

"Can you take me there?" I ask her, and she nods an affirmative yes.

"Enzio, I'd like to have a car. Can you rent one out for me?" I ask.

"Iris can take you anywhere you need to go, there is no need for you to drive in the city," he replies.

"I appreciate that." I glance at Iris, "but still, please rent me a Mini Cooper. I miss driving. I'd like to get some practice while I'm here," I insist. My college town was too small, I could get everywhere by walking. I had just gotten comfortable driving before I left for school, and it seems like a good opportunity to do it while I'm here. Enzio opens his mouth as if to protest, maybe about me driving by myself or maybe about the choice of my car, but I grimace at him, pleading, and he nods in agreement.

The one-bedroom apartment is furnished with all the necessities. Once I finish a quick walk through, I'm satisfied with the space and especially the light that comes through the large windows.

"Linen and towels are in the closet in the bedroom," Iris tells me as I stand in the middle of the room, my eyes drifting aimlessly about my new place. The dullness of the headache is still there, just annoying me enough that I don't forget about it. I feel tired. I feel confused. I thought I would never feel any concern for my father. I thought that I would not care for the life that I left behind, but now that I am back, I have a nagging thought that simmers, what if I'd stayed? Maybe my father's and my relationship could have been repaired. Maybe he just needed time to grieve. Did I rush my running away, and now I may never get an opportunity to fix the connection that we once had?

I smile at the childhood memories that float up to the surface like champagne bubbles: the treasure hunts with riddles for location hints, the puzzles that I was rewarded with for good grades. My father glowed with glee when I solved one after another and asked him to bring me more, more complicated ones. We would sneak away from my mother into my father's workshop filled with clocks, locks, keys and safes; there, we would disembowel the mechanisms and then create new ones. He would ask for my opinion on the drawings of keys and locks, and he would listen intently for my suggestions, nodding his head and rubbing his chin as if taking me very seriously. We'd come out to my mother happy, with our hands covered in grease from oiling the parts. All those memory pieces somehow didn't fit in with the puzzle of the man my father has become after the death of my mom. The intricate mechanism of our relationship is misaligned, but I have a gleam of hope that maybe now I have the strength in me to make it work again.

"Thank you, Iris, for coming with me."

"It's my pleasure. Is there anything you need help with? Groceries maybe?" Iris asks.

"I saw a grocery store downstairs, I'll go get some things, thank you. Iris…?" I pause, hesitant if I should ask the question, because the answer could be very painful.

"Yes."

"Did my father ask about me?"

She comes up to me and cups my face, "Your father isn't the most talkative man, but I know he loves you. Your bedroom in his house is as you left it. He has a picture of you in his wallet and on his desk. I've caught him many times holding his gaze on your image with such love in his eyes that only a father has for his daughter. He is complicated, but you'll come to understand him soon enough."

"Will I? What if…?" I grow silent, unable to complete the thought. Verbalizing too dreadful of an outcome somehow makes it more real and I grow more fearful.

"I'm sure he'll be found. Stay positive," she tells me, smiling softly.

We say our goodbyes until tomorrow when I'll see her again at the office.

CHAPTER 6

IRAKLIS

Six Days Before the Alignment

We pause under the cover of the building entrance. It is raining that annoying, fast, cold drizzle that pierces through your clothes, chilling you to your bones. Iris looks up to the sky, shakes her head and hands me an umbrella. I open it up and bright yellow fabric spreads over our heads like sunshine. "There is a coffee shop right there, you want anything?" She points across the street, but I just shake my head no. "Get in then." She opens the door of the black SUV for me. "I am a better driver on the road, promise, I won't make you sick." She smiles, lets me get in and slams the door shut. Iris walks around and takes the driver's seat, shaking off the rain from her bright as sunshine umbrella. She adjusts her seat so that she is perched up high above the steering wheel and we pull into the bumper to bumper traffic of New York City.

The Port Security firm is not far. The building doesn't stand out among the other steel and glass giants. Iris pulls into the garage that she accesses with a plastic keycard, the yellow barrier rises and lets us into the dimly lit underbelly of the building. The garage is quiet, expensive bright sports cars take up a row closest to the entrance, I nod in their direction.

"Portus is a car enthusiast, he loves collecting sports cars," Iris explains, looking at the mechanical beasts. "He rarely drives them anymore. He travels mostly by that one." She points in the direction of a long black limo. "It's bulletproof."

"The man is cautious," I mumble as we leave the car and get to the elevator. Iris puts her thumb to the call button, and after a few moments it turns green.

"Portus goes by the name, Olek Port. You'll need to be fingerprinted today and get your ID so you have access to the building," she tells me and we get inside.

Once we are delivered to the tenth floor, Iris tugs on my sleeve, "Come this way." She leads me into an office by the elevator where a young, skinny man with glasses as thick as my finger squints at us, and after a moment his lips stretch into a smile.

"Gabriel, meet Iraklis, he is going to be Miss Port's security, will you please make him official in this building," she introduces me and gives the young man a hug.

"Certainly, certainly, will do, Iris. It's my pleasure. Mister Iraklis, I'm glad our Miss Port will have you for her security." He comes up to me stretching his hand for a shake, he looks too happy, it annoys me. I squeeze his hand, he winces from the tightness of the grip. I chuckle, Iris throws me a disapproving glare. "Ouch, your, your shake is strong," he says, smiling sheepishly. I don't feel too bad for causing him pain.

"Thanks man." I tap on his arm. My light touch throws him off balance and he stumbles, avoiding a fall when Iris holds him up.

"Are you alright there?" I ask.

"Yes, yes, certainly, I am." He pushes his glasses up the bridge of his nose. "Right, right." He raises his finger in the air. "Let me get your fingerprints." He sits down at his desk and motions for me to come closer. I follow his prompts, and my fingerprinting is soon done. He passes me a keycard that he says will open most doors in the building. "If you ever need anything, please don't hesitate to come ask me. I certainly will try to help."

"Thanks man," I reply, this time avoiding any physical contact.

"Bye Gabriel, thank you so much, you are a sweetheart as always," Iris says, and we walk off into the main office space. The room is filled with cubicles, reminding me of a small maze.

Iris leads me confidently toward the double doors that have a sign "Olek Port, President."

"I have some things to attend to. Go inside, meet Aurora. Be nice." She smacks my arm and walks away.

CHAPTER 7

AURORA

"Miss Port, you are expected in your father's office," Helen announces over the phone. She is my father's secretary, a sweet lady of very old age. She is so small and fragile that the slightest wind would threaten to carry her off. Yet her mind is sharp, she knows by heart the phone numbers of dozens of people and will give exact directions to any destination in the city. For the time being, she works with me. It's ten o'clock in the morning and since seven thirty I've been arranging meetings, talking to the managers of every department, reviewing new client acquisitions and prospects of future growth. I make folders of to do tasks. I label. I chart and create lists. My father has always been an early riser and used to tell me that he is an example to everyone in his company. He was the first one in and the last one out, and I've decided to do the same. "Thank you, Helen, I'll be in in a few minutes."

"Yes, Miss Port," Helen replies and hangs up the phone.

"The other news of the day will make you look at the night sky." A beautiful news anchor woman with blonde hair and large breasts is reporting from the TV screen on my wall. "In six days a rare astronomical phenomenon will take place: an alignment of five planets, visible to the naked eye. Will this cause any events here on Earth? The answer is no from the astronomers. But do get out to see it in the night sky. Now we go to a commercial break."

Astronomical events have certainly been of great interest to my father lately, demonstrated by all the maps that were piled on his desk. I need to figure out what he's been obsessing about.

I step out of my office into a large room spanning the width of the whole floor. Today the cubicles are filled with employees. The atmosphere is tense; many workers are on the phones, gesticulating their frustration, and speaking in hushed and anxious tones. The onslaught of targeted efforts to break into our system has been relentless, as reported to me. The way we handle this crisis will decide the survival of my father's company.

I walk between the cubicles and the offices of the higher-ups, smiling and nodding to the staff, before I reach my father's office at the opposite side of the building. Enzio is standing behind my father's desk with a box full of broken mirror pieces, examining each one and then carefully placing it back into the box.

"It's a shame it is broken." He puts the box down on the floor and sits down.

"It's just temporary, until we figure things out," he says awkwardly getting up from my father's chair, but I wave for him to stay seated. He has been by my father's side for years, growing this company. He knows all the ins and outs, there is no one better for now to take my father's place, not until I can learn all that is needed, and I'm happy to learn from Enzio.

I imagine for a second what my father would do if he were here. He'd be sitting slouched over, his eyes covered with magnifying glasses, probably picking another lock with surgical-like instruments. Does he look the same, I wonder? Or has he gotten smaller and greyer? When my mother died, there were days when he hadn't shaved. Did he manage to start looking after himself in the absence of my mother and me? I shake my head to tuck all these thoughts away. What's the point? I can't turn back time. I can't undo what happened. *Stop imagining Aurora, it's time to concentrate on what is.*

"Aurora, it seems that your father put in some security protocols before he went missing, to protect you and the company," Enzio says, squinting his eyes.

I catch a glimpse of an article on Enzio's desk when I come closer: "Planets align. A first event of this kind known to astronomers." I feel Enzio tensing up, his gaze fixed on the newspaper. He moves it aside and clears his throat. I step right across from him and lean on the desk so I'm looking directly into Enzio's eyes. "What kind of protocols?"

"I didn't want to worry you until I had all the details." His jaw clenches and he lowers his fists on the table. "Our security detail should be here any minute."

"Wait, hold on, a security detail? You mean bodyguards? Why?"

"A law firm retained by our company delivered a letter to me this morning. It's written by your father. Here." He hands me a yellow manila envelope. "Mainly, it's you being guarded by bodyguards that he personally chose for you."

"I don't like any of this." I twist the folder into a tight roll.

"This is your father's wish. There is a provision here." He points to the envelope. I glance quickly through them, realizing that these are my father's directions in case he ever goes missing. "All operations are to be under lockdown until you agree to be guarded by a person chosen by your father. It's as if he knew he would disappear one day. You must agree to this. This is Port Security and you are the only Port left until your father is found."

"I don't feel comfortable with this at all. This is all too much. Why did he give me this burden? I don't want to be responsible for the whole company like this."

"Our clients are panicking; they want reassurance that the company can still function without your father." Enzio steps out from behind his desk and comes closer to me. "I need this company to start functioning other than in crisis mode. If the clients get any more nervous they will want to come in and check on their belongings which we've promised to keep safe for them, and we can't even access our own vault."

"Fine, fine," I say through my teeth. Enzio presses the button on his desk phone.

"Is Olympus here yet?"

"Olympus." I roll my eyes at the name.

"That's the name of the company your father chose to provide security for you." Enzio shrugs his shoulders.

Enzio opens the door after someone on the other side knocks, and after a few moments ushers in a wide-shouldered, blue eyed, bearded, blond giant in his early thirties who is dressed in wrinkled cotton pants and a white t-shirt with a low V-neck, showing off his sculpted chest. He looks like he might party all night somewhere in Miami. His shoulder length hair has natural highlights from probably spending his days at the beach. He is tan. I bet if I leaned, I would smell the ocean on him. *Daddy I really hope you were of the right mind when you chose this man to protect me,* I say to myself as the man walks into the office confidently, outstretching his hand to Enzio for a shake.

"Good to see you, Enzio," the tall man says in a deep raspy voice. Enzio's brows jump high and his mouth opens, he stretches his hand in return, stuttering for a moment. "You, you? He chose you?" says Enzio, backing away.

"He chose the best." The giant smiles wide, showing two rows of perfectly straight white teeth.

"Of course, of course, this is very good to hear. This is Aurora, Miss Port." Enzio introduces me, the muscle man turns to me and I have to look up at him before he squeezes my hand very firmly with his enormous, callused one.

"Nice to meet you. Iraklis. I'm your security detail from now on."

I pull away my hand from his tight grip and look at Enzio, but his facial expression doesn't have any signs of anger at the obnoxious confidence of this giant stranger. Enzio just nods silently, seemingly approving of Iraklis' introduction. He soon shifts his gaze, preferring to stare into the ground and not at me.

"I'm sorry. I understand that my father hired you to protect me, but it just…it just feels very strange to me to have someone follow me around." I look at the two men. Enzio shifts his weight back and forth but stays silent.

"Enzio? Is there anything else you need to tell me? I feel like you're keeping something from me. I agreed to help, but don't keep secrets from me." I stomp my foot just the tiniest bit. Enzio furrows his brows and his gaze darkens.

"I am not hiding anything, Aurora. Here is the information. We have been subjected to cyber-attacks in recent months. All of them were unsuccessful and we've been trying to understand who is behind them and what they want. It seems that they don't want what our clients have, but they are trying to simply break into our system. I have an obligation to protect you. This is what your father wanted and I will respect his wishes." A sudden shiver runs through my body when Enzio speaks of my father in past tense. My fingers find the round gold pendant around my neck, made with the etched design of a Greek key all along the border on both sides. It was made by my father and my parents gave it to me as a gift on my twelfth birthday.

I start pacing the room, "It just doesn't make sense. I am so confused by all of this."

"Aurora, Port Security has expanded its services in recent years. We don't manage just banks and private clients anymore; we provide security to the intelligence agencies, governments, and many companies. There are a lot of secrets that are locked away and protected by our keys, safes, and algorithms." Enzio puts his hands behind his back and walks away to the window. The new information is overwhelming. I didn't realize the reach my father's company has. Of course there would be people who would want to have access.

"I wish I knew all of this before," I mumble. I thought my father was happy with the size of his company, he resisted expansion. I guess he grew more ambitious while I was gone.

Enzio turns sharply on his heels and faces me. His face looks sad, "I'm sorry, Aurora. I wish your father was here, and you wouldn't have to deal with all this mess. But I'm glad that he chose Iraklis, I have no doubt about your security now." The giant who until now stood silently, raises his head, looks at me with his piercing blue eyes and gives me a corner smile. I force a small smile in return. I am not sure how this arrangement will work.

"Anyway, I'm here if you need me. I'll be trying to calm down our clients. We might have to tag team on this, because some clients will require face to face meetings to believe our reassurances. I'll send you information about a potential client that I want you to speak with today."

"Of course, I'm here to help," I say and leave Enzio.

I walk back to my office with Iraklis trailing quietly behind me. I fear his size is attracting more attention to my presence than I'd like. I try to look back without being too obvious, but all I can see is Iraklis' midsection. He opens the door for me when we reach my office.

"Thank you." I nod to him and walk in, heading for my desk. I sit down in my comfortable adjustable chair and start checking my email. Iraklis walks back and forth, checking the windows and the shelves. When he finds the remote control he turns on the TV and starts flipping through the channels. He pauses on a car auction show and plants himself into one of the chairs facing the TV. Hmm, I imagined that he would be standing over me as I go about my day. I'm scrolling through the news of the day on my computer when I feel a cold breeze on my neck. My skin erupts in goosebumps and I sense that I am being watched. I slowly turn to the window where the fog is still obscuring my view. I stare into the white, thick curtain and feel myself being pulled toward it. A small red circle appears among the white curtain of the fog, growing larger into a sphere that floats in the air, pulling me toward it. It's the color of red arterial blood, I feel my face flush from the heat that radiates from it. It floats in the air as if some invisible magician put it there as part of a trick. I scan the buildings across the street and look at the people down below, but I don't see anyone who would be controlling it. As it gets bigger, the sphere looks like a large glass ball, it spins slowly and inside of it I can make out large fires, rivers of lava, and people contorted in pain, screaming, and climbing on top of each other to avoid being engulfed by the flames. In the center of the suffering there is something dark, something or someone that wants to get out. I feel it is calling out to me. I lean closer toward the window but get startled by a heavy pull on my shoulder. I look up and see Iraklis standing over me, staring into the fog.

"Are you alright?" His brows are furrowed and his jaw tight.

"Yeah, fine, just daydreaming." I look back out the window and there is nothing but the fog. I don't want to admit to Iraklis that I am seeing things now, what would he think of me? That I am a helpless, paranoid girl. He goes back to watching his TV, and I go back to my emails. Helen calls to let me know that Gabriel, the head of digital security is here to see me. "Thank you, Helen. He can come in."

###

Iraklis

Aurora attempts to get up when there is a knock on the door, but I gesture for her to stay in the chair and get the door myself. Gabriel stands in the doorway. He pushes his glasses up the bridge of his nose, smiling when he sees me. I hold the door open just wide enough so he has to squeeze in sideways to get into Aurora's office.

"Iraklis?" Aurora says calmly with just enough disapproval in her voice to let me know I am getting on her nerves.

She then gets up and walks toward the door as Gabriel carefully shuffles past me. Aurora's eyes dart at me, there is so much distaste for my presence in them, she smiles only when she looks at Gabriel, her face softens and she shakes his hand.

"I am glad you stopped by. I was looking forward to speaking with you. Do you have any news on the attempted attacks?" she asks, leading him to her desk where he spreads papers with graphs and charts.

"I pulled the data going back three months. That's when they seem to have started to increase and they really peaked this week."

I move closer to the desk. Aurora just looks up at me and then pours over the papers.

"Each dot on the graph stands for an attacked department, the duration of each attack and the dates that they occurred is written right above. They are too random and no one claims responsibility," Gabriel continues. We all stare at the papers, Gabriel looks up at me once in a while. Aurora ignores my presence completely. Nothing in those plotted graphs gives me any information.

"They do have a pattern. Here, look, and here." Aurora points to the dots and Gabriel and I lean in closer. "Here, just small groups, two, three at a time, they are fifteen to twenty seconds longer than the rest, not more, and they target one department the most. What is this department?" she asks.

"This is our vault for private storage. It has a separate server that is not linked to the rest of the company," Gabriel replies and pushes up his glasses that have slid down his nose.

"So there is something in that vault that they want. When did the very first attack happen?" she asks.

Gabriel stays quiet for a moment, and I look up at him to see why. When he meets my gaze, he swallows hard and uses his inhaler before he speaks, "Your father increased the vault's security about four and a half years ago. I remember it actually, it was strange, it was right after…"

"What?" I nudge him.

"It was the day before your mother's death, the first attack happened the day she died." He looks at Aurora and then back at me.

She sinks deep into her chair, seemingly shocked by the revelation and stares blankly at the papers in front of her. But a few seconds later she takes a deep breath, straightens out, smiles and says to Gabriel, "See if you can track any clients who signed up for storage in the vault right before the attacks, and if anything was taken out before my father disappeared." I step away, surprised by how this girl is able to take control of the situation. She is not the softie, know it all that I was thinking her to be.

"Will do, Miss Port. I'll get right on it. By the way, you will have a personal safe delivered to the office today. Where do you want to put it?" Gabriel mentions as he collects the papers from Aurora's desk.

"My safe?"

"Yes, everyone gets a personal safe here," Gabriel explains.

"Yes, of course, it makes sense." She looks around, "Here, just put it by this wall." She points to the right wall near her desk. Gabriel nods and Aurora walks him to the door. Once it's shut her face changes from pleasant to stern and disapproving. She folds her arms on her chest and sits on the edge of her table.

"You can't be rude to people who come to see me," she reprimands. This little girl looks cute angry I think to myself. I don't take her too seriously, she is young, inexperienced, and she has no clue about her true identity. She can imagine to be of much importance, if only she knew that it is only her father who truly matters. I don't reply to her and instead take out my phone and check the time. I get a message from Enzio at the same time. It's the detail about Aurora's appointment with a potential client. His name is Mr. Black, a wealthy congressman and an antique collector. The quick search brings up pictures of a gray-haired fit man, photographed with many Hollywood celebrities and politicians. His perfect, white teeth smile beams in each photograph.

"What?" she snaps impatiently as I take my time.

"Your appointment is coming up. Enzio just sent me the details. Stay here. Let me find Iris. I will come get you." I walk out swiftly before she has time to object. I doubt that Hades will try to do anything too brazen when I am guarding Aurora. The girl knows nothing. She is just a regular human, but it's best to be prepared.

I find Iris in Gabriel's office. "I have a bad feeling," she tells me when she sees me.

"Why?"

"There is no sunlight." She walks up to the window and looks up at low, grey thick clouds covering the sky.

"Gabriel can you give me satellite images of this address for the past twenty-four hours?" I pass him the address of Mr. Black. Gabriel types fast on his keyboard and soon we get satellite feed on his computer screen. A quick review of the past day shows that there is just one visitor who came in the morning at eight o'clock, a woman. I examine the layout of surrounding streets and find that there are no hidden alleys and only one front entrance. "I am not concerned," I tell Iris. "I don't understand why Portus wanted me to be here. This girl is clueless. I'm more worried about Portus not being found yet, and Enzio is an old fool, he knows nothing himself. Were you able to get anything out of any of the employees, anything that can give us a hint?"

"No." Iris shakes her head. "But Enzio is nervous. He's concerned. He knows very well what's coming. We only have six days. He can't concentrate on anything, he couldn't even go meet this client, that's why he sent Aurora. I feel bad for her. Poor girl lost her mother. Her father pushed her away, now he's missing, and she has no idea who she really is."

Guilt peers out of the depths of my uncaring soul, for thinking of her as an entitled brat. I really have no clue about her, but I don't really care. She is of no importance. I promised Portus I'd protect her, that is all I will do and no more and then I want to be left alone.

"Meet me in the garage, I'll get Aurora," I tell Iris and walk off. My mind is preoccupied with what will be revealed in the near future. We must get the key and the helmet, and Hades will be no more.

Aurora

"I knew that," I reply as the door of my office shuts behind Iraklis after he tells me of an upcoming meeting I am supposed to have. Enzio should have sent me that information first, just then Helen walks in and gives me an envelope with our company's marketing materials inside and a business card of Mr. Black, a rich politician. There is a handwritten note from Enzio in the folder. "Mister Black is an acquaintance of your father. He is looking to hire Port Security for his personal and business security. Give him some reassurance. No details. Be vague. See you back soon. Good luck, Enzio."

When Iraklis returns I close the folder with a satisfied smile. Now I am in the know as well. I march past him with my head held high, and we walk down the hallway to the elevator. I look toward my father's office, and through partially closed blinds I see Enzio, red faced, visibly angry, staring into his cellphone. I assume he is overwhelmed by the instability and uncertain future of the company that he has helped to build. I'll talk to him once I am back from the meeting. I am still surprised he is sending me to see this client, he seems more confident in my abilities than me. I was under the impression that I would only be helping to figure out all the attacks, but I guess it is better to just jump in and learn to swim.

The elevator pings, announcing its arrival, Iraklis walks in first, and when he decides it's safe for me to go in, he motions for me to step inside. I put my hand up to press the button marked L for lobby, but Iraklis is faster than me. He reaches over my shoulder and lights up the button. I make a mental note to speak to Enzio and ask if there is a way to change my security detail to someone else, someone less intense and more polite. I blow air through my pursed lips and look as the small round circles indicating floors light up as we quickly descend to the jazzy sound of the elevator music. When the doors open up, Iraklis heads out first, his head moving fast in all directions, as I hide behind his massive persona. Once again he motions for me to follow him, this time to the black SUV with tinted windows in front of the building. He opens the door for me first and then gets into the front passenger seat himself.

CHAPTER 8

AURORA

Iris is behind the wheel and she greets me with a friendly smile as I take the back seat. She then nods to Iraklis, and he reciprocates as he sits in the front next to her. My eyes meet hers in the rear-view mirror.

"How are you today, Miss Port?" she says cheerfully, her eyes twinkle with joy.

"It's always Aurora for you Iris. I'm fine." I shoot a disapproving glance at Iraklis that Iris catches in the mirror, she giggles softly. "I'm glad you're here, Iris," I reply. She smiles at me with perfect white teeth gleaming against her dark lips. "Let's roll out. Hold on tight." She starts turning her steering wheel with one arm over the other, her head barely above it, as she manages to maneuver out of the tight parking spot and rather smoothly drives the car into the traffic. The sky lights up with occasional lightning and a distant drum of thunder reverberates through the cement and steel of New York City. Large droplets of rain start to bombard the car. The rain always reminds me of my mother, she loved it. I found her many times standing in the rain with her face toward the sky, her eyes closed, enjoying the droplets of water hitting her skin.

My mother's death was unexpected to all of us. Only after she was gone did we find out that she had heart disease and had been seeing a cardiologist for a few years. My mother's medical history was revealed to my dad in his office behind closed doors. I hid in the closet listening in on their conversation. The doctor said to my father that by the time she started seeing him he could only prolong her life. He didn't have an explanation for her heart disease. The doctor mentioned genetics and pregnancy. Her heart barely made it while carrying me. My mother had to be on bed rest for the most part of her pregnancy with me. The delivery was long and traumatic as well. She was told she would not be able to carry any more children. In the small dark closet of my father's office, hot tears streamed down my cheeks as the guilt for my own life planted firmly inside me, blooming into the idea that I shouldn't have existed. If it weren't for me, my mother would still be alive. That idea morphed into a constant guilt for my father's grief when he started avoiding me and telling me that he was sorry that I was his daughter.

A loud thunderclap and a bright bolt of lightning startle me. "He sure is angry today," Iris speaks without taking her eyes off the road. Iraklis turns his head toward her but stays silent.

"Who?" I ask.

"Zeus, of course," she states as if I should have known the answer.

"Ah! I get it. Zeus and his lightning rods. Greek myths, right? I used to love reading them when I was a child." I look up at the dark clouds. "Those Gods were a bit much, so jealous, so much bravado and attitude."

"What do you expect from someone who has so much power, Aurora? Power is like a good wine. It makes life easier, more fun. You drink enough of it and your world is better, stop it suddenly and you'll have a headache," Iris continues to theorize, managing to move in and out of traffic with seeming ease. Iraklis grunts, but I'm not sure if that is the sound of agreement or displeasure.

"Maybe. I don't know. It's fine to be drunk on your power, but don't go around hurting people just because you can. I guess that's what I am trying to say." I shrug my shoulders as I catch Iris glancing at me in her rear-view mirror and take out my phone, checking my email and then news threads of the day. We all stay silent for the rest of the ride. Iris finally pulls up and parks on a street lined with brown stones. I get out of the car and go up the steps to the address that is written inside my folder. I hear Iraklis' heavy breathing right behind me just as I am about to press the doorbell.

"What do you think you are doing?" I turn to him sharply. I have to look up at him even though he is a few steps below me.

"Doing my job," he replies, his facial expression lacks any emotions.

"No, I'm here doing my job, and you have to stay in the car. This is a potential client, no way I'm walking in there with you. How do you think it'll make me look? Forget about me. He'll think the whole company is in shambles," I berate him through my clenched teeth. But he only shrugs his shoulders and comes up onto the next step closer to me.

"No, stop it." I put my hand out against his chest. I have to lean back because his close proximity is intimidating. It makes me uncomfortable, my heart flutters like a caged bird.

I know my hand on his chest is like a touch of a feather to him and will do nothing to stop him, but nevertheless he stills. "I don't care what my dad told you to do. You work for me as well, and I'm telling you, you're not going in with me. If you don't listen, believe me, I will persuade Enzio to hire someone else."

"Fine," he blurts and I see his jaw tighten. "I'll stand right here. You call me if there is any funny business going on. Got it princess?" He stares down at me, his brows furrowed.

"Fine," I throw back at him and press the doorbell. "Don't call me princess. I have a name, Aurora or Miss Port," I say over my shoulder just as the door opens up, and a beautiful, tall woman with hair neatly tucked into a low bun greets me and lets me in, throwing a curious look at Iraklis, and then swiftly slamming the door in his face behind me when he decides to take a peek inside.

My eyes take a few moments to adjust to the dark surroundings, but all I see is the reflection of me and the model looking woman in the large floor to ceiling mirrors. She is dressed in a black tight pencil skirt and a black turtleneck. When she turns around her conservative top reveals an open back. She motions with her fingers for me to follow her and smiles alluringly with beautiful lips that are lined with red lipstick.

"Come in, Miss Port." She takes a step forward and her black patent leather heels with a red sole click clack confidently. She opens a mirrored door which leads into a large foyer with a grand staircase of dark wood and matching paneling with rosettes and heads of lions and dogs going up the height of the wall. The ceiling is overtaken by a monstrous chandelier of antlers. Maybe the owner is an avid hunter, I think to myself. As we proceed into the hallway under the stairs, I get an uneasy feeling of being watched. The space feels like a long, dark tunnel, lined with large mirrors in thick, golden frames. I glance into one as I pass by and see multiple reflections of my back and front bouncing off the shiny surface of the mirror, reflected from the one across from it. I feel a strange sensation of being drawn to it. I stop and continue to stare into the depth of the glass that keeps pulling me closer, the surface seems crystal clear, fluid. Just as I am about to touch the mirror, the furthest reflection of myself turns to face me and mouths, "Run."

"Please don't touch, Miss Port," the beautiful woman cautions in her smooth whisper like voice. "This is a very ancient mirror that can only be touched by certain people. It's a relic, you understand of course."

"Of course." I smile at her and pull my hand away from the mirror. When I look into it again, all the reflections are just as they are supposed to be. I need to check my head, maybe do blood work and go on vacation, these visions are getting too strange and too frequent.

"Follow me, Miss Port," the woman urges, and we proceed to the end of the hallway. She hums a tune as we walk. It is familiar, but I can't remember the words. We finally enter a large living room that has more of the dark wall paneling. Red rugs and curtains of a deep red color make the ambience of the room gloomy, stuffy, and uneasy. The decor completely overwhelms all the natural light coming through the tall window. The fireplace that is just as tall as I am, burns bright, making the room very warm, hot actually.

"You may sit here." The woman motions to the leather chair with a tall back near the fireplace.

"Thank you," I reply to her and sit into the warm softness of the furniture. I feel the heat on my face, the fire dances on the large log, which crackles satisfyingly, not suspecting its impending demise. I put my folder on the table next to me and smooth out my dress. The fire burns brighter and becomes taller, the tongues of the flame spread out, threatening to jump out of the fireplace. I stare into the center of the flame, it acts as if it's a live being. I wonder what it would say to me if it could speak. The log sizzles cheerfully and in the sound of burning wood I hear a whisper, "key," and a burst of sparks fly over in my direction, landing on me. I jump to my feet and brush the fiery dust off. "This is crazy," I mumble, not only am I imagining seeing things, now I am hearing stuff too.

"The fire was a gift to the people from Titan Prometheus. He stole it from mount Olympus and was punished for it by Zeus. Zeus chained Prometheus to a rock and sent an eagle every day to feed on his liver." A tall man in a dark grey suit, leaning on a black cane, comes up quietly to the fireplace. The flames dwindle to just a smolder, as if calmed by his presence. The man appears to be in his late fifties, a square chin and a sharp jaw frame his aged face with lines etched deep into his pale skin, pointing to a strong character, large dark eyes are black holes that burn into me, and I feel uncomfortable under his direct gaze.

"Thank God for Hercules, who killed the eagle. Mister Black?" I stretch out my hand and take a step forward, forcing myself to look directly into his eyes. The corner of the man's mouth goes up, he nods, confirming his identity, and stretches out his hand to shake mine. It is hot when it tightly grips mine. He pulls me in closer, heat seems to emanate from him, yet he doesn't appear flushed or to be sweating.

"Isn't it sad how the Titans have been punished by Zeus? All they wanted was a little bit of glory and…"

"And whole lot of human sacrifice," I interject.

"Miss Port, I see you are familiar with Greek mythology," Mr. Black says in a low voice, rubbing his chin.

"Ah, yes…I always enjoyed the stories." I straighten my back to make myself appear taller and not to give away that I am intimidated by this man.

"Stories…yes…" He looks into the fire, the glow of it reflects in his dark eyes, a pause grows between us. I cough, and he slowly moves his attention back to me.

"Any news of your father?"

"Unfortunately, not yet."

"I do hope that he is soon found safe and sound. Sit, Miss Port," he says in a soft tone, yet it sounds more like an order and his concern about my father is insincere. I take a step back and fall into the chair right behind me. Mr. Black twirls his cane and walks slowly around me. I take the folder from the table and put it on my lap. He looks at the colorful cover with images of locks and his thin lips stretch into what looks like a smile. He doesn't say anything, but takes a seat in the chair opposite from me. I spot a large dog, a doberman that moves like a dark shadow in the periphery of my vision. It passes by me, growls, and then proceeds to sit near Mr. Black's feet.

"Now, now, Cer. Be friendly." The large doberman lies down at the feet of his owner, letting Mr. Black pet its head.

"This is a very large dog."

"Yes. He is my biggest protector." The man's thin lips form a small smile as he looks down at the animal.

I wipe my forehead and feel my hair getting sweaty from the seemingly increasing temperature of the room. "Are you hot, Miss Port?" Mr. Black doesn't appear to be affected by the heat at all and looks completely comfortable in his three-piece dark suit.

"It's a bit warm, but I'm fine. How about we get down to business? Enzio mentioned that you might be interested in Port Security providing you with our services. Can you let me know what exactly you are looking for?"

"You see Miss Port, I'm a very powerful man." He rubs his chin, looking away from me.

"Mm-hmm," I nod.

"Besides my job in congress…" He looks at me from under his brows that arch up, and his thin lips disappear into barely visible threads before he continues, "I consider myself a collector."

I swallow hard, "What are you collecting?"

Mr. Black's face relaxes, he sits back, "Ah, things, things that…" he twirls his wrist and then flicks his finger, "Things that no longer have a purpose."

"Why do you need such things then?"

"Because for me those things are life." His eyes grow large for a moment, his hands squeeze the handle of his cane, and I can see his protruding knuckles through the pale skin that stretches tight over them. "I've lost access to much of my collection due to some unforeseen circumstances. And I came to find out that your father might be in possession of what once belonged to me. I must get it back."

"I'm afraid we don't deal in personal lost possessions. We are more of a storing and keeping it safe kind of business. If my father has something of yours, I am confident he gained it legally, and you may go about getting it back legally as well," I say with a curt smile and attempt to get up, deciding that this meeting is over. We don't have to take this creep on as a client.

"I was hoping, now that you're handling your father's business…" he begins, leaning back into his chair, his fingers digging into the armrests.

"This is temporary. Once my father is found, I'm sure you can arrange a meeting with him." I take a step toward the door and at the same time the black beast rises up from the floor while his owner stays sitting. The dog walks over to block my exit, growling and I retreat behind the chair, my eyes dash to Mr. Black who stares into the floor.

"Mister Black, call off your dog…now," I snap, my voice trembling. A drop of sweat rolls down my temple.

"Cer, please let Miss Port go. We'll have other options to get what we need," he speaks calmly to the dog. When he is done, the dog looks at me and returns to the feet of his owner.

I slowly walk from behind the chair, not taking my eyes off the animal, as both he and Mr. Black follow my every move. I never turn my back to them, not until I reach the double doors out of the room. I let out a sigh of relief once they are shut.

"Are you finished, Miss Port?" A woman's low voice behind me startles me. I turn around to find the statuesque woman who greeted me before. In the dim hallway, her thin face looks skeletal with deep lines etched between her brows and the corners of her mouth. Her bun has been undone and curled hair lies neatly on her shoulders.

"What?" I ask to make sure I heard her correctly in this strange house. I don't hear her footsteps as she seemingly floats up closer. Her breathing is labored, a slow hissing sound emanating from within her chest.

"Finished?" she whispers, and I feel the heat of her breath on my skin. Her face doesn't move, but there is slight movement in the curls of her hair in this room with no draft. She catches the direction of my gaze, strokes her hair as her lips form a resemblance of a smile and then turns around and walks toward the exit. I shake my head, bewildered by the weirdness of this building and its inhabitants. I walk behind her as she still hums the same tune from when she first led me through this hallway to meet Mr. Black, but now the words come to me. Ring-a-round the rosie. A pocket full of posies. Ashes! Ashes! We all fall down. I learned the meaning of it in high school, and I never wanted to sing it again. A dreadful children's rhyme that describes the plague sore, the herbs that people carried in their pockets to protect themselves from the disease, but finally succumbing to the grips of death and turning into ashes.

I am relieved to be out in the fresh, cool air when she opens the door for me. I jump as the heavy door slams behind me. Iraklis greets me, frowning, his hands in his pockets. Gosh, can he look any more like a bodyguard? Just then he puts on his sunglasses. "What?" he asks as I continue to stare at him.

"Nothing. It's just…" I want to tell him about the uncomfortable meeting that I've just had, but decide against it, he would probably dismiss all of it and think of me as an easily intimidated girl, or worse, he won't let me out of his sight.

"Let's go back to the office," I say instead. He nods toward the car and walks behind me until I am safely inside the vehicle. Iris is quiet, her brows are pressed together and her lips are folded in, her eyes dart toward me in the rearview window and then to Iraklis.

"What is it?" Iraklis asks her before I have a chance to do so myself. Iris leans in and whispers to him, I can only make out, "careful…bolder…"

Iraklis straightens up and without looking back at me, he says, "Fine. Miss Port, from now on, no more one on one meetings. All your trips have to be approved by me and planned out by Iris."

"Why? What's going on? Who is making all these decisions?" I raise my voice as Iris starts driving and Iraklis scrolls through his phone. "Hello? I demand to know!"

"You'll learn when the time is right. All the orders were spelled out by your father. You have a copy of his orders on your desk." Iraklis graces me with an answer that leaves me still puzzled as he continues to play with his phone.

"Fine." I lean back into the seat, sighing loudly. After looking out of the window at passing by cars, I take out my phone and text Enzio.

"Mr Black is not the right customer for us." I see that the message is read, but no reply is being typed. I then send another one, "I need to speak to you regarding my security." This one is ignored again. I decide to stop texting and instead speak to Enzio when I see him, since he is not big on conversing with me via text messages. Just before I put my cell phone away, it pings, but the message comes from the secured, ghost chat window. I've never used it before. I never thought I would use it.

When I got my first cell phone at fifteen, my father sat me down and lectured me on what I should and should not post and if I was ever in trouble I shouldn't hesitate to let him know. He would come get me no matter what. And then he grew serious, he wiped his forehead and sat in front of me, taking my hands into his.

"Your safety is the most important thing for me. I will do everything to protect you from all the evil that exists in the world, but maybe one day, which I hope never comes, I'll need to communicate with you without anyone else knowing. The message will disappear once you read it and will not be traced to its owner or his location." He showed me the shadow chat and how to use it, mentioning that he had installed the app on my phone, but it will not be displayed on my screen. I completely forgot about it. I didn't take him seriously. As any teenager would, I had a sense of invincibility, nothing could happen to me or my parents. I felt so secure in my little world that my father's words didn't concern me. I was filled with the excitement that I had my cell phone and nothing else mattered. But now I am not a teenager, blissfully unaware of the real world, and I no longer feel safe. This message means that my father's safety is under threat. "One message is waiting. Enter your password," the green window glows. I enter "lightofolympus" the password chosen for me by my father who made me memorize it a long time ago.

"Don't trust anyone. Meet me at our summer cottage. You will open the locks. Remember that my Aurora." I look up at Iris who continues paying attention to the road and then Iraklis who looks ahead, unaware of my heart racing and my mind playing out the scenarios of what has prompted my father to send me this message. He doesn't feel safe, he doesn't trust anyone but me, he doesn't want anyone else to know where he is.

I know exactly where he wants to meet, even though I thought my father sold the place after my mother's death because it reminded him too much of her. My fingers tap on the screen of my phone, rushing the reply. "Dad what is going on?" I press send and breathe out slowly. My heart drums away. I feel the pulsation in my ears, the beat is so loud I'm afraid it will be heard by everyone else in the car. But everyone stays quiet, including my father, the chat window shows that he has logged out and the message soon disappears.

I come up with a plan on how to evade my security and escape into the forest of Pennsylvania where our summer home is to meet my father. There is a small comforting feeling that my father trusts me in this ordeal. I will be able to speak to him soon, and maybe, just maybe we will be able to start anew.

We pull into the garage, Iris stays in the car, and Iraklis takes the elevator up with me. When we arrive on the floor, people are getting ready to leave for home. Enzio is pacing in my father's office, speaking to someone on the phone, his free arm flies up and down vigorously to punctuate his seemingly agitated conversation. There are no signs of any additional disaster and the company seems to be functioning. I stare into the faces of every employee, trying to decipher if they might know something, but they all smile politely when meeting my concerned gaze. I walk in the shadow of Iraklis who is always less than an arm's length away. I sit down at my desk and look around to see if there are any other messages that might be waiting for me, but everything is just the way I left it. I loudly drum away at my keyboard, glancing frequently at Iraklis who has turned on the TV and is not paying much attention to me. I get up and walk over to the door and as I reach for the handle he finally speaks, "Where do you think you are going?"

"Argh, bathroom." I roll my eyes, playing up my reaction.

"I have to go with you." He walks over to me and puts his hand, that completely covers mine, over the door handle. His touch is warm, I feel a cool but pleasant shiver running through me. I pull away quickly.

"No you don't," I snap, staring directly at him, my chin is up and lips pressed tight.

"There is no discussion," he replies.

"I need personal space."

"Wait for Iris then."

"No, I have to go now."

"Fine. Let me check the bathroom first then," he sighs heavily and opens the door for me.

"Fine." I match his tone of voice and march ahead to the ladies' room. On the way I meet two delivery men who wheel in a black safe and have to return to the office to show them where to put it. They explain that the lock will open with my fingerprint and a scan of my iris, and I can enter a password as well, as another security measure. I blow out air through my lips, tapping my foot impatiently, and quickly come up with a code word that I enter twice, and the safe screen says unlocked. I press the LOCK button and leave my office to execute my plan.

Iraklis' check reveals no enemies in the bathroom stalls and he soon walks out and nods for me to go ahead and do my business. When he leaves, I get into the wheelchair accessible stall and push on the baby changing table attached to the wall. It doesn't budge and I panic at the thought that my father has sealed this escape route that he showed to me on the plans of the building. I rub my forehead and try again, putting all of my weight into my effort, this time the table squeaks and then slides along the wall, exposing a door handle that I twist. The motion pops the wall out allowing for me to squeeze into the tight space. A narrow, dimly lit staircase runs through the building. I take off my heels and skip down the twisting steps, firmly holding onto the cold railing. I get down all the way to the garage level and peek through a door that says 'Employees Only' to those who are curious when they see it in the garage. I open it wider when my check reveals an empty and quiet garage. I pass the row of the company's Escalades and flashy cars that my father has been collecting and instead get into the Mini Cooper I asked

Enzio to rent out for me. I eyed this car for a long time, it is fast, it will keep me low to the ground and I can maneuver almost unnoticed in between motorized beasts on the road. The car starts without any hesitation.

"Aurora?" A knock on the window startles me as I am about to pull out of the spot. "Where are you going?" Enzio leans in and I push the button to open my window.

"You scared me," I whisper, the pulsations of my heart pounding in my ears.

"I was looking for you to tell you that all the access has been restored. I can finally run the company properly. Your father's conditions have been fulfilled. It's a good sign. It means he is alive. But what's going on with you? Why are you whispering?" he says.

"Nothing, nothing is going on." I shake my head, squeezing the steering wheel tight until the leather crunches under my hands.

"I got your messages about Mister Black," Enzio continues, unaware of how much I want to escape.

"The meeting went fine, strange, whatever, but he isn't the right client for us, we'll talk later. I've got to go." I press the button and my window slowly starts to roll up.

"Aurora, is there anything I need to know?" He puts his hand over the window stopping it from moving, "Your dad and now you…you seem to not be telling me something. Where is Iraklis?" His brows come together, forming a deep line.

"I don't know, Enzio. I need to go." I grip the steering wheel, looking into the rearview window to make sure no one else is seeing my escape.

"Where are you going? Have Iris drive you, or take the company's helicopter, I don't feel good about you driving this little car," he continues.

"Enzio, I need to go. Goodbye." I press my foot to the gas pedal, the tires screech, a burning rubber smell fills the air and Enzio is forced to let go as my car pulls out of the spot, leaving him behind. I will not trust anyone, even this man who has been like an uncle to me since my birth.

CHAPTER 9

AURORA

I leave rainy New York City behind and soon find myself speeding on Route 80 toward the house that we often used for summer vacations but which I haven't been to since my mother's death. The dark clouds have their hold even over the sky of Pennsylvania. The road twists and turns, up and down the mountains. Two lanes change into one and soon my little car slowly rides through the wooden bridge of the Delaware river. Tall trees sway in the wind, the leaves whisper in a language of their own as I speed through the dark tunnel of the treetops. I turn off the paved roadway and ride up the long dirt road that is overgrown with trees and bushes. There is only one house at the end of the road, a fortress with an underground bunker that my father engineered himself. It is the safest place, it will withstand a nuclear disaster and will ensure the survival of its residents for up to fifty years. I pull up to the tall gate and put my left palm on the panel of the intercom. The screen lights up, scanning my hand, "Good evening, Miss Port. Welcome! I have been expecting you, please follow promptly to the front entrance," the AI speaks in my mother's voice. My father had my mother record the commands and replies when she was alive. He was giddy with excitement installing the system and kept speaking to the AI, and when it'd reply back he would clap and skip. My mother laughed and cringed every time she heard her own voice. "You have a beautiful voice, honey. I will never tire of hearing it," my father calmed her.

"Good evening, Medea," I reply. I know the AI will need to run voice recognition before the gates open. It does so quickly, and the large gates slide open, letting me in. I pull up the circular driveway, right up to the entrance of the house. The building is dark, there is not a single light on the inside or outside that gives away any signs of life at this residence. I step out of the car, the small stones shift under my feet, and I quickly run up the steps. Another palm scan is required before Medea lets me inside.

"Dad?" I call out and my voice echoes in the silence of the large building. There is no response.

"Medea, turn on the lights," I command.

"Yes, Miss Port," she replies as the lights come on in the large foyer. The walls of the house are pure white, mosaic floor tiles are laid out with a central letter P encircled in a Greek key design pattern. Under the circular staircase there is a large solid stone engraved with images of Greek heroes battling it out against the Gods.

"Medea, locate my father," I ask, walking past the empty formal living room, as the AI turns on the lights along my way.

"Mister Port is in his study. He requires your assistance," she informs me, and I walk briskly toward the back of the house, make a sharp left near the kitchen, and push the heavy door open into my father's office. The smell of smoke is heavy in the air. My eyes dart across the room. Star maps, old books, and scrolls are sprawled across the desk and on the floor. Empty food containers and glasses are everywhere. The breeze from the open window, where a telescope is pointing up to the sky, blows the papers like helpless sails in the sea.

"Dad?" I call out, and yet again there is no response. There is one more place in this study where he can be hiding, and I walk toward the wall of bookshelves and find the leather bound book, "Homer's Odyssey". My father frequently read to me the stories from this book when I was still a child. He gave the original one to me on my twelfth birthday, this one was just a copy that had a purpose. I tilt it toward me, the bookshelf cracks open, revealing a hidden door into another study where my father used to tinker with locks. The light is on, "Dad?" I yell, just as in childhood when I yelped happily when I found my father in hide and seek. My foot gets caught and I fall over something blocking the entrance. My extended arms save me from hitting my face against the floor, but my palms are pierced by something sharp and my knees suffer, burning and aching. My hands are now covered in blood, there is glass on the floor. I look back to see what has caused my fall and the pain of my cut skin and scraped knees is sucked into a vacuum of loss that I am not prepared for.

"Dad? Dad?!" I crawl to the lifeless body lying across the floor, face down. My legs suffer more cuts, but I don't care, my lungs are gasping for air, my eyes are flooded by tears as I pull on the body to turn it over. When I finally turn him on his back, I slap his cheeks, smudging his face with my own blood, I feel for the pulse on his neck, not knowing where and what I am supposed to feel for. I hit his chest hard with my fist, but he lays still. I search for my purse, my phone falls out, evading my bloody slippery hands. I dial 911, the long beeps seem to last for tens of seconds until finally a female voice responds, unemotional on the other line.

"My father…my father, he…he is, he is not breathing." I try to force intelligible sentences through my sobbing. The woman takes down the address and calmly directs me through the steps of CPR. "It's not working…please…help me."

"Run, Aurora." Another unfamiliar voice crackles into the phone. I pull the phone away from my ear, staring at the black screen that's counting down the seconds of the conversation. "Miss? Miss?" I hear the 911 dispatcher calling for me, and I put the phone to my ear, my head is spinning, my thoughts are running like animals pushed by fear, suffocating each other by their escape.

"I…I'm here," I tremble into the phone.

"The help should be near you. Do you hear the sirens?"

"Yes," I reply, collapsing over my father's chest, the phone slipping from my hands. I grab his still warm hand, his fingers curled tight. I push them open and my fingers grasp his just like I used to when I was little. "Daddy? Don't leave me." I feel his hand growing warmer, the heat is rising, my own palm gets hot, burning my skin, a glowing light forms in our clasp, transferring into me. My heart pumps forcefully, pushing the light through into my blood supply, transferring its heat into the cells and atoms of my body. The light is a pain of being cut into small pieces, the emptiness of continuous loss, the loneliness of unwanted solitude, the knowledge of millennia of human existence. My body collapses under the overwhelming sensation as I hear the steps rushing to the house.

CHAPTER 10

IRAKLIS

This girl is testing my patience. What can be taking her so long in that bathroom? I knock on the door when I've had enough of waiting for her but hear no reply, I crack it open and call out.

"Hey? Is everything alright?" When there is no reply, I grow more annoyed. I don't have time to indulge her attitude. "Aurora?" My voice echoes inside the tiled bathroom without producing any reply. I swing the door wide and first look under the doors of the stalls, but when I don't spot any feet, I open each door only to find the space empty. Shit! I can't believe she is gone! I move my head up and down, looking for an escape route I wasn't aware of, but when I find nothing, I run out to look for Iris. When I turn the corner, Iris stumbles into me, and falls back. She frowns and stretches her arm to me, and I lift her up.

"Aurora is gone," I tell her.

"Let's go. Let's go see Gabriel." She pulls me by my sleeve. Gabriel looks up at us from his computer when we barge into his small office, he smiles at first, but quickly that smile disappears when I shut the door.

"Aurora is gone!" Iris whispers to Gabriel, her eyes are large, she is panting. I nudge her to remind her to be careful and not reveal too much.

"What, what?" She pushes my hand aside. "He is the Oracle, for your information, you muscle head. Gabriel has been put here to see who is coming and going by Zeus himself." She snickers as I lift my hands up defensively and make a step backwards.

"Alright, alright. I didn't know." I bow my head, slightly offended that my own father hasn't trusted me with such information.

"Aurora didn't take an elevator. I would have seen her." Gabriel rubs his cheek. "Let me check the cameras, first in the garage." His long fingers click away rapidly at the keys as the screen brings up small windows of cameras in different locations. A quick scan reveals only Enzio walking up to the elevator. Gabriel rewinds a few minutes back, and there we catch Aurora zipping away in her small car out of the garage.

"Something must have happened and both of us have missed it." Iris concludes.

"What? When?" I ask. "I was with her all this time. Except…"

"Except, when she went to see Mr. Black," Iris finishes my sentence. "Something must have spooked her in there."

"Where can she be going?" I ask as we lean over Gabriel, staring into his computer.

"Don't worry, I put tracking on all of the cars since we've become aware of Hades' plans. Hers has one too." Gabriel turns to us and produces his cell phone where a satellite map has a small red dot traveling the streets of New York City. "Here." He gives Iris the phone and pushes us out the door to the elevator that we take to the garage. Iris' phone pings as we get into her black SUV, she looks at the screen and then passes it to me, the message is from Portus, it reads, "Eternal flow of Meander joins by two keys, in the hand of the true keymaker the fusion will open the doors to death or salvation. Lead the morning light on the right path and it will show you the way."

"It doesn't make sense. A riddle? I have no time for riddles," I say out loud reading the text over and over again.

"He must be afraid that his messages are being read, that's why it's a riddle. Morning light is Aurora. He is trusting us to let her know who she really is. She must know where the key is," Iris explains the hidden message, not taking her eyes off the road. "Just let me know where she is going, and hopefully she'll lead us to Portus himself who will put an end to all this."

"Fine, fine," I say frustrated by the turn of the events. I track Aurora's red button on the GPS and lead Iris on the chase after a girl who has no clue about her origin and destiny.

"She stopped," I let Iris know two hours later. The two-lane road twists like a dark serpent, evading into the darkness, hiding from the headlights of the car.

"I know where she is. Strange. It's Portus' summer home, but I thought he sold it after his wife's death. Text Gabriel, we'll need entry access."

"Huh?"

"The house has an AI system, it won't let you in unless you are granted a permit."

I send a text to Gabriel, and he quickly returns a reply, "Access has been granted to both of you by someone inside the house. I'm tracking you on my computer."

"We've been cleared."

"Good."

The narrow wooden bridge over the Delaware river is barely wide enough to fit two cars passing each other. Iris slows the car down to a crawling pace as the wooden planks drum and squeak under the tires. The river below looks black in the absence of moonlight, tall trees rise like the walls of a dark fortress along its banks. When we reach the middle of the bridge, the water starts to rise rapidly. The muddy river foams, its waves crush and climb atop of each other, each one is faster than the previous one. The wooden planks of the bridge tremble, the metal frame moans as if in pain. The whole structure shakes under the threat of being swept away by rising waters. The river's violent rush is quick, it charges toward us until it creates a still, tall wall, cutting our ability to move forward or back. There is no wind, no cloud in the sky that would cause the violent tide. We are far from any ocean that might carry a tsunami wave.

"Drive! Drive!" I yell to Iris, but it's too late. We come to a full stop, the headlights of our car reflect against the liquid, muddy wall.

The water curtain parts and Poseidon himself makes an entry. He looks much like my father in height and physique, but unlike my father he has an even tan without the t-shirt lines that my father has from working in the field. His face is shaved clean, and his white hair trimmed short. He wears Speedos the size of which I only see on Olympic divers. He brushes off dirty water from his muscular shoulders, and struts toward us smiling. "Why is he here?" I ask and look at Iris who glances at me while still squeezing the steering wheel tight. Poseidon, like my father, has long decided to live a simple life, avoiding using his powers to help humans.

"I'm sure he will tell us." Iris looks at me and shrugs her shoulders. She turns off the car engine, opens the car door and takes a few steps forward toward the king of the seas. I follow her suit and step out of the car as well.

"Greetings, my day of sunshine," Poseidon rumbles and opens his arms wide, drawing Iris in for a hug. She smacks his chest. "You're wet and…" she scrunches her nose, "you smell."

"Always happy to see you, my darling. You once didn't mind my smell, splashing in the same water as me, my beautiful rainbow."

"Grrr." I clear my throat, uncomfortable learning the details of Iris' private life. She pulls away from Poseidon, instantly looking at the ground and then turning away and walking to the railing of the bridge.

"Ah, Iraklis, always there to save the day. How are you, nephew?!" he greets me, smiling. He walks slowly toward me, his arms outstretched wide, his pecs jump up and down as the wickedness churns in his clear translucent eyes.

"Don't." I stretch my arm forward, my palm facing him, but he ignores it as he comes closer. Before I can do anything he springs and wraps his arms tight around me, pinning my arms to the sides, squeezing me, laughing as I try to free myself. His hold is tight. My ribs are compressed, the air is hard to breathe in. Before he is able to lift me off the ground, I find my footing, gather all my strength, grab his waist, trip him with my leg and slam him to the ground. Now he is breathing heavy under my weight, trying to push my mass off him. I seize the moment, strategically positioning my hands around his neck, and when he thinks he can escape, I tighten my grip, choking him until he taps my back strong and fast, and then I let go. He lays motionless, flat on his back, staring into the dark sky. I watch him, expecting another attack, but only a loud laughter erupts from his chest. "Alright, bud! This was good! What was that?"

"Jiu jitsu," I tell him of the new fighting skills I've acquired over the past thirty years.

"Alright, alright, mate." He gets up and taps my knee, "You've got to teach me that."

"I thought you are more interested in posting dancing videos with pretty girls on social media." I take a jab at him.

"Don't underestimate the power of dance and how a beautiful woman can make you feel…" He takes a deep breath through his nose and throws a quick glance at Iris, "Strong, alive."

"Whatever, Uncle," I dismiss him. The man has embraced modern living, posting regular videos of his indulgent lifestyle for people to ogle. He has taken up Koi fish farming for fun, making thousands in sales from his champion fish in addition to leading a successful shipbuilding business.

"Zeus has called me." He rises to his feet, his brows come together, his jaw clenches, and hands form fists. "It's looking bad from what he tells me. The fish sense it too, fishermen haven't been catching any the last few days because they moved into the depths of the ocean." He rubs his chin and shakes his head. "I reached out to the Oracle, and he gave me your location. I'm here to help. Tell me what I can do."

I get up, but before I can say anything, Iris turns around and speaks to Poseidon, her voice is low, but soft, there is tenderness and care in the way she addresses him, but yet her arms are folded over her chest, a non-verbal cue of self-protection. "I…we need you to be prepared. We'll need everyone who is willing to take on this battle to defeat Hades."

"Alright, I will wait for your commands," he replies. Iris walks over to the car as Poseidon's gaze follows her, he lingers for a moment until Iris gets inside, slamming her door. He then waves goodbye and dives off the bridge. The waters recede like a dropped curtain, as fast and as dramatically as they had risen. The bridge stands undamaged, decorated by the droplets of water. The river falls into its channel, flowing gently between its shores and now we are free to go.

"What was that about?" I ask Iris.

"Hmm? What?" She pretends not to understand what I am asking about, firmly holding on to the steering wheel and looking straight ahead.

"Poseidon and you…I didn't know you were together," I clarify.

"You never asked."

"I didn't think it was my business."

"I ask you about your life. I thought we were friends," she zings me again.

"Yeah, I know. I'm sorry. It's not like I don't care…I…I don't know how…I forgot how to connect. You get me?"

"That's the most sense that you've made in a long time, my friend. I get you. I know you care. I know that's how you are keeping distance…so you don't get hurt…again. But man, you are missing out on being present." She glances quickly at me. I am processing her words. "It was a long time ago…we were young…foolish," she begins when I don't say anything.

"I loved him when he ruled the seas, when men still said a prayer asking Poseidon for safekeeping when they set sail. He loved me too, but I am a creature of land and sky, the light can penetrate the water only so deep. He wasn't ready to come ashore, and I wasn't ready to live in his world. Our pride and selfishness sealed our fate."

"You still love him," I state the obvious.

She smiles, but then frowns and sighs, "My love lingers, his has long passed, I know he cares about me, but I'd rather he wouldn't, it would make it less painful."

The silence grows between us as the night gets darker. We turn onto a gravel road, small stones crackle under the tires. The headlights illuminate a tall gate in front of us, Iris opens the door, and the sound of the forest fills the car with singing cicadas, the rustling of leaves, chirping of night birds. Iris speaks into the small box right by the driver's seat, "Evening, Medea. It's Iris." The box glows green, and a pleasant female voice replies,

"You are expected. You must hurry, Mister and Miss Port need your assistance. I've called emergency services, their ETA is six minutes." The large gate rumbles loudly and starts to open as Iris looks over at me, frowning, her lips pressed tight. She floors the gas pedal when she has enough space to pass, the tires spin in the soft gravel before jerking and flying past the gate. The house sits atop a hill, a large circular driveway with a central dry fountain has Aurora's Mini Cooper parked by the entrance. I swing my door open even before our car comes to a full stop and run up the flight of stairs to the entry door. I pull on the long elaborate cast iron door handle, but it doesn't budge. I am about to master up all of my strength to rip the door off its hinges when a small green box to the right attracts my attention and the same female voice from the front gate speaks, "Please place your palm onto the screen." I follow her command and the door opens softly as soon as I am done. With Iris by my side I run into the house and for a moment listen for any sounds of movement or voices, but all is quiet, only the smell of sulfur is in the air. "Mister and Miss Port are in the study. It is straight ahead and to the left of the kitchen. Emergency Services are three minutes away."

"Thank you, Medea," Iris replies to the AI as we sprint in the direction of the kitchen. I can already hear the sirens of the police and the ambulance. The smell of sulfur is getting stronger when we turn left by the kitchen and make our way into the study. We pause for a second, looking for Aurora and Portus in the large room with floor to ceiling bookshelves. "Here," Iris points to a bookshelf that is pushed aside, revealing another room behind it.

"Damn it," I growl, seeing Portus on the floor with shattered mirror glass around him and Aurora collapsed by his side.

Iris checks his pulse but shakes her head no, looking up at me, she then checks Aurora. "She's alright, she's alright. Medea hold off the emergency services."

"Yes, Iris. But someone is trying to break into my system, the gate will no longer be under my control in less than five minutes." The AI delivers the news in a calm, unemotional manner.

"His hand. Hades' work." I point to Portus blackened palm. The singed mark is from Hades' death handshake. He burns the life out of his victims when they think he is finally leaving and saying goodbye. Hades' powers are getting stronger, he hasn't been able to do that in thousands of years. "How the hell are we going to get out of here?" I yell to Iris.

"Portus is gone, but for a few hours the light will linger within the Divine body. It will be enough to transport us somewhere safe. Take Aurora," she commands.

I gently pick Aurora up into my arms, her body is limp and hot. Her long blonde hair is undone, it sticks to her feverish forehead and drapes down, releasing a pleasant smell of jasmine. She feels light in my arms, small and helpless. She doesn't yet know the weight of the knowledge that will soon collapse on her, compounding the grief of losing her father. Iris kneels down to Portus, her eyes are closed, lips moving fast in an inaudible spell known only to her. I hear the front gate starting to give out, the gravel cracking under the weight of the vehicles coming in. Soon, a light glows surrounding Portus' body as Iris continues to kneel in front of him. I wait for Iris to do her magic.

CHAPTER 11

AURORA

Five days before the alignment

"Aurora, angel," my aunt Doti speaks. I hear glass objects clink and someone puts a cool hand over my forehead. It smells so familiar, a distant memory of baked pies and cookies enters my nose. My hands are burning with pain, I feel them bandaged, small cuts pierce sharply as I try to bend my fingers. I cringe. My head is hurting from the loss, I search in the emptiness of my mind for answers to what has transpired and where I am.

Suddenly the temporary wall of amnesia shutters, I gasp at the sharp stab of the memory of losing my father. I open my eyes and sit up into the embrace of the woman who was like my second mother. "Shhhh, child...I know...I know...shhhh." She pulls away from me, her own beautiful blue eyes are red and puffy. Her porcelain skin is glowing, lacking any spots or wrinkles that would give away her age, her dark brown curls are a flowing waterfall over her shoulders. Aunt Doti wipes my tears as her full lips quiver before she says again, "I am so sorry, Aurora." She presses her hand against my cheek and I lean into it, closing my eyes, comforted that she is next to me. I place my hand over hers, finally seeing white bandages covering both my hands.

"Hold on, how…how did I get here?" I look around, recognizing the apartment that is located near Central Park in the heart of Manhattan. My aunt frowns, bites her lips, twisting her slender fingers, and then looks over my shoulder. I follow her gaze to Iraklis, a tall cold figure that is looking out of the window. "What are you doing here?" I sniffle, asking him. He turns around slowly, hands hidden in his pockets, a deep frown is settled between his brows, he avoids looking at me.

"Have some tea, Aurora," my aunt offers and pours hot water into a beautiful porcelain cup.

"Wait…how…why am I here? My father…Did you call the police? Ambulance?" My eyes dash from Iraklis to my aunt.

"Aurora…" My aunt puts her hand over mine, her gaze still avoids mine, "Have some tea. Rest, angel." She brings over the cup from the table to my face. The steam rises up from the hot liquid, releasing the sweet smell of mint, orange, and bergamot.

"I don't want any tea." I push the cup away, "What is it? Why are you not telling me anything?" Their silence makes my heart pick up the pace.

"You're tired…" Aunt Doti tries to touch my forehead, I pull away and get up, rushing toward the mountain of a man who hasn't said a word so far.

"Tell me!" I say through my teeth as my eyes fill up with tears, but he just takes a step back. "Tell me!" I hit his chest with my fists. My palms burn under the bandages, but Iraklis doesn't move.

"How did I get here? What happened to my father!" I raise my fist to hit him again but he grabs my wrist. I lift my other hand, but he swiftly gets hold of that as well. My tears roll slowly down my cheeks, the heat of anger rises, and all I can do is scowl at the man who overpowers me. "Let me go!" I bark. At that moment the bandages over my hands start to smoke and catch on fire. Iraklis lets go of me, stepping away. I tear the bandages off and stamp the flames out with my feet. When I look at my palms, they glow. The light grows brighter, it expands, forming a warm spherical luminosity between my palms. I feel it as if it's physical matter that I can control. Iraklis makes a small step toward me, I slowly move back, staring at my hands. I shake them, but the light lingers, stuck to my hands, its warm glow is a perfect translucent yellow. It moves when my hands move. It's not painful, it feels like a warm stream of energy flowing through my veins. "What...what is happening?" I wipe my hands on my clothes, but when I lift them up the light is still there. My chest begins to tighten, I breathe fast, but fail to pull in enough air. I start to get dizzy.

"Aurora, stop." Iraklis walks slowly toward me, his arms outstretched with his palms up.

"I...I can't...I can't stop...what is happening to me?" I manage to say in between gasps, staring at my glowing hands.

"Angel, breathe." I hear my aunt Doti behind me. Her soft voice is full of care, but her not telling me anything about the dramatic and mysterious events of tonight makes me feel caged.

"No, no...I have...I have to go." I spin, looking for an escape route as Iraklis and my aunt close in, their outstretched arms almost touching, encircling me.

"You just need to rest, angel, come with me, you need to rest. I will tell you everything when you rest," she continues to plead with me as I step back, avoiding her touch, only to bump into the hard, tall wall of Iraklis. The escape is impossible, the events of tonight are incomprehensible. Air…I need air. I pull hard through my nose, but the oxygen fails to stop the blurriness that overpowers my brain. I tilt and stumble, everything goes black, and I collapse into the weightless darkness.

Iraklis

"What was that?" I whisper to Doti after I put Aurora to bed. I have no explanation for the surge of power that came from within her hands. It terrified her so much her body gave out, and now she is unconscious, recovering in the guest bedroom.

"That, that wasn't supposed to happen." She walks back to the living room shaking her head.

"Cut the bullshit, Doti, what was that? She has been out for the whole day and now she is like this?" I press her as she is pacing the room, twisting her fingers. Her eyes dart to me.

"Her powers… Portus wasn't sure if she had any, and he hoped that she'd be just like his wife, simply human. I guess, maybe now that Portus is dead, what was hidden is breaking through. She is now a keymaker."

"Why the hell wasn't she told any of that, she should have been prepared," I growl. This girl is under my protection. She is my responsibility, entrusted by her father. I couldn't save him, but I will do everything in my power to keep her safe.

"Portus had doubts about the realm of Gods. He began to think that a simpler life without any powers was a better life. He thought having any power would be a curse, a burden. He asked me, Artemis, and Persephone to create protective spells so if Aurora had any powers they would never realize, that way her life would be easier. He loved his daughter." Doti stares at me, biting her lips. She cocks her head as if asking for redemption, but I am in no mood to justify what she and others did. They had no right. They altered Aurora's fate. When will they learn that they can't play games with people's lives and make decisions for them?

"What now?" I say loudly in my frustration. Doti gets startled, her cheeks blush, she starts pacing again.

"If she is now the keymaker, she is the only one who can unlock and release the Titans or keep them locked away forever. We have to make sure we guard her so Hades doesn't get his hands on her. And I have to, I have to get Artemis and Persephone here. We have to undo the spells completely, or the energy of the power will cause harm to Aurora." She rushes to the table and grabs her cell phone, typing frantically something on the screen. A few seconds later, the phone pings twice. She taps on the screen. "They'll be here before sunrise." She looks up at me.

"Good. And Aurora? What if she's up before then?"

"She will not be. I will work my magic." She gives me a small smile.

"I'm not so sure your magic has much power over her," I say with sarcasm.

Doti doesn't show if my comment stings, instead she puts her hands on her hips and squints her eyes. "Would you like me to try it on you?"

"No, no." I lift my hands up and chuckle. "Do your magic on her. I need to rest." Doti is a knockout, a gorgeous woman, most men wouldn't be able to resist her charm. She commands love and admiration, but I stay away from her charming and flirtatious ways. She is like a sweet that will give you a belly ache and tooth decay if you eat too much. I don't enjoy such a dessert.

"You can take the spare room over there." She nods in the direction, "The bed is made. Let me know if you need anything."

"Thanks. Good night," I reply and walk off to the bedroom. I pull the sliding doors closed behind me, take a deep breath in and close my eyes for a moment. I feel tired, exhausted, guilty. The feeling pushes down on me. I rub my eyes and decide to take a shower. I get undressed and turn the water all the way to hot, the steam fills the room fast. I step in and put my face to the shower head, letting the water burn my skin. When I can no longer handle the heat, I turn the cold water up and wash my scarred, sore body. I finish in a few minutes, dry myself up, and climb into bed. My muscles relax when they hit lavender scented linens over a perfectly firm mattress and soft pillows. I groan, because my brain continues to work through the details of the day. It keeps zinging me with what ifs and my failure to find Portus sooner. It brings up images of Aurora, her small body draped over her dead father. She looked so helpless, demanding answers from me today, answers that were not for me to reveal. I took the job to repay Portus for a favor he did for me thousands of years ago. But now all I want is to make sure Aurora is safe. I shut my eyes but her honey colored warm eyes linger, refusing to stop asking, demanding me to tell her who she is. When she hit my chest, she looked frightened, frightened of what she didn't know, but she wasn't scared to stand up to me. The girl is a fighter, a beautiful one at that. Her golden locks of hair undone, fell past her shoulders, when she lifted up her bandaged, wounded hands to me. I wanted to hug her at that moment, to tell her that I would protect her, but I pushed the thought away. I drift off into restless sleep thinking of Aurora. She is not mine. She is a job I need to finish. I cannot like her, people I care about get hurt. I must hold my distance. Tomorrow her life will change. Tomorrow she will find out who she really is.

CHAPTER 12

IRAKLIS

Four days before the alignment

The rain didn't let off throughout the night, drumming away at the window as the wind howled. I groan, get up, and get dressed, wondering if Aurora is up already. Outside on the streets, the cars are honking. I glance out the window, New York City is grey with low clouds resting on the skyscrapers. There are occasional people with umbrellas dashing in the streets, a brave runner, determined to get his workout, sprints through the puddles, disappearing into Central park. I hear dishes clinking and head out toward the sound that leads me to the modern white kitchen.

"Good morning!" The southern twang is too cheerful for the weather. I turn around to find C sitting at the table. He has long preferred to stay in the south of the country, Texas, where he enjoys dazzling high society gatherings. I guess Doti summoned him as well.

A large gold ring decorates C's pinky, so big that if C was standing up, he would probably tilt under its weight. He is the largest owner of dating sites and services for different religions, ages, and marital statuses and it has made him very, very rich, because people are as desperate as ever to find the one.

"Morning, C."

C stands for Cupid, the mischievous God of love. I turn my back to him and head to the counter which is set up with a variety of breakfast foods. I pour myself a cup of black coffee and pile a plate full of scrambled eggs and bacon.

"Why so grim, Iraklis? Your heart is so heavy. Come, come here, sit with me, darling," he calls out to me in his high pitched, raspy voice. He used to shoot arrows into the hearts of his victims, making them fall in love. But over the ages he has become cynical, turning his skill into a money producing machine.

"Don't pretend you don't know what's on my mind, C." I ignore his invitation and sit at the counter directly across from the table. He slides down from his chair, picks up a champagne flute filled with orange juice with his ring adorned pinky pointing straight out, and struts, hips swinging, toward me. He pauses in front of the high counter chair, as if estimating the effort it will take him to climb it, and instead pops his hip out, puts his one hand into his pocket and takes a long sip out of his glass, his eyes squinting, staring at me.

"I know, darling, Doti told me. We have a new keymaker, there seems to be a world in danger, et cetera, et cetera, nothing that we haven't seen before." He puts his glass on the counter, takes out his handkerchief, and blots his mouth.

"Mm-hmm," I grunt, taking a sip of my coffee.

"She is a beauty, Portus' daughter, Aurora that is." He snaps his fingers. "Aurora, the morning star, the northern light, how poetic."

"Yeah," I say as I stuff my mouth with food so that I don't have to get more involved in the conversation. I don't like C, I find him highly pretentious. People worshiped him, believing that his arrows were the only way that someone could feel love. But that *love* was a poison, eating at the person's self-worth and confidence until he or she got all consumed by the other, who they thought they were in love with. But alas, they soon figured out that they didn't need C to find love, true love, that is.

"Good morning!" Doti walks into the kitchen, stunning as ever in her floating, silk robe, her long brown hair undone, reaching her waist. She doesn't wear make-up. She doesn't need to. Her skin is beautiful and smooth like polished sea glass: rosy cheeks, dark long eyelashes and perfectly lush lips. Her steps are light, she doesn't rush, she walks confidently, she knows everyone always looks at her. She comes up and gives C loud air kisses on the cheeks.

When she looks at me, she hesitates and then just gives me a small smile as I stuff another fork full of eggs into my mouth. "Hey," I mumble. I am not a morning person.

"Morning." In marches Artemis greeting everyone loudly. She is dressed in black leather pants, with thick soled boots and a long sleeve black shirt. She hasn't changed. At her height of over six feet and a face with a permanent scowl, it would be hard to look much different. Her short blonde hair slicked back, brows pressed together, she doesn't smile, ever. She spends much of her time in impoverished countries assisting women. She goes for the coffee, makes it black, takes a sip, and just for a few seconds her brows part as she takes a deep breath and closes her eyes. We all nod, acknowledging her presence. Her scowl returns as soon as she looks up from her coffee.

Artemis is followed by Pia, she shortened the name from Persephone. It's more hip, goes better with her personality, she has informed everyone. The last I heard she lives somewhere in the north of Europe, eats vegan food and recycles to the point that she doesn't have any garbage. Her hair is a mess of ribbons, dreadlocks and jewelry, a long wrinkly dress hangs loose on her thin body. She lifts both her arms up, stretching and yawning, Doti and C gasp.

"Darling, what's with the hair?" C points to Pia's armpits, his lips turn downward. She looks at her hairy underarms, smiles, and shrugs her shoulders.

"What? It just grows, it's natural. Morning, everyone." She hops and skips to Artemis first, their embrace is tight, then it's Doti's turn. Pia hugs her, trying to press close, but Doti just pats her awkwardly on the back, not returning the squeeze. "C, it has been ages. How are you?"

"I'm well, good to see you." He extends his hand for a shake, catching Pia's fingertips, but she pulls him in for a hug. "Don't be so grumpy, old man. I'm not a yeti, just a woman with hairy armpits, I promise I won't hurt you."

"You should look into lasering it off, darling. I had it done and it's wonderful, just wonderful. This, what you have going on, it's not a good look, darling." He scrunches his nose and smiles that wide smile that stretches your lips but doesn't show your teeth. Pia throws her head back and laughs. I don't know if she finds what he said funny, or she is laughing at C himself for being a miserable prick. I hope it's the latter.

"It's good to see you, Iraklis." Pia comes to me now. "How have you been?" She cocks her head and smiles, her eyes twinkling with kindness. We embrace each other. She is an old friend, trusted. She smells of mint, parsley, and rosemary, pleasant, I take a deep breath in. "Same old, same old. It's good to see you too."

"I presume, Aurora hasn't awakened yet." Artemis gets straight to the point. I release Pia from my hug and everyone comes closer to the food laden counter.

"She had a tough night, the ritual took much of her energy. It drained me as well, actually. I feel like I have a wrinkle now, right here, look C, do you see it?" Doti turns to her short confidant and points to a smooth forehead with an invisible to everyone wrinkle. C squints, "No darling, there is nothing there, you are beautiful." She likes his reassurance and smiles.

"You have taken down your spells, her powers are free?" I ask, and all three women nod.

"Whatever was left of them," Artemis replies.

"What is the plan?" Doti sits down, her silk gown parts as she puts one leg over the other. She doesn't rush to cover up, instead she stares at her long, beautiful legs for a moment, and only drapes them with her robe when Artemis clears her throat.

"It's clear to me that when Aurora wakes up, we need to prepare her. We only have four days, Hades will need Aurora to release the Titans, so she has to find and destroy the key before the alignment happens," Artemis lays out a straightforward approach.

"I don't know, guys," Pia shifts, speaking quietly, we all have to lean in to hear what she is about to say. She bites her lip, "Has anyone asked Hades not to do that, not to release the Titans? There is goodness in him, I know."

"Don't tell me you still love that…that," C smacks his lips, unable to find a fitting description.

"Cruel, ugly, jealous monster," Doti finishes for him. Her stare is blank, the corners of her mouth are turned upside down, the look of disgust is evident.

"He is not that bad, I know." Pia clasps her hands and presses them to her chest. "Yes, I love him, I love him very much. We just, we just have different lifestyles, that's all."

"Darling, darling, you being vegan and him eating meat, that's a difference in lifestyle, but you wanting to make this planet better and him looking to destroy it, that is a non-compatible, futile affair." C paces, wagging his finger up in the air and when he is done he points it directly at Pia. Her eyes dart to each one of us, she tucks her neck in and bites her lip. "He is not that terrible, I don't believe it," she says in a barely audible whisper, lowering her gaze.

"Stop picking on Pia, C," Doti says sternly. "She loves him." She smiles, and I don't know if it's a condescending or a sympathetic smile. C bows his head slightly and sits down at the table.

"This is nothing to do with the relationship of Pia and Hades," Artemis takes control of the conversation. "Hades is looking to release the Titans, he needs two things to do that, first he has to get back his invisibility helmet, second he needs the key." The room is silent.

"So what's the problem?" I sound loud and obnoxious.

Doti and Pia get startled. Artemis' brows come closer together, she takes a deep breath in. "First, we don't know where the helmet is, second, we don't know where the key is, and third, we don't know where Hades is," she punctuates slowly all the bullet points.

"We have Aurora, she is the keymaker. She will keep the Titans locked up. Portus said he'll give us the helmet if we protect Aurora, so he must have had it, we just have to find it," says Iris. Everyone turns around to find her standing at the entrance to the kitchen, leaning on the wall nonchalantly.

I smirk and take the last bite of my breakfast. I find it satisfying that Iris and I know more than these Gods.

"I'm worried about Aurora," Pia says. "Is she ready for all of this? I sensed trepidation in her heart when we were unlocking her power."

"We need time to prepare her," says Doti.

"We don't have time. The coming of the Titans is upon us. She needs to be ready now. I'll talk to her. I am the only one who went through what she is going through. Human one day, then a demigod the next," I say to everyone and they nod.

"Good idea."

"That's right."

"You're right."

"Give her another half hour for rest. She will need all her strength for what's coming, and be gentle with her, Iraklis. This kind of news can be shocking." Pia grabs my hand.

"I'll do my best," I reply and give her a small reassuring smile.

CHAPTER 13

AURORA

I wake up to the hushed voices of Iraklis, Doti and someone else in another room. It's dark, the rain drums against the window. I have no idea what time of day it is. I glide my arms around me, trying to feel my surroundings before I open my eyes, but all I feel is the soft covers of a large bed. My hands are still sore. I feel new bandages wrapped around them. I open my eyes just wide enough to see where I am. I recognize the room right away. I am still at my aunt Doti's apartment, but this time instead of the living room, I am in a guest bedroom where I've stayed many times. I know if I look outside, I will see Central Park. I frequently sat on the windowsill watching people below, wondering about their lives and where they were going. But today I am wondering about my life and what has happened to me. I lift my hands and stare at the bandages, this time there is no light or glow coming from them. I shake them, but nothing happens. I touch all my fingers to the thumbs on both hands, sensation is intact. I unwrap the white dressing to discover that both of my palms have two circles, one within the other as if burned into my skin, but the circles are not formed with a solid line, instead they are short interrupted lines. Questions flash in my mind, hurting with their speed and possible answers, all adding further confusion. How did I get these marks? Did I have a bad dream? Was I so distraught about my father that I imagined my hands glowing? My father! I sit up and look at the foot of the bed, where I find my purse. I quietly slide down to the floor and grab the phone out of my bag. Battery is only one percent. My fingers dial 911, after two long rings, a female picks up the line,

"Nine one one, what is your emergency?"

"Hi...hi!" I hesitate, unsure of what my actual emergency is, the death of my father, my glowing hands, or my appearance in my aunt's apartment.

"My father, my father is hurt," I say.

"Can you please tell me what happened?" she replies in a steady voice, I hear the clicking of the keyboard as she speaks to me.

"I...I don't know. I found him...face down. I think someone hurt him."

"Are you with your father now, ma'am?" The woman continues as the fingers click away.

"No, no," I whisper into the phone.

"What is the location of your father, ma'am?"

"He is in Pennsylvania. 203 Snow Ridge. Please hurry," I whisper into the phone as my own voice trembles.

"Ma'am, please hold, I'll send police to the location." The dispatcher's voice gets muffled as there is more fast clicking on a keyboard. She speaks to someone over the radio, alerting police to go to my father's house. "Ma'am, police are on their way. Do you require any assistance?"

"I...I..." the phone goes dark, my battery loses its charge, and I feel abandoned. Do I require any assistance after all? Where do I go? Whom do I ask for help? Aunt Doti and Iraklis are hiding something from me. I have to get back to the firm, I need to get into my father's office. I'm sure I will be able to find some answers there. I put my bare feet on the floor and slowly get up, listening in to the voices that sound like they are arguing about something.

"We need time…" I recognize Doti's voice.

"We don't have time…we must, we must act." Iraklis sounds angry. I hold my breath, afraid that it will be heard by people in the other room.

I then tippy toe toward the exit with my purse over my shoulder and my shoes in my hands. I slowly open the door, hoping that the hinges don't squeak, giving away my escape, and carefully step on the hardwood floor. My heart is pounding on my chest wall, its pulsations pressing on my eardrums. I reach for the doorknob, praying that there are no complicated locks. My hand slowly twists it, the door gives and as I pull, it squeaks treacherously. I shut my eyes tight, freeze, holding my breath, the tingle of nerves is felt in my scalp. I listen to the people in the other room, but they stay preoccupied with their conversation. They must be eating as I hear utensils clinking against glass dishes, someone turns on the water in the sink, a whistle startles me…it is a teapot coming to boil. I let out a long, steady breath through my pursed lips. I don't pull the door any wider and manage to squeeze my body into the narrow opening. I pull it softly closed behind me and run the long hallway of the building toward the elevators. I press the elevator call button and to my luck the doors open up immediately. I get in and put my shoes on. Once I am delivered to the ground floor of the marbled white and gold lobby, I dash across to the exit as my footsteps echo in the empty space.

I open the door to the outside and am greeted by a wall of water coming down from the skies. There are a few people running from cover to cover, trying to stay dry in the downpour. I scan the street, deciding which way I should go to catch a cab. The elevator pings loudly, the screen indicates that it's going up. I can't wait any longer. I run into the cold rain that drenches me in just seconds. I head down the street, trying to spot a cab, while covering my head with my purse, but it doesn't prevent cold, stinging droplets hitting my face.

"Miss Port!" I hear a man calling me. I turn around and see Mr. Black in a rolled down window of a black town car. His gaunt face and dark eyes are menacing, the man terrifies me. Why is he here? "Miss Port," he yells again as I step back away from the car, "you have to come with me. You are in danger. Come with me." He opens the door, but before his foot touches the ground, I turn away and start running again. *Trust no one,* my father wrote to me. I have to get answers, and this man is not my friend. I keep hearing him calling my name until I turn the corner. It's a one-way street and Mr. Black's car will not be able to drive against traffic. I begin to shiver from being wet, my head is burning with fear and lack of answers. I decide to keep going down the street, hoping to see a cop or a cab. Just then I hear, "Aurora!" Breaks screech, and I dart first right and then left, looking for a place to hide. "Aurora, it's me, stop!" A tall man jumps out of a car, and I am relieved to see Enzio.

"Enzio." My voice trembles, "Enzio, I…I… Dad, he is dead, something happened. No one is telling me anything," I gasp as the tears start rolling down.

"Come, Aurora. My goodness, I will tell you everything. Come." Enzio opens an umbrella over me, puts his arm around me, and leads me into his car. I take the back seat, and he gets into the driver's side. He adjusts the mirror, and presses the gas, the engine revs up, and we pull away from the curb. I look back to check if Mr. Black's car made it around the block. But all I hear is a loud honking in the distance as the road is blocked by a delivery truck.

"What is happening Enzio?" I lean toward him.

"Let's get you somewhere safe and dry, and then I'll explain everything." Enzio doesn't take his eyes off the road.

I lean back into the seat of the car and look through the window at the grey, wet buildings of New York City that don't care about getting drenched by the cold rain. I look at my palms, the circular wounds are not sore, they are turning into pink, smooth, raised scars. I clasp my hands and when nothing happens, I open them, and stare at my skin again. *What do these marks mean?*

CHAPTER 14

AURORA

"We are here," Enzio tells me as he makes a turn and pulls into an underground garage right across from our company.

"Why here?" I sit up and stare out of one window, then another, but all I see is a garage, as plain looking as any other New York City garage.

"Your father owns several apartments in this building. He never told you, but we also have a division where we provide security for people. It is convenient to have a safe space in close proximity to the offices."

"I keep getting surprised with how much I don't know about the internal workings of the company. It's as if I never knew my father."

"He didn't want to have secrets from you. Your mother's death changed him. He became fearful. He wanted to protect you, and he thought by pushing you away he would keep you safe. But he built the empire that is Port Security and his dream was to see you heading the company he created. You've yet to learn much about it." Enzio pulls into a parking spot with a tag that says "Reserved."

"What was he fearing? What did he want to protect me from?" I ask as we get out of the car, our steps echo in the emptiness of the garage.

"I'll tell you everything soon enough." Enzio walks briskly to the elevator that takes us up. Enzio leads the way confidently to one of the apartments that he opens with his own key.

"Come in." He holds the door for me. The apartment looks like a fashionably furnished hotel room without any personalized touches. The large living room has floor to ceiling windows and a direct view of the Port Security building right across the street. I can make out my father's office just a floor below. I stare at his desk and instantly remember the smell of that office, cigars, aftershave and bourbon. I hold my breath, hoping that I will see my father open the door, shuffling in, tinkering with yet another lock or puzzle, but he doesn't. I gasp, and my eyes fill up with tears. I wipe them away, take a deep breath, and turn to Enzio who has brought out a few shopping bags.

"Here, I think these should fit you."

"Where did you get the clothes?" I frown.

"We, Port Security, retain personal shoppers. I texted one to send some clothing up when we were driving." He shrugs his shoulders and passes me the bags.

"Oh, I didn't know we had those…" I cringe at how little I know about my father's business.

"Bedroom is over there," he points. "I will order some food, when you are done, come out, and I will talk."

"Okay," I say and head to change. I close the door behind me and throw the contents of the bag on the bed. I choose a dark pair of skinny jeans and a grey t-shirt. After, I neatly fold the rest of the clothes, and put them back into the bag.

I take everything with me to the ensuite bathroom and turn on the hot water. I step inside and raise my face toward the water, forceful drops pleasantly massage my skin and warm me. I don't linger too long, I wash my hair and get out. I get dressed into my new outfit that fits surprisingly well and hang my damp clothes over the foot of the bed. I glance at my palms where the circular marks appear faint, I rub them on my shirt, and head out of the room to see Enzio who is sitting by a table full of food.

"Sit, eat something." He motions to the chair and takes a sip out of a cup which probably contains black coffee, the only liquid he ever consumes.

"What time is it?" I ask as I grab some French toast, a bowl of cut up fruit, and fill a cup of coffee with milk to the exact imagined line that I myself draw on every cup.

"It is ten in the morning, Thursday," he replies.

"Wait…Thursday…? No, how, how can it be? It was Tuesday, when my father…when I was in PA."

"Yes, you've been gone for almost two days. The police think it's you who did that to your father."

I put my elbows on the table and lean my head into my hands, my fingers digging into my scalp, "Two days…I…I didn't do anything…I didn't do that to my father…I found him."

"I know, Aurora, I know."

"We have to go to the police, I'll tell them…I'll explain what happened, Medea, Medea has recordings, let's bring them to the police." I get up from the table and start pacing.

"Medea has been hacked, there are no recordings from the time your father arrived at the house." Enzio continues to sip his coffee.

"Why is this happening, Enzio? Who would want my father dead?"

"Sit down, Aurora, eat." He moves the plate and motions me to sit. I grab the French toast from my plate and take a bite as my stomach growls, but continue walking back and forth.

"You are making me dizzy, Aurora."

"Sorry." I sit down and take another bite. I align the fork and spoon with my free hand so they are parallel to each other and move the cup to the right of the plate, close but not touching.

"What I'm about to tell you will shock you. It might sound unbelievable, and I wish your father was the one to tell you all of this, but please just listen. I'll answer all your questions." He puts his cup on the table and stares directly into my eyes. I nod with my mouth full and move my chair closer to him.

"Your father was no ordinary man. Truthfully, he was no man at all," he chuckles, but then his face grows serious again when he sees me frowning. "Do you remember, when you were little, you loved to read Greek myths?"

"Yeah."

"Those Gods, the myths, they are not just stories, they are based on beings who had special skills, who lived among regular folks. They still exist, hiding, pretending to be regular humans."

"Haha, Enzio," I throw my head back laughing. When I look at him again, he doesn't have a glimmer of a smile, his jaw is tight and he cracks his knuckles. "Enzio? You can't be serious."

"Why? Because it's hard to believe that there are those who possess special powers? Think about it, Aurora. You've heard the stories, you've watched the movies, and you've read the comic books. It doesn't matter what they are called, Gods, mutants, superheroes, magical beings. They are not made up, they lived and they exist now."

100

"You are telling me that my father was a God?" This time I whisper.

"Yes."

"And he could do things? He had special powers?" I lean closer toward Enzio.

"Yes."

"What were they?"

Enzio takes a long sip of his coffee before he answers, "Your father's name is Portus. He was a God of locks, a keymaker. He had the power to unlock any lock, solve any puzzle, he was also the one who created unbreakable mechanisms to keep the secrets of others. That's why he created his company. He was sought out to keep treasures safe. He was the best one at locking things away, and no one else but him would be able to open his locks." He takes another long sip of his coffee without taking his eyes off me.

I take another bite of my food and chew slowly, trying to process what he has told me.

"Mm-hmm, mm-hmm." I nod. "You expect me to believe this…this…I don't even know what to call it, bullshit."

Enzio slowly puts his coffee cup on the table, clears his throat, cocks his head to the side, blinks fast and smiles with one corner of his mouth. I return a smile back, squinting my eyes, and in an instant the man, the person I've known since I was little, disappears. There are no clothes, no shoes that are left over, only the cup from which Enzio drank his coffee lays broken on the floor. Instead of Enzio sitting at the table a moment ago, now there is a bird, a falcon. The dark brown bird is massive, as tall as I am, its sharp claws grip the chair which squeaks under its weight. Its curved beak is open as it looks at me. It cocks its head to the side, and its black eyes stare at me, blinking as I fall back out of my chair. It flaps its wings and the power of generated wind pushes me back. I crawl away hastily from the table until I back myself against a wall. I stay there, unable to move. I try to speak, but there are no words. I try to think, but my brain pathways are fried, it only manages to signal my body to collect itself from the floor and head toward the door.

"Don't be scared, Aurora. You don't need to run. Trust me, I was just trying to make you believe me." I turn around when Enzio speaks. He has taken on his human form again. He leans, picks up broken pieces of his coffee cup off the floor and places them on the table.

"This...this is not...just can't be...it's impossible." I slowly approach Enzio, pick up my chair and sit down in front of him. "How did you do that?" I lean in and stare into his face, his small dark eyes, his hooked nose. He looks just as I've known him to be, but these features resemble the bird that I just saw. He stretches his hand to me, and I extend mine cautiously. He clasps it firmly and pats it with his other hand.

"My power is that I can transform into a falcon. Before there were planes, cars, and the internet, I was the messenger to the Gods. Since the population of humans has grown and technology has advanced, my skills are no longer needed. I was fortunate to have your father as my friend. I was by his side when he formed his company, serving as the communication expert, if you will, to both Gods and humans who wanted to use the services of Port Security," he explains, holding my hands in his warm hold, his arthritic joints remind me of the bird's claws. I pull away and lean back on the chair, rubbing my eyes and then massaging my temples, a chuckle escapes my lips before I speak.

"So you're telling me that my father was a God, that you are a God, that there are many Gods living now?"

"Yes."

"Was my mother a God?"

"No. Your mother was a mortal, but she knew of our true abilities. Your father had no secrets from her," Enzio replies.

"So what does it make me?"

"A demigod, of course," he replies without any hesitation.

"Do I have any abilities?" I ask as my heart begins to beat faster, anticipating either a disappointment or a weight of responsibility that will manifest itself when Enzio answers.

"We have yet to find out the full extent of it, but I would imagine you'd inherit your father's gift," he replies and walks up to the window, leaving me dissatisfied with his answer.

"What do you mean?" I come up to him as he looks across the street at my father's office.

"Your father and your mother decided to protect you, from you. From the abilities that may be too much to handle. From others that may decide to harm you. They used spells to keep your skills hidden. Even they didn't know what you are capable of." He turns back, towering over me.

I walk back to my chair, and sit down hiding my hands, not to reveal the circular marks, I don't yet know if I should reveal them to Enzio.

"So how do we undo the spells? Is there someone we can call?"

"We need to get back in there," he motions toward the Port Security building.

"Why? Is the answer in there?" I stare at my father's office, bewildered by all of the information has been revealed to me.

"Your father must have left you a note, a letter, something to let you know what is happening. Did you receive anything from him? A package perhaps?"

"No, nothing."

"Aurora think," Enzio says loudly, startling me. He then quickly rises from his chair, rushes towards me, kneels besides me and grabs my arms, giving me a few slight shakes. His fingers digging deep into my flesh, his eyes are moving fast across my face as if searching for an answer.

"Ouch, Enzio. You're hurting me. I told you, I didn't get anything, just a dusty office and a safe I have nothing to keep in."

"A safe?"

"Yes. Gabriel says everyone gets one. It was delivered before I left to see my father."

"A safe?" he mumbles, rising up from the floor, rubbing his chin slowly. "Did you look inside it?"

"No." I shake my head and bite my lip, blaming myself for not doing so.

"We have to check it out. Maybe your father left a package inside it. It takes several weeks for a safe to be ready for a new hire. Maybe your father somehow knew you'd come and he had it ready for you in case…in case…" he chokes up and turns away from me, but in just a few moments he clears his throat, composes himself and proceeds to tell me in his matter of fact tone of voice, "That package may be the key to unlocking your abilities."

"So let's go, what are we waiting for?" I turn and start marching toward the door.

"Wait, Aurora, remember, the police think that it's you who murdered your father. They found your car in the driveway of his house and your fingerprints near his body. You'll be arrested as soon as you cross the street. We must wait for the nighttime when there will be less of a chance of you being seen. Trust me."

"Of course, of course, you make complete sense. Wait, but what about Aunt Doti and Iraklis, why wouldn't they tell me all of this? Are they, too, you know, Gods?"

"Yes, they are. Your aunt Doti is the goddess of love."

"Aunt Doti is Aphrodite?" I gasp.

"Mm-hmm, she went by the name of Venus as well." Enzio nods. "Iraklis is…"

"Hercules," I finish his sentence for him as I make the connections.

"That's right."

I walk back to the table to sit down, and we stay silent for some time as I stare at the wall, mulling over the revelations. "We are old, very old. We came to be at the same time as humans, but we don't know why we have the skills that we have. Gods used to be united as we guided the humans, teaching them, protecting them, saving them from the disasters that they themselves caused. But soon, the time came when a divide grew among us. There are those who no longer want to lead humans, to show them the right way, the better way of living. They want people to fight for their own existence, but there are some of us who still think that we were put on this Earth for a purpose of creating order, peace, prosperity. I'm afraid Doti and Iraklis belong to those who no longer care for the fate of the ordinary people, that's why they haven't told you anything," Enzio finishes. I look up at him, his body is tense, he is breathing fast, his lips are pursed, and fists clenched. He looks like a person who is passionate about the subject. What he says is so complex and large that I have trouble comprehending its enormity. I wish my father was with me so I could tell him all of it. His harsh words make so much sense now, "I wish I wasn't your father. I wish that you would just disappear and no one knew where you were." Those were the words of a father in pain for the future that his daughter would have just because of his blood inside of her. He didn't despise me. He loved me and wanted me to be safe. It is all so clear now.

Maybe if I'd tried contacting him, maybe he would understand that I would have been better off by his side. I wish he would have sat me down, poured himself a glass of scotch, lit his cigar, and pulled out the chess board. He wouldn't say much. He would grunt occasionally, pulling in the smoke and then masterfully blowing it out in rings that bounced and floated until disappearing into the air. When my hand would reach for a figure that would make a questionable move he would mumble, "pa-pa-pa-pa" as I would stare him down. "Think, Aurora, not of the immediate step, but all the other steps that will follow. To have the key is to understand the mechanism of the lock. Think, my girl."

My brain churns as I try to align my steps. I just have to have a plan. I need to find out who killed my father, why they killed him, and I need to clear my name. I am now the owner of Port Security. I will untangle this mess. It's just a puzzle, a complicated one, but I've yet to find a problem that I couldn't solve. Enzio has been my father's friend for years, I know him. He saved me from Mr. Black. I can trust him.

"So, let's get into the building around ten o'clock. We'll find the package and hopefully it will explain why my father was killed and by whom and then we go to the police, right?" I lay out the plan.

"I'll go into the building first. Once I'm in your father's office, I'll give you a signal, and that's when you'll come over through the garage. I will override the security locks to let you in."

"Do I no longer have access to my own company?"

"I'm afraid not, the police requested to be notified when you try to get in, they will immediately be alerted if you use your biosecurity. I decided it would be best if it was deactivated. Trust me."

The dull pulsation of a headache begins to slowly pound in the back of my scull, "Yeah, I guess. Argh. I have a headache. I'll go lay down," I tell Enzio and he nods.

I go into the bedroom and drop across the bed face down, then I turn and lay on my back, and a few moments later onto my side. I stay there, staring out the window at the grey building across the street, the view is blurry as the rain drums at the window, cascading down the glass. I feel beaten down, tired, weak, and alone. The realization of loneliness overcomes me as I gasp, and tears start running down my face. I feel as if I am not prepared to be on my own just yet. I have so much to learn. I need to understand this new knowledge, and I have no one in my corner who is looking out for me just because. Everyone needs something from me, Enzio as well as Aunt Doti, and Iraklis…he was just doing his job. I have doubts that they have my well-being in mind. They are Gods, they are worrying about humanity, saving the world from destruction; and Iraklis, I am sure he will have no interest in being my bodyguard now that my father is dead. I cover my face as my body shudders, stifling my crying, a loud thunder erupts in the sky and lightning strikes somewhere, it's blinding, the electricity clicks and its humming stops.

"Aurora?" Enzio calls out after he knocks softly on the door.

"I'm fine, Enzio." I wipe down my tears and try to sound chirpy.

"The power is out. I'll step out to get lights and batteries in case the outage lasts long. Don't go anywhere," he tells me through the door.

"Yeah, yeah, that's fine. I won't go anywhere, don't worry." I have nowhere to be. No one to care for me. I am alone. The realization is crushing, I no longer have a clear purpose. My life was a straight path, but now it is dark and full of obstacles that scare me and I don't know if I want to follow it. But do I have any choice? The bright flashes of green light erupt in my head. I press my palms over my eyes, my migraine is setting in.

CHAPTER 15

IRAKLIS

I am not a talker, I am not skillful in stringing words into pretty sentences. I don't know the right way to tell Aurora who she really is. My replies are limited to snarky remarks and calls to fight. I never had the patience to explain. I clear my suddenly dry throat. I need to come up with answers about what Aurora's existence means? I turn into the hallway, heading to her bedroom, but a firm, rapid knock on the front door announces the urgency of a visitor on the other side. I look at the door with some hostility as if it's an enemy interrupting my mission, but turn to see who the visitor is regardless. The knocks don't stop, not until I swing the door open. I recognize the face, it's the client that Aurora saw on her first day, he looked like an ordinary man in the picture that I had. But now when this man looks at me from under his eyebrows with his almost black eyes, and his thin lips stretch into a menacing smile, I know instantly it is Hades hiding behind this gaunt face. My body's reflexes respond with rage.

"Hades," I growl, lifting him up off the floor with one hand, then dragging his body into the apartment only to slam him into the wall, breaking the sheetrock. I let go and he falls, but there is no sound of objection or pain. He doesn't fight back or try to get up. I reach and lift him by his tailored black jacket. I raise him high to the ceiling, my fingers digging into his neck, his throat collapsing.

He manages to gurgle out "Aurora is gone. I'm here to help."

"What?" My hand relaxes, and Hades' body drops with the loud thud of a bag of bones to the floor.

Artemis rushes to my side. We tower over our enemy. He sits up and lifts his arm in defense. Pia runs up and helps him get up. C stands aside, loudly slurping orange juice through a straw. Doti evaluates the damage that I've done.

"What did you say?" I breathe out the words to Hades through my clenched teeth, but before he answers I order C to go and check on Aurora. He doesn't rush, he strolls to her room. It takes him a few seconds to reach it. He peeks through the door, calls her name, but when there is no response, he turns to me and shrugs his shoulders, "She's not here."

"Where is she?" I bark and put my face right into Hades', my hot breath reflecting off his face, he keeps his gaze down, his body pressed tight against the wall. He looks weak, sickly. His skin is grey, deep lines are etched across his forehead and between the brows, his eyes are red, his grey hair is wet, sticking to his face. He used to be a good looking man with raven hair and a devilishly charming smile, always thin, but dapper, a lover of dark humor, and always quiet, observing everyone and everything.

"Get in there." I nudge him lightly, but it sends him flying down the hall toward the kitchen.

"Stop it Iraklis," Pia pleads, helping Hades to get up from the floor once again. He leans on her and smiles. "It's alright, Pia, I deserved that." Her eyes dart at me, full of anger, and then back at Hades, filled with compassion. She has long tolerated his antics, the grandeur of world domination, always fighting with Zeus. She, as many women, have hoped that she will be the one to change the bad boy into the perfect doting husband, but Hades only cared about one thing, more power, more souls to collect, more people to worship him. But now people are living longer, and they don't believe, nor are they scared of him. Pia left him. She gave up waiting for Hades to change, since then he has been growing weaker, which fed his idea to release the Titans upon the world to instill the ancient fear of the Gods.

We all crowd around Hades as Pia helps him sit up at the counter. Artemis impatiently taps her foot, her hands folded across her chest. My own hands are tight fists in my pockets. Doti is calling someone to arrange for the repairs, and C continues to drink his orange juice, watching all of us quietly.

"Where is she?" I growl, my breathing is fast, my heartbeat is even faster.

"She came out of the building just as I pulled up. I tried to stop her but was foiled by Enzio who scooped her up, and I'm sure he is telling her lies as we speak." His voice is hoarse and weak.

"Enzio is a friend you liar." Artemis slams her fist on the counter. "Iris call him, tell him to bring Aurora here. Tell him we are trying to help, and he can join us." Iris nods and steps out, dialing her cell phone.

Hades smiles, his eyes travel from one person to another who crowd around him. He then throws his head back, erupting in loud laughter. Pia doesn't leave his side, stroking his arm, her face growing serious.

"You fools. He has tricked you all. You are calling me a liar. Yet you've lied to yourselves all these years that you are special, that you can help the world, its people. You've grown so stupid that you haven't seen treachery right in front of you," he manages to say as he continues to laugh loudly. The sound of it is not joyous, no, it's the sound of doom, terror, and fear. Hades freezes when someone from behind me throws water into his face. I turn around to find Iris holding an empty glass, her eyes meet mine, and she just shrugs her shoulders. "Enzio is not picking up," she says.

Hades wipes his face, pressing hard on his skin, his expression is now calm and collected. Pia passes him a napkin with which he blots his expensive suit.

"Speak of your intentions now…" Artemis towers over him, her voice booming in the large apartment, "…or I'll help Iraklis send you deep into the ground where you will languish until the end of times."

Hades looks up at her sheepishly and takes a deep breath, lifting his arms up in surrender. "I know I don't have the best reputation. I am the evil one, the collector of souls, the ruler of the underworld, thirsting for power, always competing with Zeus to rule the world."

"Yeah, we know."

"True."

"Mm-hmm."

"Yes you are, darling."

Hades' head hangs lower with each of our responses. "I guess I've been on a path of seeking redemption."

"You'll find none here," I snarl at him.

"You are just scared to disappear, to live an ordinary, mortal life," Iris chimes in as she fills up a glass with water, Hades watching her every movement.

"Yes, I'll admit, I'm still selfish. I'd like to be stronger again. That's why I've come to the keymaker to get my helmet. He made a deal with me that if I let him see his wife just one more time that he would return the helmet."

"Why did he have it in the first place? And why would you promise him the meeting with his dead wife. You know too well that this would cause her soul to be restless, tortured, the memories of the life she had will disturb her. She is in a beautiful peaceful dream, living what she thinks is a real life," Doti finally speaks, her beautiful face is full of sadness.

"I didn't think the keymaker was such a selfish prick. I'm surprised," C mumbles.

"To answer your first question, I traded my helmet, for a loan, a large loan. I gambled and lost, lost a lot to demons. I needed to pay them or they would…" his eyes travel to Pia and his face relaxes, he tilts his head and his mouth quivers, "I'm sorry Pia. I had no choice. I couldn't bare seeing you, always looking at me, lovingly, tenderly. You're a mirror that I couldn't hide from and I hated my reflection." He finds her hand and clasps it.

"You did it on purpose? You made me leave you." She sniffles, her eyes swell and turn red. "Why didn't you explain? Why? We could've overcome anything, anything." Her voice gets quieter and she pulls her hand away from his and walks off to the opposite end of the kitchen. Doti joins her, rubbing her back, whispering something indistinguishable.

"I'm sorry my love," he says quietly which she doesn't hear. "I've wondered myself, why would the keymaker want to see his wife, knowing that it would disrupt her spirit. I found out that it wasn't Portus that I spoke to, but Enzio."

"Enzio? Are you sure?" I repeat to make sure I've heard correctly.

"Yes." Hades confirms.

"He revealed that he has grown tired of the current affairs, not just in Port Security, but among Gods and people. He has grown weary, sensing that the time of Gods is coming to an end. He missed the grand times, when people served us, admired us, feeding our powers. He started to hate Portus and the others who had decided to mix with humans. He feels that it's the ultimate betrayal. According to Enzio, we are special, put on the Earth to rule, we need to keep our blood pure. We shouldn't help people, but let them succumb to their own demise."

"So what did he want with Portus' wife?" Iris asks, her brows pressed together firmly, she rubs her cheek waiting for Hades to reply.

"He wanted to know about the key that can release the Titans. He couldn't ask Portus, he was sure his wife knew all the secrets," Hades speaks, tapping his long, bony finger on the counter.

"I hope for your own good you didn't go through with that," I whisper through my teeth as I grab him by his shirt, lifting him out of the chair and bringing him close to my face.

"Stop it."

"Put him down."

"That's enough."

"Iraklis, let go of him," the chorus of female voices erupts. Hades looks straight at me and I think I see a flash of a smirk on his face that changes into a solemn, almost helpless expression for everybody else to notice.

"I'll be watching you," I say into his ear before I sit him back down into his chair.

"I haven't gone through with it. Enzio called it off. He found out that Portus was hiding in his summer home. Enzio wanted to use Aurora as a bargaining chip, so he went there to threaten Portus. Enzio thought that it would be an easy bargain. But…" he pauses and looks down at his bony long fingers as they stop their drumming.

"Portus is dead…" Iris finishes.

"He was murdered. I was there. I smelled the sulfur in his home. You treacherous snake. You were there too and for all I know you killed him and are now blaming Enzio." I get close to his face, trying to catch any twitch of a muscle fiber that would give out his guilt.

He doesn't move, looking directly at me, his breath is calm and steady, "I went there to warn him about Enzio, hoping that he would return the helmet to me in gratitude for the warning. But…"

"But what?" I cut him off impatiently.

"Enzio flew in and attacked us. I was able to escape through the reflection tunnel, I was holding Portus' hand to pull him with me, but Enzio shut the tunnel. I lost my grip on Portus. He stayed behind."

"What a convenient story," I say while everyone else stays silent.

"Who is the person that told you it is I who is seeking the release of the Titans?" Hades challenges. I step back from him, not knowing the answer.

"It is Enzio, Enzio. He spread the lie and you all took the bait so you wouldn't pay attention to him," Hades speaks fast.

"Why did you have Aurora visiting you?" I ask.

"I wanted to find Portus first. I thought he'd be watching her and would reveal his location to speak to her. Enzio was just too smart and figured out where she was going before she got there."

"Darlings, darlings," C screeches, stretching his words. "So, Portus is dead, Aurora is missing. Hades' helmet is possibly hidden somewhere in Port Security and we don't have any clue how to defend ourselves and the world from the potential release of the Titans, in just four days. Did I get it right?" He then proceeds to take a long sip from his cup, looking at all of us from underneath his brows.

"We need a plan," Artemis breaks the silence of the room. "Do we know when the planets will align exactly?"

"Portus was tracking the movements of the planets. I saw the charts on his desk, it is happening just as you have heard, in just a few days." Iris speaks up.

"OK. Good. Do any of you know the location of the Titans?" Artemis asks the room.

"I do." I raise my hand and everyone turns to me. C coughs, choking on his drink. Doti raises one of her brows up and Artemis frowns.

"What?" I challenge their looks.

"I thought only Zeus knew that," Artemis says her brows pressed in a tight knot.

"Yeah, I thought only the Gods by birth were privy to the information," C chimes in.

"No shit. So all of you here are Gods by birth and I am the half breed who knows the secret location of the Titans' prison?" I throw my head back and let my laugh rumble. My father told me where it is centuries ago. He predicted there would be an attempt to release them. He said he had no interest, strength or enough rage to fight like he used to. He made me promise that I will be the one who will protect the world, he trusted me, his son from the human mother. He trusted me more than he trusted his brothers and sisters. The realization makes me feel a deep sense of belonging that I haven't felt before.

"It doesn't matter who knows this information," Pia interjects. "We need to work together, see the bigger picture. The world is in danger. The Titans' rage will have no limits. They will burn the ground. They will murder people and those who survive will die suffering because there will be no food or shelter for them. We are the ones who will need to prevent their coming."

"I think we need to get into Portus' office. Look around. Do we know where Enzio is?" Iris says.

Everyone shakes their head no.

"But I know who might help us." I get my phone and dial. Gabriel the Oracle picks up right away. I bring him up to speed on the current events and he informs me that the building has been on lockdown since the news of Portus' death, but he could get inside.

Iris and I decide to go to Port Security as soon as it gets dark. Artemis will send out a message to be on the lookout for Enzio. Doti and C don't want to leave the comfort of the apartment under the pretense of staying in in case Aurora shows up.

CHAPTER 16

IRAKLIS

Iris drives me to meet the Oracle and to break into Port Security. All the glass and grey steel of New York City is pushing down on me. I rub my forehead, processing everything that is happening, everything that can happen. My thoughts are interrupted by our arrival at Port Security. The Oracle dashes to us from underneath a bodega across the street. I let him inside the car, he is wet, his glasses are fogged up. He rubs them with his tie and pushes them up his nose. "Enzio ordered for all exits and entrances to be locked, all the employees were told to stay out and take personal days. The only access would be through the sewer system up to the garage. There we'll be able to take the hidden elevator."

"I'm not going into the sewers." Iris scrunches up her face in disgust, shaking her face vigorously. "No, no, no. It's all you guys. I'll be waiting for you here or wherever you want me to wait."

"Fine," I tell her. It will be better that she doesn't come, three people will be too many in this covert mission. "Where do we go in?" I ask Gabriel. He nods toward the building across the street from which he came from.

"Good luck," Iris sends us off and we leave the car, covering our heads with our jackets. The wind is blistering, turning the drops of rain into icy pellets. I am happy when we reach the awning of the bodega. Gabriel wipes his fogged up glasses and motions for me to follow him into the Chinese Restaurant right next door. He walks into an establishment that is empty of customers. He nods to the waiters, we pass the dining area and the kitchen where two young men are cooking something in the woks, the steam is whooshing and the oil splattering as they masterfully shake the food so it cooks evenly on the fire. They acknowledge us with a nod and we enter the storage area behind double doors and then into the small back alley with garbage containers. Gabriel pushes one of the large and rusted metal containers, but it stands its ground refusing to move.

"Let me try." I nudge him aside. I grab it with one hand, my fingers dig into the metal, bending it. The container screeches, pleading not to be moved. My fingers dig deeper, warping the metal until a few seconds later the container moves reluctantly, uncovering a manhole. Gabriel bends down to lift the cover only to fall back as his fingers give out without lifting the heavy metal lid.

"Let me do the heavy lifting here," I tell him, holding back my laughter at his lack of strength but respecting his attempts. I bend down to see how I can lift the lid, if there are any grooves or notches, but see none. The manhole bears the emblem of Port Security, a large PS within the circle of a Greek key pattern along the edge, the alphabet of small Greek letters filling the empty space. I rub my chin thinking about how to proceed.

"This is not a usual manhole," Gabriel states the obvious.

"No shit," I mumble under my breath. "Don't you know how this is supposed to open?"

Gabriel pushes his glasses up his nose, his hair is wet and he is shivering, "No, Portus mentioned this during my briefing. He said that I'll know how to use it if it comes to it, but I never thought…I never thought…"

"It'd come to it," I finish for him and wipe rain drops from my face. "If Portus said you'll know, then come here and see if it comes to you. There must be something here, on this lid." He comes closer to me and we both stare at the iron circle.

"PS stands for Port Security…" The Oracle begins.

"I got that much," I reply impatiently.

"Yes, yes. It's quite obvious. This pattern, all around. That's Greek key. It stands for the eternal flow, a serpent. Portus used it a lot in his drawings of puzzles and he even had it engraved on his and his wife's wedding bands and on Aurora's medallion." Gabriel runs his hand along the pattern.

"It used to symbolize the river, Meander, I traveled its twisted channel many centuries ago."

"Yes, of course!" The Oracle presses on the imprints of the letters. The Greek key pattern starts to turn and the PS symbol moves and slides down revealing a keypad with a screen.

"What did you press?" I nudge him, leaning toward the blue glow of the buttons.

"I spelled Meander in Greek." The Oracle smiles at me. His fingers type feverishly on the keypad, "This part is easy. I recently updated the security codes myself." The manhole circle slides, revealing a well-lit shaft disappearing into the depth of the ground. I lean in to look and hold back the urge to yell so I can hear my echo. I hear the water running, but I can't see the bottom.

"Let's go." I get into the tight space with my back almost rubbing against the cement wall and slowly start climbing down. Gabriel hesitates; he circles the manhole several times, appearing confused at how to begin his descent.

"Just get in already," I bark at him, he startles, but places his feet on the ladder and starts climbing down as well. The ladder brings us down where there is no light and we step into ankle high water.

"Which way?" I ask my companion.

"Wait." He is looking for something in his pocket and when he takes his fist out, it's glowing. He flicks his hand and a string of light travels ahead of us, illuminating the long corridor ahead. The Oracle looks at me, another satisfied smile is plastered on his face, "It's a gift from Helios, a sun ray in case of an emergency."

"Nice. So, it's that way?" I nod in the direction that is now well lit.

"Yes, of course." He steps in front of me and takes the lead. "Have you kept in touch with Helios?"

"No."

"I'm married to his sister you know, Selene," the Oracle continues to chat, pushing ahead.

"Mm-hmm."

"Helios comes by once in a while, he keeps pretty busy touring. He loves performing. I don't know what he is going to do once he has to stop." Helios has become a singer, popular during the sixties, soul and rock. He's managed to stay relevant, drawing crowds of fifty and sixty-year-old women who want to relive their youth through his songs. He shines on stage, literally. Everything from his socks to his jacket is sparkling with beads and stones. His house, well even his house glistens in the shiny gaudy surfaces. The man has a golden toilet in every bathroom, crystal chandeliers and large portraits of himself with his blinding white toothy smile. He is nauseating and self-absorbed.

"Good for him." I keep my answers short. Gabriel seems to understand that I am not interested in pointless chit chat and continues to lead down the humid tunnel in silence. My thoughts drift off to Aurora. I wonder how she is. Is she scared, is she safe? Her head must be filled with so many questions. She doesn't yet understand the enormity of her powers, but she'll have to adjust. I hope she is not like me.

I remember when Zeus first told me I am a demigod and his son. It got to my head. My ego grew by the minute. I pushed away people who truly cared about me. Instead I surrounded myself with willing pleasers who told me what I wanted to hear. I was happy to pursue any challenge, there was no equal to me in strength and endurance. Megara, a beautiful princess was given to me as my wife. She changed me, her love made me see what's truly important. If only I could have made her as happy as she made me. If only I didn't murder her.

"We are here," Gabriel says and his voice echoes. I put my finger to my lips telling him to be silent. I don't know if Enzio can hear or is watching us. Another large metal door is in front of us with the same engravings as the manhole cover and a keypad. Gabriel presses the buttons quickly, they beep, the light glows green, and the loud mechanism churns within the door and then it screeches open. We both slide into the opening.

Chapter 17

Aurora

Enzio returns with a flashlight and batteries. We go over the plan again and at around ten o'clock he heads to the Port Security building. I watch through my window and when I see him in my father's office giving me an OK sign, I go downstairs and sneak into the building myself through the garage and then up the hidden staircase that I took to escape in order to see my father. I meet Enzio in my father's office. He is shuffling through the papers on his desk, but as soon as he sees me he nods for us to go to my office. The building is dark and quiet, the generator runs to support only the essentials, security cameras, servers, alarms and locks. I tippy toe behind Enzio when just a few days ago I walked confidently. Now I am afraid to be seen or heard. I don't want to be arrested before I solve the mystery of my father's death.

"Okay Aurora, go ahead." He motions toward my safe. I press my thumb first into the little screen, then my retina is scanned before the keypad is activated and I am able to put in my password. I never chose dates of birth, or the digits zero, one, two, three in a row and not the very obvious spelling of the word PASSWORD. My passwords usually contain names of famous scientists, artists or philosophers of past and present. The current one is Socrates. The safe clicks and opens. I reach out and grab an ordinary brown carton box, about the size of a Happy Meal container from McDonalds. It feels light. I was expecting it to be heavy for some reason, filled with something big that would explain the death of my father. I carefully walk with it to my table as if I am carrying a bomb that needs to be disarmed, Enzio by my side. I place the box gently on my desk and open it with a box cutter. The brown paper guts pop out and I move them aside, searching for the contents, with Enzio digging in as well.

"Where the hell is it?" I hear him mumble under his breath.

"Here." I find another small box. I open it to reveal my mother's wedding ring. I stare at the small polished circle of the shiny metal. The design was created by my father himself to match his ring. The large Greek key pattern occupies the width of the ring. The inside bears the engraving "Eternity is Not Long Enough." My father's ring has an engraving as well "Looking Forward to Forever." I remember asking my mother what these words meant. She told me they picked them out for each other's rings and got to read them when they were married. It was sweet. But why did my father send me my mother's ring? It is puzzling. I put it on my right ring finger for now. I shuffle through the stuffing of the box and find a note written in the miniature, messy, almost illegible writing of my father.

> One lock, two keys.
> One keymaker to set the Titans free.
> In the depths of Tartarus your power will shine.
> Forgive me daughter for your pain.

You've always been my light.
Seek way among my lines.
Beware of friendly lies.
I send you to the God of War.
To find what you are seeking for.

I pass the note to Enzio. The writing doesn't make sense. My father loved riddles, he often wrote them up, sending me on searches to find a gift that he had gotten for me from his travels. I loved them, they were fun. I always figured them out. But this one, it doesn't sound fun, there is something ominous. My father has sent me a message that no one would understand except for me and this time I am scared I won't figure it out.

"I don't understand it." Enzio crumbles the paper and throws it on my desk. "Why would Portus send this? I was looking for…"

"What Enzio? What is it that you wanted to find here?"

"I was hoping to find God damn answers." He slams his fist on the desk. He then rushes to me and grabs my arms, his fingers digging painfully into my flesh, his face is contorted in anger, no it is rage. His eyes are dark, he shakes me, "Where is it? Tell me!"

"I don't know Enzio. Let me go! You are hurting me!"

"Let's go!" He grabs me by my arm and starts dragging me out of my office. Just then the door swings open and in rushes Iraklis. He grabs a chair and lifts it as if it were a weightless feather and throws it at Enzio who ducks and the chair hits the floor to ceiling window behind us breaking it. The cold wind rushes in before we hear the chair hitting the pavement below. Enzio springs to his feet and grabs me from the back holding something cold and sharp to my neck.

"Don't make me do it Iraklis," Enzio says, his voice is low and steady as he pulls me toward the window.

"Let her go." Iraklis follows us. His steps are soft and careful as if a lion on a prowl for his prey. Enzio makes his way behind my desk, inching closer to the window. The sound of cars on the wet roads, the beeping horns, the chorus of raindrops hitting the pavement is getting louder. The cold sharp wind burns my skin and sends the papers flying all over the room. Enzio keeps pressing something sharp into my neck. I try to keep up and not lose my balance. My heartbeat is throbbing in my ears, my chest is moving too fast, pulling in little air.

"You are a fool Iraklis. I'll bring on the change. And you…I'll make you bow to me." He extends his free arm, pointing his long finger at Iraklis. His tight grip shifts, exposing his wrist and I take my chance and sink my teeth deep into his flesh. He jerks his arm and yelps loudly, when I don't let go, he hits me hard with a fist on the back of my head. I release him from my bite and take a small, unbalanced step back. I feel that Enzio's body is no longer behind me. I hear the flap of wings disappear into the distance and I lose the firm ground underneath me as I fall out of the broken window. In slow motion Iraklis' eyes expand as he leaps after me, grabbing my hand to save me from the fall. I dangle out the window, screaming, the tears obscuring the street view below me. I shut my eyes tight, grabbing feverishly for Iraklis with my other hand.

"Aurora," he says in a soft, steady voice, "Look at me." His calm voice draws me out of my panic. I listen, I listen to his voice and open my eyes. The sharp glass that remained in the window frame is dug into his arm, piercing his jacket. I see deep red blood dripping down but despite his injury

Iraklis effortlessly pulls me up and into the office without me touching any sharp edges. We collapse onto the floor, and I keep grabbing him, pressing tight, pulling my legs in, I want to be small, I want to be safe, I want to hide.

"It's alright. You're safe." He wraps his large arms around me, speaking in a warm, comforting voice. His embrace is like a weighted blanket, lulling me, steadying my breathing as I calm against the warmth of his chest rising slowly.

"What is happening? What is happening?" I mumble through the gasps for air, my body starts to shake uncontrollably from adrenalin rush. I feel Iraklis squeezing me tighter, my body warming up, my shivering subsiding. He continues to rub my back and my arms until I am completely still.

"We should go," another voice says. I look behind and see Gabriel's spectacled face, his clothing is drenched and he shuffles from one foot to the other.

Iraklis' lips form a small, but warm smile. He looks tired. "We have to go," he urges me gently. I nod, hypnotized by his stare. I feel like I am a paper boat rocked by the waves of the spring. Monsters and storms fighting for who will bring my demise first. I have no strength. I am confused. I have nowhere to go, so I decide that I might as well go with Iraklis. We are almost in the doorway when I turn around and on my soft, shaky legs, run to grab my father's note.

Iraklis waits for me, his hand extended, welcoming me and I grab it, grab it tight and then squeeze his arm with both my hands clinging to him.

Chapter 18

Aurora

I don't know how we get out of the building. I let Iraklis and Gabriel lead me through stairs and tunnels and then some backstreet alley. We get into the car, and I lean my forehead on the cool window, watching the outside, but if I'm asked what I've seen I will not be able to answer.

When Iraklis opens the door for me and I step out, my feet buckle, unable to carry my own weight. My body is exhausted, I can't process anything around me. I don't notice if it is dark or light outside or if it is still raining. I can't even form a sound. All I do is just look up at Iraklis, and without a word he scoops me up and lifts me off the ground. I hide my face on his chest, closing my eyes, listening to the beat of his heart. It tells me it's going to be ok, thump-thump, you are safe, thump-thump, and I have no strength to think otherwise.

I feel my body detach from Iraklis' warmth, and I am placed on something soft. A familiar scent enters my nose, I've been here before. I open my eyes, and concerned faces are staring at me. I know these people. They are my aunts Doti, Artemis, Pia, my funny uncle C, Iris, and of course Iraklis, and Gabriel. I try to recollect what has happened and what needs to happen.

Aunt Doti has her hands clasped over her chest. Aunt Pia puts her cool hand on my forehead, she stares at me with deep concern, moving strands of hair from my face. Aunt Artemis is frowning, talking to Iraklis in a low voice. I can't make out their conversation. Uncle C is rubbing his chin.

"My goodness, Aurora, you scared us all with your disappearance. We were all so worried. You need to rest. I have some tea, let me get it for you," Aunt Doti says. She turns around to walk away, and in that moment rage resurfaces inside of me. I am angry at all of them for keeping secrets from me.

"No, I don't want tea. I don't want to rest. I don't want any of that." My voice is surprisingly loud and stern. "I don't want, I don't want you to behave like I had some normal life accident. Stop, stop it! You...you have to tell me. I need to know... I need to know the truth. I can't, I can't live like this," now I plead.

They all straighten up, glancing at each other.

"Just tell her, damn it!" Iraklis barks, startling Aunt Doti. Aunt Pia sits on the floor beside me and takes a long breath, Aunt Artemis sits next to me, leaning her elbows on her thighs with everyone else getting comfortable in the chairs or against the wall.

"You are not a regular kind of human, Aurora," my aunt Doti begins. "None of us are in this room."

"Yes, yes. I know that already. You are Gods, superhumans. Enzio told me that, but he also said that you were trying to stop him from helping people, regular people, to get on the right path, that he is the one who is trying to make everything better," I say. Everyone in the room frowns, exchanging glances, only Iraklis chuckles.

"Enzio wants to bring back our domination over humans. He wants people to bow down before our powers like in the old times. He thinks it's what's best for them. He takes them for stupid sheep that need to be shown the way, and he sees himself as their shepherd," Aunt Artemis speaks. "Do you think that's righteous?"

"No, no, I don't think that." I shake my head.

"We've long decided not to use our powers to interfere with the lives of humans," Aunt Pia chimes in, rubbing my hand. "We live our lives among regular folks, and we let them live the way they want to."

"I'm so tired." I press my palms into my eyes. "But tell me more. I need to know more," I say, not asking anyone in particular.

"Well, I am the one who you might know as Persephone. I have the power to make plants bloom, my touch of crops will make the harvest bountiful."

"I am Artemis," my aunt speaks. "I have a gift of healing. In old times I was the best hunter. I am fast, strong, stronger than most."

"I am Aphrodite. I'm sure you know about my set of powers," my aunt Doti adds and smiles. "C is Cupid. He is the mischievous God of lust, my helper. We bring people together. We make them feel the sparks." Her eyes grow big, twinkling with joy.

My eyes travel to Gabriel, he raises his hand and gives me an awkward wave, "Hi there! I am the Oracle, I, well, in simpler terms, I provide situation analysis and come up with possible outcomes based on the information at hand." He pushes his thick glasses back.

"And you? You are Hercules, aren't you?" I look directly at Iraklis.

"I am," he replies, his face is calm, not giving away any emotions.

"Are the stories true about your strength then?" I continue, drilling my eyes into his.

"They are." He doesn't hesitate under my stare.

"Is it true that you killed the nine headed Hydra?"

"Partially." His lips form a smile. A smile that is of complete satisfaction.

"How so?" I demand, ignoring everyone else in the room.

"Those were ancient times. People were scared of many things that they couldn't explain, so I suppose they might have made the details a bit more colorful than they were. I helped those who asked for my help," he says.

"I see. Then what am I?" I put my hands palms up and look at the faces that stare back at me. "What am I?" I repeat, my voice is a barely audible whisper.

Pia nods and both Aunt Doti and Aunt Artemis sit closer to me and each takes my hands.

"You are a descendant of Portus, a God of keys, a keymaker. Your father died, unleashing the power within you. You are a keymaker, Aurora," Pia says as she stares at my hand. The two circles on each palm are formed by pink raised flesh of interrupted lines, a smaller circle within a larger one. They do not hurt, they have completely healed. "These circles are the keys to unlock any lock, physical or otherwise, you will soon learn to control your powers." She runs her fingertips along the now permanent marks on my palms and then closes my hands with hers.

When she sits back and lets go of me, I open my hands and stare at them, then close them, and then open them again. I touch the raised, healed scar tissue and remember the glow that formed when Iraklis held me and wouldn't let go. What was that power, that energy? How do I control it? How do I summon it? How would I be able to open locks? It seems I have more questions than answers.

"Enzio told me about my father," I say without lifting my head, continuing to stare at my palms.

"He bore the same marking as you on his palms, although his have become almost invisible. He expanded into digital security as was demanded by the modern times and formed Port Security first to protect our secrets, but soon began to feel that he could work with people as well. He saw our powers as our limitation. Your father wanted a regular life, but at the same time he couldn't ignore his gift. He hoped that you would not inherit his powers. He made us put a spell on you just in case, so you would not be aware of who you are. He didn't want you to be burdened by the responsibility you had no choice in, but last night we took down our spell," Aunt Artemis says.

"He took away my choice. I wish I knew before. I wish I could speak to him. I wish…" my voice breaks, and I begin to sob.

"He loved you, Aurora, more than anything." Aunt Doti rubs my back gently, slowly. "You were his world. He just wanted to protect you."

"What about my visions?" I ask and then tell everyone of my reflection that told me to run, the red dot that grew into a sphere that pulled me toward the fog and the voice on the phone that told me to flee. Everyone exchanges glances, some shrug their shoulders and only Pia offers an explanation. "There is something unique about you Aurora. It seems that fate itself is looking out for you. Your power is of great importance, that's why you are having these visions. Listen to them, trust them."

Sobs shudder my body, taking away my ability to speak, and no one in the room says anything until I calm down.

"Who killed my father?" I ask.

"Enzio," Iraklis blurts.

"We don't know that, I still don't trust Hades," Artemis replies sternly. She is holding my gaze, her back turned to Iraklis.

"No, it can't be. He is my uncle. He was like a brother to my father. No, no, don't say that." I get up and come closer to Iraklis.

"He almost killed you today." He leans in close to my face, his blue eyes peer deeply into me.

I press my lips tight and fold my hands into fists, angry at Iraklis for the way he is speaking to me. He thinks that I am a spoiled child.

"I know that," I say through my teeth but then soften, remembering that Iraklis saved me. "I'm sorry, I never said thank you for saving me." I touch his right arm lightly and then notice that his hand is covered in blood. "You're still bleeding."

"Yeah, it's nothing." He stares at his hand and shakes his head.

"Let me see, there is a lot of blood." I put my hand on his arm, searching for the injury. He tries to pull away, but I hold his arm firmly and look him in the eyes. "Please, let me see."

He gives in and takes off his jacket, the sleeve of his shirt is soaked with his blood. I raise his large and heavy arm up and turn it out to discover a rip in the shirt and a deep gash wound still slowly pulsating with a stream of thick, dark red blood. In the corner of my eye I notice his face cringing in pain. I seem to be the most concerned with his wound, others don't show any worry. They don't rush to assist me. But I don't care what everyone else is doing, all I care about is making Iraklis feel better.

"Sit down. It needs to be taken care of." My voice suddenly takes on a firm tone as I take charge of this situation.

"Don't worry." Aunt Artemis moves me aside and evaluates Iraklis' wound. "He will be just fine." She rips the sleeve off his arm with both of her hands.

"I'm going to the living room, I just can't stand the sight of blood," C mumbles and disappears, Iris and Gabriel follow him.

"Call us if you need anything, we'll just stay out of your way," Iris says over her shoulder, but no one replies to her. Aunt Doti stays on the couch, quietly observing everyone. Aunt Artemis places her hands over his wound and starts to rock gently with her eyes closed, her voice humming something indistinguishable. Aunt Pia comes up to me and hugs my waist, laying her head on my shoulder and we both stare at Artemis. I glance occasionally at Iraklis to find that he is looking at me. Every time I catch his gaze, I get that ticklish sensation in my stomach as if I'm coming down from the top of a roller coaster ride. I like the thrill.

Aunt Artemis' masculine face softens, there is a barely there smile that graces her lips, she looks maternal. Aunt Pia has her eyes closed as she slowly rocks back and forth. I look at these women, their ancient knowledge fascinates me, but I feel lonely, I am a human with powers that only few have.

A soft glow emits from under Artemis' hands, and when she takes them off and opens her eyes she smiles wide. "All fixed," she says. When I look, there are no signs of the injury, not even a scar.

"Wow. That's incredible." I reach out and touch his arm. His skin is warm under my fingertips. I don't linger on it too long. I don't want to make him uncomfortable. "You can heal anyone?" I ask.

"Yes," she replies.

"Are you…me…are we immortal?"

"Kind of," Artemis and Pia answer in unison and Iraklis nods.

"A long, long time ago we could only die at the hand of another God. Our immortality was fed by the belief of people in our divinity. But since that time has long passed we are now weaker and can succumb to a profound injury," says Artemis.

"We live until our power leaves us or we give it up voluntarily. We have tools to transform ourselves, so that we don't stand out among humans, but we bleed if we are cut and we can die," Aunt Doti says as she comes up to me and rubs my arms, looking at me lovingly.

"We can get rid of the powers? How?" I ask.

"It's a process, a painful process," Aunt Pia puts her arms on my shoulders and makes me turn toward her. "You don't want to know about that."

"OK. So what do we do now? We need to find Enzio, he has to pay for what he did to my father."

"Your father was afraid of another coming of the Titans. We mistakenly thought that it was Hades who wanted to release them, but now we know it was Enzio, we need to make sure we are one step ahead of him," Aunt Artemis says.

"The coming of the Titans?" I ask.

"They are monsters who have been locked up in the depths of the underworld. Enzio will try to unleash them in four days and then everything as you know it will be no more.

There will be only pain, suffering, and darkness. Zeus put them in Tartarus and became the Supreme God himself and you will have to keep them locked away," Pia Explains.

"But what about Zeus?" I ask.

"Zeus is no longer strong enough to fight them. They will destroy everyone they once loathed for their hate has grown during their imprisonment. Earth will become hell and Enzio its ruler. People will be tortured, enslaved, and murdered. We cannot fight them, we are too weak," Artemis adds.

I sit back down on the couch and lay my head back on the headrest, closing my eyes. "It cannot happen then," I say first inside my head and then out loud. I get up and begin to pace the room, organizing my thoughts, my next step, my options.

"Enzio was hoping to find something in my safe." I frown, remembering his nervousness and urgency.

"He needs the invisibility helmet, for the Titans to recognize him as one of the supreme Gods, and he needs a key," Iraklis informs me.

"We have to find it first then. Look, my father left me a note." I show them the message that came with the ring. Everyone crowds around to read it, and I whisper the already memorized riddle to myself,

> One lock, two keys.
> One keymaker to set the Titans free.
> In the depths of Tartarus your power will shine.
> Forgive me daughter for your pain.
> You've always been my light.
> Seek way among my lines.
> Beware of friendly lies.
> I send you to the God of War.
> To find what you are seeking for.

When they are done reading, Pia says, "It's clear he is talking about your brother." She turns to Artemis.

"Yes, I got that much, but why would Ares be involved with Portus?" She rubs her chin.

"So, let's go and find Ares?" I say.

"It's not so easy," Aunt Doti says. "He is a warlord, he moves a lot, his whereabouts are hard to trace." Uncle C and the Oracle return to the room and Persephone shows them the note.

"He is in Moscow, taking a break," Aunt Artemis replies.

"So we need to go to Moscow then, only…" I stop, realizing that it might be difficult with me being a suspect in my father's murder.

"I can arrange new documents for you," the Oracle tells me.

"I'll call to prepare Pegasus," says Iraklis.

"We're gonna fly to Moscow on a horse?" I ask, trying to imagine a mythical creature and most likely an uncomfortable multi-hour trip.

Iraklis throws his head back and laughs loudly, when he is done he reaches for his phone. He presses and taps on the screen a few times and shows me a picture of himself near a sleek white, small plane. Pegasus is written on its tail alongside the image of the horse's head. "We do use modern technology," Iraklis zings me.

"Of course, I don't know what I was thinking." I rub my forehead, embarrassed.

"It's all right. I know you are overwhelmed." His voice softens, and he winks at me. He dials his phone and tells someone on the other end to prepare the plane, he then glances at his watch and says that he and a companion will be ready by eight o'clock, and that we need to be taken to Moscow.

"It's all set. We'll fly out tomorrow morning. You need to rest," he tells me. I nod and suddenly feel tired, my head begins to throb, my muscles feel weak and heavy. I rub my eyes and giggle, "We get tired, right? There is no magic to get rid of it?"

"Sleep, my dear. Go ahead, you've had lots of excitement, you need to rest," Aunt Doti tells me and nudges me toward the bedroom.

"Yeah, I'll go rest. Thank you, for everything," I tell everyone, turn around to face Iraklis, grab his hand, and give it a squeeze, "Thank you." I feel a squeeze in return and notice a fleeting smile on his lips.

CHAPTER 19

IRAKLIS

Three Days before the Alignment

Aurora comes out looking like a femme fatale and not like the girl I met a few days ago. The women have cut her hair shorter and dyed it red. For the first time I notice little specks of green in her eyes that now stand out against her fair skin. Doti has dressed Aurora in a black tight jeans and a turtleneck.

"Here is your passport." I show her. "Gabriel arranged for it." She looks at me so daringly, she is not taken aback by my short fuse and my grumpy temper. But Aurora can't like me. I have to make sure she doesn't like me. She will forever be in harm's way if the wrong people find out that there is something between us.

Iris drives us to the airport where a small private plane is ready for us. The sun is still hiding under a thick blanket of clouds, an eruption of a volcano in Iceland and the rain over Europe prevents her from using her powers to transport us, but we can fly around it in the plane which Iris will copilot with me today. The flight will be turbulent, the weather conditions are unfavorable. I take Aurora to her seat and help her buckle up. I can't tell if she is worried or excited. I feel she is smiling when I tighten her belt to make sure it is secure. I don't make eye contact with her, instead I just show her how to call the pilot's cabin in case she needs anything and then walk away to start the pre-flight check without saying another word.

We take off as soon as the check is complete, like we've done so many times before, and when we reach cruising altitude Iris sends me to check on Aurora.

"She's fine. I'd rather stay here," I reply, hiding the fact that I want to see her.

"I know when you are lying, go talk to her, she'll appreciate it," Iris replies, smiling without looking at me. She knows me too well. She's been my friend for way too long. Iris is the one who saved me when I was ready to take my life after the tragedy, after what I did. She's stayed by my side since then, always watching out for me. I grunt and hesitate, making it appear as if I don't like her idea, and then step out of the cabin.

Aurora is looking out the window, her forehead pressed against the glass. When she looks up at me I see her eyes are red and puffy, she tries to smile, but then looks away, brushing off the tears. The note from her father is in her hands.

"I feel like there is something else to this note. It's too obvious. My father always loved hidden messages and meaning. But I can't figure it out. I feel so guilty. I should've been by his side. I shouldn't have let him send me away." The sudden turbulence shakes the plane, and I fall into the seat opposite from her, a small table separating us. Her eyes are large, and she squeezes the armrests of her chair tight.

"Don't worry, we'll have some turbulence, but we can handle it," I reassure her and reach for her hand across the table. She places her small, delicate hand into mine and I squeeze it lightly, her skin is soft and warm. I feel bad for being a brute to her before. I smile at her and she relaxes, letting out a long sigh.

"Isn't Zeus your father? Can't you ask him to stop the storm?"

"It's not that simple." I let go of her hand and lean back into the chair, looking out the window where thick clouds cover the sky as far as the eyes can see, occasional lightning strikes in the distance.

"I'm sorry. I didn't mean to make you uncomfortable."

"Zeus is my father, our relationship is…err…it's complicated. He can't help us right now. He can only control lightning that's within his proximity."

"It seems we have one thing in common," Aurora says and takes my hand again.

"What's that?"

"A complicated relationship with our fathers. I tell myself that my father loved me in his own way. I felt his love when I was little. I have memories of being confident in his adoration of me. But then it all changed when my mother died."

"He did the hardest thing," I start.

"What's that?"

"He pushed you away even though he loved you. He made you dislike him, even hate him, so you could be safer. He must have known the danger you'd be in staying by his side. He wanted you to be plain, to have no value to his enemies so they wouldn't think of using you against him. I know it's complicated, but he simply loved you," I tell her. She looks at me with her eyes filled with tears, her lips are red and swollen, quivering. She covers her face and sobs.

"I should've known. I should've known." She rocks, her voice is a whisper.

"If you knew, you wouldn't have left. He did what he thought was best." I lean forward, pry her hand from her face, open her palm and kiss it. She looks up at me, startled. Her cheeks blush, her hand lingers under my lips for a few seconds, and then she slowly closes it and takes it away.

"Don't feel bad for me." She frowns and casts her gaze down.

"I don't. I'm sorry, I shouldn't have done that." Why the hell did I do that? I can't keep my hands to myself around Aurora, and all I can think about is her, when I absolutely shouldn't.

She looks back at the note, the plane shakes again, and Aurora reaches for my hand across the table and grips it tight. I come around and take the seat right beside her to make her feel safer. My leg touches her, my arm next to hers. Her proximity feels pleasant, comforting. Shit! I have to control myself. I will put this girl in danger.

"I'll head back to the cabin," I tell her and attempt to get up, but she grabs my hand.

"Wait. I think I got it. There is something hidden here, of course, how could I have forgotten. Do you have a lighter?

I pat my pockets. I carry a lighter for emergency situations and for an occasional cigarette if I get stressed out. "Yeah, here." I pull it out from the pocket of my pants. She grabs it and tries to light it up. Aurora doesn't look like she has had much experience with lighters, the spark wheel spins without igniting the flame. She bites down her lower lip and tries again, and again, and again, without any result. I extend my palm to her, she looks up at me and puts the lighter back into my hand. My thumb strikes the spark wheel, and the flame appears right away. Aurora raises an eyebrow, her lips pucker up, and I hand the lighter back to her.

She puts the note a few inches above it, moving it slowly over the flame. A few moments later her eyes light up. "I knew it. Look. Right there. You see it? Look." I lean in and stare at the piece of paper. At the bottom of the already familiar verse the blank space now has letters, they appear brown as Aurora moves the light underneath. "He wrote a hidden message in milk, it becomes visible when you hold a flame to it," she says. Now I can make out the writing.

Simple mind makes swift decisions.
Let him fly to a faraway land.
The warlord is just a diversion.
Now you are a few steps ahead.
Seek guidance in the summer palace,
Where to take you I promised,
To waltz the day away.
There sacred water will fill you with knowledge.

"Who does he refer to as simple minded?" Aurora mumbles. "Is he talking about Enzio?" she keeps talking to herself. "Is he?" She looks at me.

"He must be." I shrug my shoulders, "Enzio only knows the first part of this message. He will fly to find Ares thinking he has the helmet, but what is the rest of the stuff?" I ask.

"We have to go to the summer palace. That would be…what?" She bites her lips again and looks at me, but her gaze doesn't concentrate on me, rather it is somewhere far away, searching for the meaning of her father's message.

"I hate puzzles. Why wouldn't Portus just be clear about his intentions?"

"This is his way of protecting information from people who shouldn't have it, can't you see that?"

"I'm a straightforward kind of a guy," I reply. Her face softens and she smiles.

"Sit down, we'll figure it out together."

I move again to the seat across from her and put my elbows on the table between us, resting my chin on my fists. She returns to the letter, her lips move slowly, silently pronouncing the riddle over and over again. I get to look at her delicate features, a small light brown beauty mark that rests on her right cheek, her eyelashes are dark at the ends, but light at the base. She has a small gap between her front teeth, it makes her look so real, authentic. Her dyed red locks fall forward and her slim fingers quickly fix them behind her small ears. I rub my eyes. Shit. What is happening to me? I can't have these thoughts.

"I got it!" She looks up, her eyes lit up from the discovery. "It's so simple. I can't believe I didn't get it right away. Waltz, that can only mean Vienna. And he did promise to take me there. He once brought me this, this chocolate cake, and it was the best cake I ever had. He said he would take me to Vienna and we would eat it together there and he would teach me how to dance the waltz. He promised, but we never had the chance." Her voice becomes sad, her eyes glisten, but she shakes her head and tears never flow, she gives me a small smile.

"Then we go to Vienna." I reach out to her and put my hand under her chin. "It's going to be all right. You'll figure it all out, and I'll be here to protect you."

The plane jolts, and we are thrown up into the air. We land awkwardly in our seats, the sign to buckle up turns on. A loud screeching sound of the metal being crushed is deafening.

144

"Iraklis to the cockpit," Iris transmits over the loudspeaker. I glance at Aurora and she nods for me to go ahead.

"It's just turbulence. Don't worry." I give her a reassuring smile and walk back to the cockpit as the plane shakes. The metal sounds as if it is giving out under the pressure forces.

"What's going on?" I ask Iris as soon as I take my seat and look over all the data.

"Something is wrong. Something is very wrong. We are losing fuel, look." She points to the screen; we are almost at quarter tank when we should still have more than half. The plane is thrown harshly again, and when we look up, a large beak comes and strikes the window, cracking it. The falcon glides next to the plane, its black eyes are like small holes of death. It shrills so loud that I have to cover up my ears. It then quickly flies up and disappears somewhere above the plane.

"Enzio found us," Iris gasps. Just then the plane tilts uncontrollably, and we watch as the falcon grabs onto the left wing and with its beak tears off parts of it and throws it into the engine which chokes and coughs and then goes silent. Flames burst through the turbine and then thick smoke streaks along the wing. The bird flies off again as I lean against the window trying to find it.

"Switch to manual," I tell Iris.

"Done. Where is he?"

"I don't know. I don't know," I reply, trying to anticipate where he might land.

He does so on the right wing and the plane tilts under the bird's weight and Enzio the falcon immediately starts shredding it. The metal rips easily under the curved claws of the bird until only the bare metal carcass is left. When the bird is satisfied with the damage caused he flies off again.

The plane starts to lean to the left and I know it is just a matter of seconds before we start spinning. I call for May Day and reach out for the parachute under the seat only to find that I don't have one. I reach out under Iris' seat, relieved that hers is there.

"Iris. Take your parachute! Now!" I pass it to her as she is still trying to overpower the lever. Now I need to make sure that Aurora has one.

"He will catch us as soon as we leave the plane." She shakes her head.

"We have to try. I don't see any other option. We will have to deal with Enzio, but we also have to leave this plane. Put it on."

Iris follows my command and straps on the parachute.

I unbuckle and try to walk back to the cabin, my walk that of a drunken man in the violently thrashing plane. I check all the compartments to find that there are no parachutes. When I reach Aurora she is breathing through the oxygen mask, her eyes are large, she is holding tight onto the seat.

"What is happening? Are we going to crash?" She grabs onto my arms.

"It's Enzio. I will get us out. Bend down and hug your knees," I say to Aurora and show her what position she has to take. When I look at her, she is frozen, she doesn't blink, her chest is rising fast. "Look at me. Look at me. Listen. Aurora. Trust me, we will be ok." I grab her by the arms and squeeze them tight. Aurora nods and follows my instructions. I race back to the cockpit where Iris is radioing our coordinates. I buckle in and watch as we pass the blanket of thunderous clouds and head straight for the wall of steel grey ocean. The plane spins, I know we're going to hit the water nose first. Hitting the water at this speed will be like crushing into a cement wall. None of us will make it.

"I have no light, the sun is covered. I can't get us out of this plane, we will crash." Iris stares at me, and I see my friend terrified like I haven't seen in a long time.

"We have to get the plane from the nosedive. Engine two is still working. We might be able to glide using the wind."

"It's impossible. Both wings are damaged. The plane will be ripped apart," Iris replies. It seems like we are moving in slow motion, but my heart is drumming away and the spinning of the plane is getting faster.

"We'll have to jump!" I yell to Iris and we both unbuckle and slowly proceed out of the cockpit, our bodies fighting the power of G force that is trying to pin us against the wall.

"Where is your parachute?" Iris finally realizes that I don't have one.

"Don't worry about me." I pull Iris to me.

"No, no put mine on. I will hold on to you. We can make it." She undoes her parachute and starts putting it on me. I hesitate for a moment considering if this is the best option. "Take it," Iris urges and I nod, taking the parachute out of her hands.

I leave her by the exit door and go for Aurora. She is in the same position as I left her, only now she is shivering. I unbuckle her and pull her up, her eyes are wide, looking at me. I don't have time to explain, the situation is dire. I strap on the parachute to her back, lift her up and throw her over my shoulder. She doesn't object. I get us to the door and turn the lever, but it doesn't open. I pull Iris behind my back, "Hold tight." I grab the handle, kick the door and it dislodges from the plane. The pull of the atmosphere is strong, we only have a few minutes before we hit the water. It looks bad. I see the falcon's shadow pass over us. I know he will pluck Iris and I off one by one, tear us to pieces, and carry off Aurora to fulfill his plan. But we either die in this plane or hope for a small chance of survival if we jump.

Aurora's body is limp and I keep a tight hold on Iris. I leap as far as I can out of the plane, holding both women. I look up and see the falcon dive after us. His small eyes are black beads, fixated on us, his beak is open, ready to bite, his sharp claws are spread to grab. I begin to spin fast in the blistering wind. It's hard to breathe and my eyes tear up. I just have to make sure I don't let go of Iris and Aurora.

"I will use my light," Iris whispers into my ear.

"No, no. You can't do that. We will make it. I will not let you do it!" I object to her offer with every cell of my body, holding her tight as we are plummeting toward the ocean. This would mean death to Iris.

"Find me in Tartarus, Iraklis. I will be waiting for you. Goodbye, my friend."

"No, Iris." I press my forehead against hers, shaking my head. The falcon releases a deafening high pitch scream and I feel the bird gaining on us but I will not let Iris go. I will keep her close. We will make it, I just have to hold on to her. She smiles softly at me and leans against my chest. She starts to hum a silent spell, her own death sentence. Her voice is steady, unaffected by my protests trying to silence her. She releases Aurora's parachute and the force of it pulls Aurora and I up while Iris breaks away from my hold and continues to free fall.

"No Iris! No!" I can't reach her and before her facial features become indistinguishable below me I can make out that she is smiling. The falcon gains on Aurora and I and grabs the parachute with his beak, ripping it and throwing us violently to the side. I lose hold of Aurora. All I can see is her terrified eyes as she screams and reaches her arms toward me. The falcon gains on her but a bright beam of light flashes from somewhere beneath me, hitting the falcon. It screams, blinded, releasing Aurora, his attack foiled. It flaps its wings just to stay in the air. He can't see us anymore. I know the light is coming from Iris, it's her life force leaving her body. She sacrificed herself to save Aurora and me.

Our fall slows down. The wind is no longer blistering or cutting my skin. I am basking in the warm glow, we are floating. The light from Iris has saved us, it doesn't matter that we don't have the parachute anymore, I know this light will not let us fall. My throat tightens as I choke on the grief of losing my best friend and just then we gently land in the water.

The plane falls and blows up several hundred feet away from us.

When I make sure Aurora can swim I tread water toward Iris. Her body is floating on the surface, a soft glow pulsating and dimming around her, as if she is a star that has fallen. Her face is peaceful. She is smiling, but I know she is dead. She is dead because of me, because I couldn't figure it out, because I didn't come up with a plan to save us. I pull her toward me and put my forehead on hers. I feel breathless. This is my friend, the only friend who I could trust, who looked out for me, who saved me from myself, but I couldn't save her today. She sacrificed her life and now she is doomed to the underworld, wondering without aim or purpose in the darkness.

"Thank you, my friend," I whisper. "I will find you and bring you into the light. I promise." Just as I utter the last words, the water around Iris bubbles into the foam, lifting her up and then rests her in the arms of Poseidon who comes up from the depths of the ocean. His face is contorted in pain, wet from the ocean water, but I can see his eyes are filled with tears. He brings her to his face, sobbing loudly and unashamed as if he is a wounded animal. I look over my shoulder and find Aurora right behind me, her lips are blue and shivering, but she doesn't say anything, she just watches, silent in her own sorrow and letting us grieve. I stretch out my arm to her and pull her toward me, she must be tired swimming in this cold water. I myself start to feel my body chilling and weakening as the current is pulling us in an unknown direction. I stay silent and just wait, wait until Poseidon has shed all the tears. He finally pays attention to us when Aurora goes under and struggles to resurface. I pull her out as she coughs up the water and tries to float on her back.

Poseidon kisses Iris on the lips, the water bubbles over her, and her body disappears under.

Chapter 20

Iraklis

Poseidon takes his trident that floats up to his extended hand and churns the water, forming a funnel that we fall into. The water covers us, and we are in a large bubble of air that travels fast through the depths of the ocean. Aurora clings to me, she is cold, her body is shivering. I wrap my arm around her and hug her tight. Poseidon twists his trident and the water forms a bench on which he sits in front of us.

"What happened?" he asks, covering his face with his hands, rubbing his eyes as if rubbing away a bad nightmare that terrifies him.

"Our plane was attacked. We couldn't get out in time. Iris…she sacrificed herself to save us," I tell him.

"Who attacked you?" Poseidon growls and uncovers his face, his brows pressed together, his jaw clenched tight.

"Enzio." Aurora's voice is barely a whisper. I bring her closer to me and rub her arm as her shivers are getting stronger. She takes my hand into hers, her eyes full of sorrow; another person in her life is gone in such a short period of time. I don't think I can console her, because my own grief for losing Iris is immeasurable.

"Is it true?" Poseidon looks at me, and I nod. "Then I'll make sure she didn't die in vain." He lifts up his hand and slowly forms a fist, watching it as if it was Enzio's neck that he is squeezing. His own face is twisted in pain, red from rage, every muscle is trembling. He allows one single tear to escape and run down his cheek, and when it's gone, Poseidon closes his eyes. When he opens them again, his face is blank, void of any grief, it's indifferent, and I don't know if I like it.

"I'll take you to my island where you'll dry and rest and then I'll make sure you get where you are headed, but you'll need to tell me more." He points his trident at me and I nod in agreement.

I tell Poseidon all that has happened from the moment we found out that Portus was dead as we continue to move in the large air bubble through the depth of the ocean. By the time I am done, I feel that the water around us has gotten warmer and clearer, colorful small fish dart around our air bubble, and larger ones swim slowly past us, uninterested in our peculiar presence. Aurora stays quiet, clinging tightly to me. Soon the water above us breaks, letting in warm humid air. I look up into the cloudless sky and close my eyes for a second. Aurora does the same, salt water has evaporated on her beautiful skin, her long eyelashes are still stuck together, but her lips are turning bright pink. The water gets shallow, it parts around us, and we are able to stand on the sandy surface.

Poseidon takes the lead, and we walk up the long stretch of perfect white beach. Lush greenery of palm trees and shrubs act as a live wall separating tropical overgrowth from sandy dune. Beyond it, hides a large house, seemingly built of just glass. Water is heard everywhere, it is coming from small and large fountains, an infinity pool that has a waterfall cascading down to a lazy river that shimmers in the sunlight.

"Wow!" Aurora breathes out.

"Yes, it's serene here. I wanted it that way. It's where I get away from the world." Poseidon stands proudly, looking over his tropical getaway, but there is no smile of satisfaction on his face. He runs his fingers through his hair, his head hanging low. There is no getting away from the loss of Iris, not even in this paradise. "Come, I'll show you your rooms," he says in a low raspy voice. Poseidon walks quickly away from the main building, we pass the infinity pool, and take stone steps down to where a smaller replica of the main house is located. It has a pond with pink flamingos and a smaller pool in front with hammocks hanging right above the surface of the water. "You'll stay in this guest house. Living room and kitchen are on the ground floor, and two bedrooms are at the top. Iraklis, I'll send over some of my clothing for you. Aurora, I'll have my maid bring some clothes for you. Dinner will be served in the main house, I'll send for you when it's ready."

"I appreciate it," I say.

"Thank you," Aurora replies and Poseidon salutes us but doesn't look directly at us and sprints away.

"I am so sorry," Aurora whispers and grabs my hand. I stare at her, puzzled by her strength and compassion. Here she is, a young girl, who is so naive about life, but has so much experience with loss, yet she finds it within herself to express her sympathy to me. I am grateful for her generous and kind courtesy. My throat tightens. I can't verbalize what I am feeling at this moment. All I can do is nod and squeeze her hand tighter.

"We just traveled across the ocean in a bubble, with Poseidon," Aurora mumbles, forcing a laugh, but her eyes are filled with tears. When she smiles, they roll down her cheeks, but she quickly rubs them away, continuing to smile. I am glad for the change in topic of conversation. Aurora lets go of my hand and walks into the house, taking in her surroundings. "I still can't quite come to terms with all of it, this power in all of you, you know?" She has her back turned to me.

"You're still new to it. Give yourself time," I tell her. I make a hesitant step toward her to give her a hug. An embrace might make us both feel better.

"I don't think I'll ever get used to this much loss. Does it stop being this painful?" She turns to me, leaning her whole body in my direction. Her eyes are seeking an answer, a drop of hope that there will be less pain, less loss in her future. I step back for I can't give her any solace nor hope for the better. I feel anger starting to slowly twist in my chest. I know it will soon form into full on rage. I'm angry at these powers that kill everyone I love. I hate the Gods for being so vengeful, so merciless, so unkind. I hate, I hate myself for being one of them. I can't bear Aurora's gaze any longer and go straight to the fridge. It has no food, to my disappointment, only beer. I open one and take long gulps until it's done. It neither takes away my hunger, nor dulls the pain from losing Iris. I take another and finish it quickly. And it still has no effect on me. So I get another one and gulp it and slam it loudly on the counter, shattering the glass bottle into pieces.

"I am sorry," Aurora says softly, and that voice breaks me. I collapse onto my knees and start to sob, like I haven't sobbed since I was a child. She rushes to me and grabs my hands. "You're bleeding," she says, looking at the hand that was holding the beer, a piece of glass cut deep into my palm. It doesn't hurt. I wouldn't care if it did. I don't want Aurora to see me like this, broken and weak. I jerk my hand away from her. "I want to be alone," I bark at her, get up, and storm upstairs.

I get into the first bedroom I see and slam the door shut behind me. The glass windows shake. It's so sunny in here. I hate this light. I want it to be dark. I want no sounds. I want…I just want to be alone with my pain. I go inside the bathroom and run the cut under the water. I say the prayer taught to me by Artemis and look at my flesh heal without leaving any noticeable mark. I slide down on the cold marble floor and close my eyes. I remember the same coldness that I've felt before.

###

Iraklis

I was kneeling on the floor of the cave. It was dark. I had a knife in my hand, the sharp point of it pressing against my chest, one push, and it would go right through my heart. One push, and I would no longer be alive. One push, and it would no longer be painful. One push and I would have my family back. One push, and no other God would have power over me. I told myself that I would count from ten, and then I would do it when I said one. Ten… A thin streak of sunlight appears through the tiniest hole above in the ceiling of the cave. Nine… It moves like a bunny, hopping joyfully. Eight… It stops right in front of me. Seven… Iris is sitting by my side, lit up by the glow of sunlight, her hand over mine and over the knife's handle. Six… She is crying, tears running down her cheeks. Five… "Stop, Iraklis, you don't have to do this," she whispers. "This is what she wants. She wants you dead. If you take your life, no one else can stand up for people." Four… "I'd rather be dead so I can be with my wife and children." My voice cracks, and I press on the knife, it enters my flesh slowly. Three… "Your wife and children are walking the

Elysian Fields. You are here because you have a purpose. Don't you see all the suffering? Don't you know that you are needed here?" Two… "Look at me, Iraklis. Look at me." Iris grabs the handle of the knife with her other hand and is trying steadily and calmly to force it out of my hands. "If you die, Hera lives, and she may kill other wives, sons, and daughters." She lets go of the knife and grabs my face, staring into my eyes as I battle with pain, rage, and the thirst for revenge. One… The knife drops onto the stony surface, the sound of the metal echoes in the cave as I press my hands onto the cold floor and take a deep breath, and then another. I sit back and raise my head to the darkness and let the last tear dry up on my cheek. The thirst for revenge has won that day. I think Iris hoped it was my calling to help others. I never told her otherwise. I didn't want to disappoint my friend, who for some reason insisted on seeing only the good in me. I never told her that I made Hera pay for what she did. She is imprisoned in the underworld and Portus made an unbreakable lock to keep her there forever. I promised him a payment for that. "When time comes, a request for protection will be asked. Promise you will not abandon me or mine when I need you the most." He gave me the contract and I signed it. He could have asked for my life, my powers, then or now. I would have given him whatever he requested just to avenge my family. I am bound by that promise forever. Even the death of Portus will not free me. If I refuse I will be cursed with the same punishment as I bestowed on Hera.

CHAPTER 21

IRAKLIS

I am wondering what Aurora is thinking of me as soon as I wake up from my nap. Why do I care this much? I take a deep breath and head to the shower. It's no use to be stuck with so many thoughts about this girl. By the time I get out, there are folded clothes for me on the bed. They are new, tags still attached. I put on the jeans and a t-shirt. Even the shoes fit just right. I head out and linger by the door of the other bedroom. I raise my hand to knock on the door but decide to face her when other people are around us so I can keep our conversation less personal. She doesn't need to know about me, she will not like me for the things I've done. I step away from the door and head toward the main house.

When I get there, Aurora is sitting with Poseidon on the couch, they are both looking at a large album. Poseidon slowly flips the pages, pointing and saying something indistinguishable. They both smile occasionally, sometimes Aurora gasps and covers her mouth. I like watching her reacting to the discoveries of the world she knew nothing about until just recently. I know the album they are looking at very well. It's the collection of drawings, pictures, letters, and memories left behind by the guests who've been to

Poseidon's house. Over the centuries it has collected amazing pieces of historical value. There are pictures of Gods, politicians, scientists, artists, inventors and Aurora's father and mother who spent their honeymoon on this island. Poseidon is one of only a few Gods who has managed to keep a balance of having his powers and socializing with other Gods while maintaining a relationship with many regular people. He is rich which protects him from unwanted attention. He is in the ship business; Poseidon says that it is boring and uninteresting to the general population. He donates large amounts of his fortune to ocean cleanup. He is considered a reclusive, eccentric billionaire.

I spend a few minutes just standing and watching both of them, until Aurora lifts up her head and sees me. Her smile disappears, she frowns and looks at the album again, but Poseidon gets up and puts the book away. "I'll show you more next time, Aurora. I'll tell you lots of stories about your father, but now let's go eat, you must be famished." He stretches his hand out and pulls Aurora from the couch. She is dressed in shorts and a turquoise t-shirt that compliments her red hair and her eyes that are getting greener. She glances at me quickly but turns away and heads toward the dining table, led by our host, while I trail behind. I feel a pang of jealousy that Poseidon can be so easily personable with everyone, especially her. I want to be the one whose hand she takes. I want to lead her, but lately my heart and my brain are not agreeing on what's best for me.

"The fastest and most inconspicuous way to get to Vienna would be to take my submarine. We'll dock in Italy, and from there we can take my plane to Austria," Poseidon says as we are served a meal of a salad, followed by filet mignon and mashed potatoes, all washed down by a few bottles of wine between Poseidon and I as Aurora sticks to just one glass.

"A submarine? We can't take the bubble?" She asks.

"The bubble is just for short distance travel and you will be wet if we take it. The submarine is much more convenient. Don't fear, I've been using submarines for many, many years for traveling under the radar. It's quite safe," Poseidon tells her. "What is your plan in Vienna?"

"We have to follow my father's message. He mentioned the summer palace. I guess we'll have to find the palace, and hopefully we'll get our answer there," Aurora says to Poseidon and glances at me. I nod, agreeing with her plan of action.

"The summer palace is called Schonbrunn, it's a museum now. It actually has quite a lovely fountain dedicated to me. They chose to name it Neptune fountain. I always preferred Poseidon, it sounds…I don't know…" He shrugs his shoulders, and his eyes drift to the ceiling for a moment, and then back to the fork with a piece of juicy meat on it, "…strong. Oh well, it doesn't really matter what the name is." He waves the fork in the air, chewing. "I know that Clio is hosting a gathering of the deities tomorrow to celebrate the upcoming planetary alignment. She is the one you'll need to speak to."

"Clio, the goddess of history?" Aurora asks.

"She is a muse." Poseidon shakes his head, and his mouth forms a smile, but it disappears quickly. "What she lacks in beauty, she makes up for in unimaginable volumes of knowledge. She'll help you. Come to think of it, they were friends, you know, Clio and your father. She is the one who introduced him to your mother. I'm sure she'll be able to help you."

"That would be great," Aurora replies and takes the last sip of her wine. "Please excuse me, but I'd like to return to my room. I think I'm still rather exhausted from today's events." She gets up, and Poseidon waves to her as he pours himself another glass of wine.

"Of course, dear, go rest."

She glances at me as I watch her move so gracefully. I think I see her blush, but she turns away too fast. I listen how her steps disappear into the evening before I chug the last of the wine from my glass.

"You're in trouble, my man." Poseidon wags his finger, squinting one of his eyes at me. "It's about time you found yourself a woman."

I slam the glass down on the table and pour it full of wine again. "She is no woman for me," I growl.

"Don't make my mistake, Iraklis." Poseidon leans forward and looks at me from under his eyebrows. "When you find a special girl, you don't push her away because of personal insecurities. You hold on to her and make her happy. She is the one who will accept you as you are. Time with her will be a slow swim in the warm waters of happiness. Push her away, and you'll forever struggle to stay on the surface."

"You don't look like you are struggling," I zing him with drunken sarcasm. He stays quiet, not breaking off his direct stare, then he leans back and takes a deep breath.

"I know. I've learned to hide my unhappiness. I always thought that we'd have time for us, but now her time is up, and I, I have nothing else to look forward to." His head hangs low as he rubs his hands, then suddenly he gets up and sways, "I'll go for a swim." And he walks out of the house into the darkness.

A man and a woman, dressed in white button-down shirts and black pants, enter silently and start cleaning off the table. I take my cue and head back to the guest house. The air is thick with humidity, bats dash in the darkness between the trees. The island is loud with the sounds of birds and insects. I look up and see Aurora's shadow pacing the room behind closed shades. I pause and just stare. My heart starts to beat faster and the sound of it overtakes my logical thought process, drowning it out in the beat that pushes me to her. I run up the steps and knock on her door.

She opens it, and we just stand there looking at each other. I'm waiting for her to tell me to leave her be, but she says nothing. I don't know what I should tell her. So I stay quiet. I can't explain why I'm here. I just feel the need to be around her. I'm drawn to her presence, and I can't resist it. I don't want to, actually. I prop myself up on the doorway, I'm about to push off and walk away, but she reaches for my hand and puts it on her cheek and closes her eyes, letting me caress her beautiful face. My fingers slip into her hair, and then she opens her eyes, the emerald green fires of sweet wickedness flicker, pulling me in closer, and no godly strength can resist their force.

"Aurora, I..."

"Don't..." she whispers before she throws her arms around my neck, and her lips are on mine, soft and yearning, impatient, and I am thirsty for hers. I pick her up and she closes her legs tight around my waist. She pulls the t-shirt off me as I am walking us to the bed. My hands move all over her body, pressing and touching, taking off her shirt and bra, sinking my fingers into her hair. Her warm skin electrifies my body, sending chills that evaporate into the hot waves of desire that is leaving me breathless. We collapse onto the bed, and I pull down her shorts, finding to my delight that there is nothing else for me to take off. I take her long leg and rest it on my shoulder, and I start tracing it with kisses, teasing her impatience with quick flicks of my tongue. Her other leg hooked tight around my hip, her body gyrating slowly as I move higher to her inner thigh. She is stunning, her fiery locks spread like a wild crown and her cheeks are burning red. I grin in satisfaction. She licks her full lips and flashes a big smile, then pulls her leg away and wraps it tight around me, her hands undo the buttons of my pants and she drags them off me with her feet and then pulls me right on top of her. She is small under my mass, my body pressed tight against hers and I feel her heart beating fast, and mine responding, following her pace. She licks my neck, and then her teeth bite down gently on my earlobe, her hot breath reflecting off me. "You're mine," she whispers, and in this moment nothing else matters.

CHAPTER 22

AURORA

Two days before the alignment

I wake up next to Iraklis. The sunlight is creeping in above the treetops. Its soft and gentle glow fills the whole room through floor to ceiling windows. Tropical birds are singing their morning greetings, and the sound of ocean waves crashing against the shoreline soothes in a whooshing whisper, "Relax, relax, relax."

I lay still, enjoying the sounds. The steady breathing of Iraklis changes as he turns behind me and wraps his arm around me, pulling me closer.

Yesterday was overwhelming, the crash, the death of Iris, our unconventional travel through the ocean, all of it culminating in the surrender to my suppressed desire for Iraklis. Was it the right decision? It certainly felt like that yesterday. He stirs again and nuzzles into the back of my neck and then stills. I hold my breath, waiting for his next move that will determine our relationship. He sighs, and I know last night's good decision is today's big regret, at least for him.

"Aurora…" he begins as I lay there looking at the sunlight moving across the floor, not turning to face him, "are you awake?"

I give him a slight nod and wait for him to continue. He clears his throat and pulls me to face him. When I turn, I stare directly into his eyes, he is frowning, his eyes moving fast across mine, "Last night…it was amazing…it's something I was trying to resist…the attraction I've felt for you. It was wrong of me to act on it. Your father entrusted your security to me and…shit…I screwed up. You are not safe if someone finds out that, that we have something."

"You realize that you were not the only one who made the decision that led us here?" I finally speak. "But anyway, you don't have to explain why you can't be with me. We are adults. One-night stands are often mistakes." I try to downplay what has occurred, and hopefully it will ease the awkwardness between us. I need his help to finish the quest, we only have a couple of days.

"Aurora, I want you to know the reason, to understand that I care about you. I have many enemies. They'll stop at nothing to hurt me, and they will hurt me by harming those that I care about." He caresses my cheek, but I don't want him to touch me, it will only make my heart ache more if he prolongs this. I turn away from him and get up, the floor is warm from the streaming light, the rays have moved onto the bed and blind Iraklis when I get up. He moans, covering his face. When he finally looks up at me again, I am already dressed and heading out the door.

"C'mon, we have another big day," I throw over my shoulder and leave the room.

Iraklis meets me in the main house a few minutes later. The breakfast spread is plentiful, it can easily feed fifteen people. I make my plate and stare out the window where Poseidon is practicing yoga salutations. I feel Iraklis' gaze burning into me. I don't want to talk more about us. It's clear, he can't be with me. I just have to limit our conversations.

I take my plate, leave the room, and sit on one of the lounges by the pool. It gets hot, and the birds retreat into the depths of the jungle, only the ocean waves rustle, beating against the shore, whispering to me, "Fool, fool, fool." Damn it! I walk back into the house, Poseidon soon follows. He is dressed in just shorts that sit low on his narrow hips. His body is young and muscular, but his head is completely grey. He eats fast, humming something under his breath, and when he is done, Iraklis and I follow him to the dock where a speed boat awaits us.

"Climb in. The submarine is on the opposite side of the island in a deep lagoon. We'll get there in a few minutes." Poseidon gets in first and stretches out his hand to help me. The boat rocks, and Iraklis offers his arm to prop me up, but I ignore it completely and give my hand to Poseidon who smirks but says nothing, pulling me inside.

Once we are all on board, Poseidon starts the boat, and it quickly gains speed. The ride is a bit bumpy and I have to hold on tight to the railings not to lose my balance. Iraklis stays in the back. I know he is looking at me, I feel it, but I will not give him the satisfaction of looking back.

The boat curves around the island and slows down to enter a lagoon guarded by a mountain rising out of the water, covered in tropical overgrowth. Right in the middle of the water there is a beautiful, multilevel super yacht, white and sleek, like an alien ship. We pull up to a ladder in the back and two short, skinny men dressed in all white uniforms with skin dark with tan help us up. One of them then gets into the boat we came in and speeds away.

"Wait, this is a submarine?" Iraklis asks and Poseidon nods, rubbing his hands.

"Yes, yes, yes! It's one of a kind, no one else has it. Come, come with me. I'll show you everything." Poseidon is as giddy as a little kid with a new toy.

Poseidon introduces us to the staff, and all of us are ushered inside by Naomi, a petite woman with short hair. She is dressed in white pants and a button-down shirt that is gleaming in the light, the rest of the staff is dressed the same. The yacht is spacious. Luxury is felt in every detail. Redwood paneling and white leather on the inside are inviting. It rocks gently on the calm waters. It feels airy, and I take deep breaths in. Naomi leads and we follow behind Poseidon a few steps down where she points to the two doorways right next to each other. She opens one and says it will be my bedroom. The small, cozy room has a queen size bed made with white linens, redwood paneling from floor to ceiling, and a desk with a TV over it. I step inside and see that it has a bathroom attached to it.

"Wow. Look," I point to the ensuite bathroom to Iraklis. He smiles and Naomi says, "Yes ma'am, this yacht can accommodate ten people. It has a gym, a spa room, and a swimming pool in the back with a sun deck at the top."

I mouth wow again.

"Once we are out in deeper waters, we will dive, come below. I'll show you everything. Naomi, prepare for the dive." Poseidon says.

We take narrow ladders down, deeper and deeper where the ceiling gets lower and hallways narrower. It feels suffocating. I glance at Iraklis, he has to bend down to avoid hitting his head on different pipes and machinery. He looks like a caged animal and the cage is rather too small for him. I feel a pang of sympathy for his discomfort. The boat submarine starts to move as we get deeper into the bottom of the ship, but I don't hear the engines. Poseidon moves effort-lessly in this closed off space, ducking and turning his body sideways to pass in the narrow tube-like hallway. There is an aura of excitement emanating from him, he is almost skipping toward what I assume is the front of the submarine. "Here is the kitchen for the bottom crew and here is the bath-room," he points to the small spaces, "Here is the room you can share with Iraklis if you want to experience sailing as if we are in a regular submarine until we get to Italy, mine is right next to it. I actually prefer sleeping down here. And here is where it all happens, here is my command center as I like to call it," he says, showing us a small space with no windows, just a semicircular surface filled with buttons, levers, and screens where two crew members sit with their backs to us. In the middle of the small space, there is a periscope that Poseidon taps on proudly. "OK. Get ready, we will dive in a few minutes." He rubs his palms and puts on a white cap-tain's hat, standing in the middle of his command center.

"Already?" I say, feeling anxious in this closed off space as my chest gets tighter.

"Why? Aren't you ready? Stay here, you can go up to the higher level once we reach the necessary depth. I promise you'll enjoy it." Poseidon cocks his captain's hat to the side. He looks quite ridiculous half-naked, in only his shorts. I shake my head vigorously. "Don't worry, dear, it will take just a few hours, we are not that far off."

"That's one fast submarine you have. What is it, nu-clear?" Iraklis asks, looking at all the dials.

"No, no, mate. I don't deal with nuclear. It's a mix of solar and hydrogen, but I use my water powers to make it move much, much faster than it would have on its own."

"How do you deal with radar detection and military?" I ask.

"It helps to have friends in various military forces around the world, plus, don't forget, I command the seas and the fish. It's quite easy to trick the radar when you have those powers." He winks at me and fires off commands to the two-man crew.

I can hear the water beating against the metal. It moves higher and higher until the sound of it disappears, and now there is only the noise of the machine as the propellers start. There is an occasional knocking on the metal casing as we go deeper, the water compressing the submarine yacht and us. I feel the pressure building in my ears, I have to swallow hard, and then I open my mouth wide and press on my ears to release the pressure. I glance over at Iraklis, and he is pinching his nose, I guess he is subjected to the laws of physics as well.

"Sir, we've reached eleven hundred meters," one of the crewmen reports.

"Go ahead to the kitchen, guys, there are some snacks and booze there, enjoy while I perform my captain duties." Poseidon waves us off. I go ahead first, squeezing by Iraklis, trying not to touch any part of him. He towers over me, seemingly trying to make my attempt more difficult, and when I pass, he follows me.

I sit down on the hard, uncomfortable bench at one of the three tables and play with my fingers, thinking how best to pass the time. Iraklis sits right behind me, his back right next to mine.

"I had a wife once," he begins suddenly, and I tense up, listening, making sure I heard correctly through the noise of the propellers. "I had two children, Rhea and Alexander." I make an attempt to turn. "Wait, I can't tell you this if you are looking at me." So I nod and just stay turned away from him, letting him tell his story.

"We lived in Greece." He stops to chuckle. "Everyone seemed to live in Greece at that time. It was the center of the world. People flocked to learn the arts, to meet the scholars, to witness its richness and beauty. There is some truth to the myths. My father loved the women, and his wife Hera, hated all of them. And when she didn't succeed in destroying them, she made sure that no illegitimate descendant of Zeus stayed alive." He pauses and clears his throat, and after a deep breath continues, "Hera put a spell on me. It drove me mad. I had visions I was battling beasts and demons. I killed them all. I was victorious, but when my mind cleared, I saw the destruction I'd inflicted. My house was in shambles. My children…" he whimpers, "my wife, they were dead…I'd killed them." He takes a deep breath and then slowly breathes out. I make an attempt to get up, so I can sit next to him, so I can see his face, but he stops me once again, "Don't. I couldn't imagine my life without them, the guilt, I couldn't forgive myself. I stole a dagger from Apollo, a dagger which causes wounds that cannot be healed, and I attempted to take my own life. Iris was there. She stopped me."

"I'm so sorry. I didn't know. I can't imagine the pain you went through."

"Yeah," he sighs.

"I locked Hera up in the underworld to pay for what she'd done." His voice is tense and deep. "But I am still afraid, afraid that one day if I get close to someone I will be their biggest threat that they never see coming."

"You can't punish yourself like that forever…" I pause, looking for the right words. "It wasn't your fault. You weren't yourself."

He sobs, and then I hear him take a deep breath before he speaks again, "Every time I shut my eyes, I see their faces. How terrified they must have been…I can't…I can't forgive myself."

This time I get up and sit down across from him. His head hangs low, he doesn't look up at me. I grab his hands and he doesn't pull away. "You have a gift, a power, there is so much you can do. You need to know that. Your strength is not your curse. Our lives don't always play out the way we imagine. But it's up to us to either sail with the wind of change or against it. Hera is locked away. For all we know, the world as we know it will end in two days, if Enzio gets what he wants…" I stop and listen, waiting for his reply. I just gave him an opportunity, will he take the chance? Iraklis stays quiet, his fingers stroke mine as he stares at our inter-locked hands. His chest rises, he lets out a long stream of air through his pursed lips and looks up at me, "We have to be careful. I don't want our relationship to be in the open, not just yet." He shuffles through his backpack and takes out a dagger. Its handle is an intricate work of engravings of Greek Gods adorned with jewels. "Take it." He forces it into my hands. "Take it," he repeats when I push it away. "This dagger is your protection if…if I am not myself."

"It won't happen. I know."

"Please, Aurora." There is such sorrow in his eyes that I can't object any longer. I nod and put it away in my bag.

My ears pop again, I don't know if we are going deeper or if it's the opposite. My head feels heavy, and there is a sour taste in my mouth.

170

"I think I'm seasick," I blurt and dash to the bathroom. When my bout of vomiting ceases, I rinse my mouth in the tiniest of sinks and open the door. Iraklis is waiting for me, ducking under the doorway.

I manage to wave to let him know that I am fine before bile comes up again, and I turn to the toilet just in time.

I don't know how long I have been inside the tiny bathroom. I feel tired, my head is heavy, filled with the whooshing noise of the ocean. I know soon I will start seeing the green light, and my migraine will set in. My eyes are burning from the tears I can't control, my nose is running, and I feel I will vomit again.

"How can I help?" Iraklis' voice is muffled as he knocks gently on the door.

"I'm, I'm just gonna stay here for a while." My back arches again, the muscles of my stomach contract, twisting painfully, and I dry heave over the toilet.

"I'm going to be right here," Iraklis says, staying behind the door.

"Okay," I whisper and close my eyes before my head hangs over the toilet again. I feel weak. My body has nothing else to purge. My hands shake as I pull myself up to the sink and rinse my mouth. I open the door and find Iraklis standing there just as promised. I manage to give him a smile.

"My God, Aurora, you're so pale. Go lay down. Come, I'll help you." He scoops me up into his arms and has to shuffle sideways to carry me to the bunk bed down the narrow and low hall. He lays me down and puts a bucket on the floor. He puts a bottle of water to my lips, "Here, take just small sips so you can stay hydrated." I try to gulp it down but he quickly takes it away. "Small sips, otherwise you'll get sick again." My eyes grow heavy and after a few more small sips I drift off to sleep as Iraklis stays seated by my side.

###

I wake up as Iraklis moves hair from my face.

"How are you feeling?"

"Like shit. Are we there yet?" I reply, feeling groggy.

"We just resurfaced."

"That's good to hear!"

"Come, I'll help you. Poseidon is waiting for us to get to a higher level of the boat."

Iraklis gives me his hand, and I use it to pull myself up to sit.

"Argh! Can't we just come ashore?! I'll never go sailing again after this." To which Iraklis just chuckles.

When we finally climb up to the deck, the sunlight is blinding, the breeze is warm and pleasant. Our boat is anchored in a bay surrounded by other small and large white vessels that rock gently on the calm water. The seagulls' squawking is deafening as they fly to and forth between the ships and the town perched up on the green hill in front of us. Life is happening just as it always does and no one can even imagine the threat they are under.

Naomi greets us, smiling, "Once you rest and refresh, you can come to the dining room to get some food." She gives us a quick nod and smiles before leaving us.

"I'll see you in a little bit, I just need to take a shower," I tell Iraklis and playfully move my brows up and down. He frowns at first, but then smiles, "I'd love to join, but it would be best to not make us obvious, remember?"

"I know, I know. I'll see you later." I go to the bedroom that Naomi showed us before, close the door, and fall face first on the bed. The sheets smell divine of sweet citrus and mint. I take a deep whiff and then go and take a shower. I feel refreshed after it, and when I come outside, Iraklis is standing by the railing looking into the water. He turns his head slightly when he hears me coming, but then turns back and says, "It's so peaceful, isn't it? Everything just goes on, people are completely unaware that their lives are in danger. Does the weight of responsibilities pull you down, Aurora? Do you feel burdened?"

I come up to his side and stare into the horizon, "I don't know. I don't feel the burden. It's just something that needs to be done, and I believe that we can do it. I can't even think of failure, it's not an option for me."

Iraklis looks at me and smiles, "I like that about you. You are all in, fully committed to whatever you do. Come on, let's see what news Poseidon has for us."

CHAPTER 23

AURORA

Iraklis and I find an elevator and take it to the top deck. The staff members point us in the direction of the dining room, which is spacious and glamorous. Its walls are a dark grey color, a black, glass top table for sitting ten has black chairs around it. There is a crystal chandelier that illuminates the room, and the table is already set formally for just the three of us. There are two large windows on opposite sides making the space light and airy.

Poseidon walks in right behind us. He is now dressed in white linen pants and a long sleeve shirt unbuttoned almost to the top of his abdomen. A large necklace of shells is on his neck, he stretches out his arms and inserts himself between Iraklis and I.

"Friends, let's eat." He walks us to the table, where he sits at the head, and Iraklis and I sit opposite each other. Three male crew members also dressed in all white walk right in, bringing trays of food and place them on the table. They keep going in and out bringing more, finally leaving us after topping our glasses with water. My stomach rumbles, protesting at the sight and the smell of anything edible. I take a sip of water, then a deep breath, hoping that my nausea will not return.

"So, let me tell you about your plans for tonight." Poseidon's eyes drift slowly from me to Iraklis, making sure he has our attention. "Schonbrunn is closed today for a private event, the gala of the divine. The only way for you to get in is to have invitations, which were generously offered to me as I am one of the largest donors for arts and historical venue preservation. I have arranged for Aurora to be styled, have your hair and make-up done at a hotel not too far from the palace. Iraklis, you will have a tuxedo and please have my barber do his thing. You look like you spent months at sea without access to a comb or a blade. When you are at Schonbrunn, you will look for Clio…"

"Will she be expecting us?" I interrupt.

"I don't know. The news of your father's death must have reached her, but the relationship between you and your father was known to be rather, how I should say it…cold. So I don't know if she is expecting to see you," Poseidon explains.

"If the news of me being a suspect in my father's killing has reached her she will not trust me."

"You have a point," Poseidon strokes his jaw and his head bops side to side. "Your father trusted Clio, she has been the keeper of the Divine history, there is no one else who knows more about it. He knew she is wise and will do the right thing. You have to make her trust you. I see no other way," Poseidon says. "We will take my jet to Vienna in two hours, be ready. I'll arrange everything with customs, you need not to worry."

When we finish eating, Iraklis and I both go to the back deck, where two comfortable, large, sectional couches are arranged so we can sit facing each other. Right behind us is a swimming pool and a hot tub with clear blue water.

"How are you feeling?" Iraklis asks when we sit down.

"I'm good." I touch my stomach that is quiet and not causing any discomfort. "I'm a bit nervous actually, what if Clio won't tell us anything, what if I can't persuade her, what then?"

"If Clio was a friend of your father, I think we have nothing to worry about."

"I hope so," I reply.

In about fifteen minutes Poseidon comes for us, and we all get into a small boat that takes us to the shore. A black Mercedes awaits us with a driver dressed in a sharp black suit, white dress shirt, and a black tie. His eyes are hidden behind dark sunglasses. He doesn't say anything, just nods to each of us, and holds the door for me.

The drive through the city's small, cobblestone streets filled with cafes and tourists is slow. We get to the airport in forty minutes, a small jet plane with a dolphin painted on its tail waits for us with its engines already running. The captain and his copilot greet us with handshakes and as we are taking our seats Poseidon talks to them about the flight details. Once the plane starts to move, my heart begins to beat faster, my fingers dig into the armrests. I haven't recovered from the earlier disaster. What if scenarios play out in my mind, and I shut my eyes tight.

"Hey!" Iraklis grabs my hands, and I open my eyes. "It's going to be alright. Just breathe."

I nod my head vigorously, but my heart and lungs are not persuaded, continuing the fast pace. I forcefully breathe out slowly through my mouth and breathe in through my nose. Iraklis turns my palm up and strokes it in circles with his fingers. The sensation is pleasant, the spiral of his movement helps disperse my anxiety. He touches my scars and frowns. "If you connect these little lines, they will form a

176

meander, an eternal flow, a convoluted path of infinity. It is a symbol of love and friendship."

"A Greek key," I whisper, and Iraklis nods, smiling. I touch my medallion, the outer circle of which on both sides consists of the Greek key pattern. I take it off and put it on my right palm. Suddenly the lines on my palms light up, and the medallion floats in the glow. The engraved pattern on the medallion illuminates, and the circular ridges pop out of my medallion. I glance at Iraklis who looks into the glow of my hands frowning. I move my hands slowly, the medallion floating in between them.

"It looks like it's a…"

"Lock," I finish Iraklis' statement. "Look at these ridges, if this is the lock, there must be a key that fits it. What did my father say? Do you remember?"

"Eternal flow of Meander joins by two keys, in the hand of the true keymaker it will open the doors to death or salvation. Lead the morning light on the right path and it will show you the way," Iraklis recites.

"What are the two keys?" I ask out loud, but Iraklis just shrugs his shoulders.

"You are the only one who would know that."

I close my hand over my medallion and the metal of my mother's ring hits it, the idea pierces my brain. I open my hand where the glow appears again and I stare at the medallion and then my mother's ring.

"Take it off," I say to Iraklis and wiggle my ring finger with my mother's wedding ring on it. Iraklis obliges, removes it, and inserts the ring on top of the medallion. The Greek design on the ring comes alive, moving and flowing until it untwists from the ring and attaches to the edges of the medallion as if the two were magnets.

"It fits, it fits perfectly," I exclaim.

"Look on the other side, I think you need another ring to go here." Iraklis points to the other side of the medallion where the ridges came out of the surface.

"That's the place for my father's ring. It all makes sense. He said it in his message, 'two keys, one lock'. This is it, we have it." I close my hands, the glow stops, and when I open my palm, the ring and the medallion lay detached, back to their original form, as if just ordinary pieces of jewelry.

"Now we just need to find my father's ring and the helmet, and everything will be ok," I murmur and put the medallion around my neck, hiding it under my t-shirt, and the ring back on my finger.

"Keep it safe. Don't tell anyone. Do you know where your father's ring is?" Iraklis asks. I shake my head.

"We need to find it. We have to destroy it forever, so it can never be used again. The Titans will forever be a threat. They are powerful beyond your imagination, thirsty for revenge and will stop at nothing to destroy everyone. Nothing and no one will stop them once they get out." Iraklis takes my hand and twirls the ring around my finger. I nod, but inside I feel sad at the thought of destroying my father's creation, which connects me with my parents. I lean back and close my eyes.

Soon the captain announces our descent, and before long we softly touch down on the runway. Another black Mercedes delivers us to the hotel. The grand hall inside the hotel is busy with shine of baroque style. The walls are decorated with mirrors in thick, ornate, gilded frames, many statues are displayed throughout. The ceiling is painted with nude men and women, angels, and clothed old men whispering something on the sidelines.

Poseidon is greeted by all the staff we meet with cheers and hugs. He laughs rumbustiously, waving and throwing fist bumps. We linger a few feet behind him, trying not to attract much attention to ourselves. When he is done, he leads us to an elevator that takes us to a penthouse. When the doors open up, Poseidon stretches out his hand and strolls in lazily, nodding his head approvingly.

A butler appears quietly by our side and shakes Poseidon's hand. Poseidon pulls him in for a hug and loudly pats his back.

"Welcome Mister Don. We are happy to see you. Everything is arranged to your liking and we have followed your instructions and request for the visit. I presume this is Miss Kleidaras and Mister Dynamis?" The butler gives us a bow.

Poseidon covers the side of his mouth and says to us, "I go by Mister Don." I say hi and give Iraklis a puzzled look about our introduction. He stifles laughter and extends his arm letting me pass ahead. Our butler shows us the rooms that fit my imaginary fairy tale castle description. On the bed I find a gown and an invitation to tonight's event. I lift up the dress and put it up against my body. It's the color of deep green, with open shoulders, and a high slit in the front. Several shoes and purses are lined up for my choosing.

"Miss Kleidaras, your hair and makeup team will arrive shortly, I will send them up here if it is alright by you?" the butler says.

"Yes, that's fine, thank you," I reply.

He then takes Iraklis to his room, but after a few minutes Iraklis is back, chuckling, "Is everything to your liking, Miss Kleidaras?"

"What's so funny, Mister Dynamis?"

"These names, they have a direct translation in Greek, would you like to know them?" He comes up close and wraps his arm around my waist, leaning in close to my face, smiling wickedly.

"Yeah, tell me." I lick my lips as if he is a delicious meal that I am about to feast on.

"Kleidaras means keymaker." His lips are barely touching mine, tantalizing me, challenging me to make the first move.

"Clever." I smile, not giving in to his teasing. "And what does Dynamis mean?" I move my hair to the side and expose my neck. Iraklis is not giving in either, so I pull him down and kiss his neck, my lips barely touching his skin. His Adam's apple moves inside his throat as a moan escapes his mouth, and I smile in satisfaction. He throws his head back and laughs again, it's so contagious that I pick it up and laugh as well, wrapping my hands around his neck.

"It...it means power," he chuckles. When he finally stops, his brows come together, he clenches his jaw, his fingers slip into my hair, he tugs me gently back, "Which I seem to lack when I am around you," he whispers, before his lips finally meet mine, but a knock on the door interrupts us, and we pull away from each other. I go toward the bed, while Iraklis walks off to the window. I clear my throat before replying in an unnatural to me high pitch, "Come in."

Chapter 24

Aurora

"Your beauty team is here, Miss Kleidaras," the butler announces as he opens the door. He is quickly pushed aside by a very well dressed, handsome man in a perfect dark suit with a sheen, a large purple tie, and a matching pocket handkerchief that looks like it was tucked in with a purposeful messiness, and somehow it looks great with his bright pink shirt. His salt and pepper hair is perfectly slicked back, and has a trim beard cut with sharp detailed lines. When he smiles, his white teeth shine against his tan skin.

"My God! They didn't tell me you were this beautiful. Bella, bella." He walks confidently in wide strides extending his arm for a shake, "I am Massimo. I will create your look for tonight's evening." He shakes my hand and then twirls me around, murmuring while rubbing his chin, "Fantastic, bella." He then snaps his fingers, and in walk more well put together men and women. They chat in Italian, touching my hair, turning my face side to side, looking at my fingernails. Some shake their heads in displeasure, some nod in agreement. Others walk out and come back with rolled up objects. When they are unrolled on the bed they contain hair products, brushes, hair dryers, nail polishes, makeup, hair extensions, and jewelry.

Iraklis has been quietly standing, observing all the commotion, but suddenly he sneezes, and the small crowd of people who have been paying me all the attention stop and look at him. No one moves or utters a word until Massimo snaps his fingers and everyone starts working on me again. Someone is filing my fingernails. I feel my hair being curled, teased, sprayed, and brushed. Another person is applying makeup, and someone else is brushing a shimmery powder on my arms and décolleté. Massimo walks over to Iraklis, "Who is this gorgeous giant?" he asks no one in particular, "You look, so…so magnificent." He twirls his hand in the air, slowly walking around Iraklis as if he is a beautiful statue to be admired. Massimo's mouth is slightly open, his eyes shine, "You must let me cut your hair and trim your beard. I can't possibly let you go with your hair, like…what's the word?" He snaps his fingers searching for a term to describe the state of Iraklis' hair, "…like, like this. You look like a savage that will carry off this beauty with you."

"What's wrong with my hair and my beard?" Iraklis touches his face and runs his fingers through his hair.

"There is nothing wrong with your hair if you want to live in a cave, but it doesn't, it just doesn't work for this ball. Look at you, you must show off your divine features. Look at that jaw, my God, come, sit, sit right over here, trust me." He nudges Iraklis toward the chair pulled up to them by one of Massimo's assistants. I have to close my eyes for the makeup to be applied as Iraklis' face is wrapped in steaming white towels that seem to appear out of nowhere.

When my makeup is applied, I am pulled away into the bathroom to put the dress on. When I return, Iraklis is gone, and Massimo is gazing out the window.

I clear my throat, and when he turns, his brows go up, his mouth opens and Massimo prances toward me, clapping fast with satisfaction, "Bella, bella. I love it. You will be the queen of the ball."

"Thank you, Massimo." I smile and feel my cheeks burning. I hear the door behind me open. Massimo's face lights up even more, and I turn to find that it is Iraklis dressed in a tuxedo, his beard is trimmed and groomed, but the biggest change is his hair.

"You look…," I gasp.

"Doesn't he look like a Greek God?" Massimo breathes out. I bite my lip trying not to smile.

Iraklis comes up to me, his blue eyes capture mine hostage, and my heart starts to beat faster. I feel a heat wave rise as he takes my hand and kisses my palm without taking his eyes off me.

"You look stunning, Aurora," he says.

My skin erupts in goosebumps, "Thank you."

"Alright, you beautiful people. I've had enough of you." Massimo claps his hands high up in the air, and his team promptly collects their belongings and orderly march out of the room. Massimo bows slightly and takes my hand into his, placing a kiss on my knuckles, "You will conquer them all with your beauty."

"Thank you," I reply.

Massimo then straightens up and measures up Iraklis while pushing his chest forward. A satisfied smile forms on his lips, and he nods in approval, "You, you, just look at yourself." He brings his fingers to his lips and kisses them loudly in a chef's kiss. He then grabs Iraklis' hand and gives it a firm shake, holding his chin up high. When the handshake is over, Massimo takes Iraklis' arm and wraps mine around it.

"Go, go now." He waves us off, looking away as if we are his children leaving to a prom and he is a proud parent.

"Goodbye, Massimo."

"Thank you."

Iraklis and I bid our goodbyes and leave the room.

CHAPTER 25

AURORA

We arrive at Schonbrunn in a stretch limo with Poseidon, who is dressed in a tuxedo as well. I look miniature walking between the two of them, I feel so protected. We walk up steps that are dressed in a red carpet while photographers take our pictures, screaming out for us to turn and face their camera. There is a famous model with her billionaire husband walking in front of us, a recently divorced actress that made headlines with her tell-all book about her cheating ex-husband, a power player in Hollywood. A couple of reality show stars that pose to each photographer. They do not smile, each gesture, each turn of their body seems to be calculated and adjusted to show off the best version of them.

"Are all of them, you know, like us?" I lean in and whisper to Iraklis. He nods, "They are Gods and Goddesses and magical beings." As we continue moving up the stairs. Poseidon excuses himself and says that he has to do interviews for a few publications, and that he will meet us inside soon.

Once inside, we are offered Champagne, which I and Iraklis accept. We are then directed to the white and gold rooms, which are simply that, white walls with golden branches and vines draping over them, a simple yet luxurious elegance. Waiters dressed in black and white walk slow with their hors d'oeuvres. Most of the beautifully dressed women decline the food offerings, but my stomach rumbles from hunger, and I already feel the effect of champagne as my head starts to feel light. I motion with my index finger for one of the waiters to come over and when he lowers the serving dish and announces that he has mini crab cakes, I take two into my napkin. As soon as the waiter walks off, I stuff one inside my mouth and close my eyes chewing the delicious food slowly.

"Thanks," I hear Iraklis say, and when I open my eyes, I see him reaching out for the second piece, I frown and slap his hand away. "Ouch, woman," he says in a low voice, his lips stretch into a smile.

"Don't mess with me when I am hungry." I say and eat the second piece of crab cake.

"Come, you have to see this." He takes me by my elbow and leads me toward the double doors that open to the outside. I gasp at the view. The immaculate garden is divided into large squares that run parallel to each other with wide pebbled pathways in between. Each square is a green carpet of grass; each like a canvas, painted with pink and purple patterns of carefully arranged flowers by a masterful gardener. White statues are standing as a frozen audience to the beauty of this space along both sides of the garden.

"Who are these statues of?" I ask Iraklis as I pull him to explore the gardens of Schonbrunn up close. He shrugs his shoulders, "They are people from the myths."

"Did you know them?" My curiosity peaks as we stroll straight through the center of the garden. My head turns right and left taking in all the details.

"I knew some, I've heard of others," he replies with a slight smile. I wonder what he is thinking about. Is he remembering the long gone past? Is it possible to have memories from that long ago? "Greece was vast. It took months to travel from one end to another. Gods were drunk with the power, the fascination of the regular people. None seemed to question the longevity of that order of life. The Gods thought they would rule forever, and people relied on the Gods to be there for them, always. I believed it too."

"Why did it change?"

"I don't know, maybe because people changed. They realized they didn't need Gods, and at the same time the Gods realized how much they needed people."

"Hmm," I exhale as we stroll along the path toward the fountain at the end of it. When we reach it, I carefully examine this piece of art. At the top of the rocky composition, Poseidon stands erect, grasping his tall trident in his left hand. His nudity is covered by a carefully draped piece of cloth; he is looking at a woman at his right foot. I can't see her face, but her posture tells me she is asking Poseidon for something. Below Poseidon and the woman are large shells and men with fish tails instead of feet who are reining in the horses. The fountain exudes power and strength.

"Poseidon looks like he is a proper ruler of the seas here," I say out loud.

"This is Neptune fountain, actually," a female voice interrupts Iraklis just before he is about to say something. We turn around to see who the voice belongs too. She is a woman who is not afraid to show her age. Her hair, completely grey, untouched by hair dye, is neatly pulled up. Her dark eyes are curious, piercing deep without giving out their own emotions, lines fan from the side corners of her eyes. She smiles and looks at us with curiosity.

Iraklis lets go of me and walks into the embrace of the woman who is stretching out her arms to him, "So good to see you, brother." She cups his cheeks and her eyes examine details of his face, trying to decipher what he has been up to.

"Hello, sister. It's been a long time." His head hangs low. I can't see his face, but his voice sounds soft and kind. The woman is a bit taller than me, but even she only reaches up to Iraklis' shoulder. She puts her head on his chest and her arms come under his giving him a hug.

"I'm so happy to see you," she says, pulls away from him, and smacks his arm lightly. "Where are your manners?" She steps out and looks at me.

"Please forgive me, Clio. This is Aurora, she is…"

"The keymaker's daughter, of course," she interrupts him. She then comes up to me and grasps both my hands and lifts them up, looking me up and down with a smile of a long-lost aunt who is seeing her niece for the first time.

"I am Clio, my dear Aurora. I'm happy to finally meet you." She lets go of me and brings her clasped hands under her chin as her eyes fill up with tears. "I'm so sorry for what has happened to your father, he was a very close friend of mine, and your mother was like a sister to me." She tilts her face up to not let the tears roll down and ruin her makeup and after a few seconds she shakes her head, spreads her arms and embraces me, laughing softly.

"Hi," I reply. When she releases me from her hug, I glance at Iraklis and back at Clio again, wondering how these two completely different looking people can be related.

"We have different mothers," Clio explains, following my gaze. "But he is still my little brother. You both look stunning by the way. Why didn't you tell me you were coming?" She smacks Iraklis on the chest.

He cringes in pretend pain, but soon his face grows serious, "We believe Portus gave you something, and we are here to get it."

"Mm-hmm, mm-hmm." She nods. "I love you Iraklis but why would you think I'd give you something I was entrusted to protect?" She raises her chin up and folds her arms across her chest. Clio is clearly no pushover.

"Enzio betrayed Portus, he wants to release the Titans. We need Hades' helmet before Enzio gets his hands on it and goes down to the underworld to unleash the Titans."

"But he needs the key to unlock their cage. Does he have it?" her eyes dash to me.

"No, nobody knows where the key is." I decide to avoid telling her the truth that we have the partial key right on me. I am not going to trust a woman who I just met even if she is a muse and Iraklis' half-sister. She will have to show me that I can trust her.

"Well, if you don't have the key, you should worry about that first. If you don't have it, then Enzio is out there looking for it as well."

"Clio, Enzio killed Portus. He will soon figure out who Portus might have trusted to hide the helmet. He tried to kill us on the way here. Iris died. We are all in danger, nothing will stop Enzio," Iraklis speaks in a low, slow paced but soft tone. Clio shakes her head, stepping away from us.

"What is hidden should stay hidden. Portus trusted me to protect the helmet, Enzio will not find it, he can't."

"We need to destroy it, so it never gets into the wrong hands." Iraklis comes up to Clio and places his arms on her shoulders looking directly into her eyes. But his words don't seem to move Clio. She stays silent for a moment, looking into the ground, frowning, and then takes a step back away from Iraklis' hold.

"I am the keeper of history, and history always repeats itself no matter how much Gods or people interfere. We have to learn to let go and let fate decide the way it ought to be. The helmet stays hidden. Please excuse me now, I have to attend to my guests." She turns around swiftly and walks away from us. I step forward and open my mouth to try to persuade her, but Iraklis shakes his head, "Don't bother. I know my sister. She will not change her mind."

"But we have to get the helmet, the alignment is happening tomorrow. And why didn't you tell me she was your sister?" I nudge him into his ribs with my elbow.

"My father has a lot, a lot of children. We are brothers and sisters in title only. I haven't seen Clio in ages. I know her now just as I know many strangers in this room." He nods toward the palace.

"She didn't make it seem so," I wonder out loud, but Iraklis just shrugs his shoulders.

"Women's behavior is frequently a mystery. I don't know why the sweet pretense. Let's go inside and eat, we'll try to speak to her again together with Poseidon, she always had a soft spot for him," Iraklis says and curls his arm, offering it to me. I wrap my arm around his and smile at the tightness of the tuxedo sleeve around his bulging muscles.

Inside, the guests are directed into the grand gallery. There are a few hundred people there already when we get inside. I couldn't have imagined there were so many Gods and Goddesses, but here they are in this spacious ballroom, strolling and conversing with one another. I observe men and women with curiosity, trying to distinguish a peculiarity or an unusual feature that may give away their magical powers, but all of them look like ordinary, dressed up people.

The grand gallery is large, with tall ceilings, it basks in the golden glow emitted from multilayer candle shaped cones on the walls and two large gilded chandeliers. I can easily imagine this room during royal balls, filled with women dressed in beautiful ball gowns, elegant couples paired up, dancing the waltz. The light reflects from the large mirrors on the opposite from the windows wall, glistening in the golden stucco decorations. Many guests are looking up at the three beautiful frescoes depicting angelic like figures floating in the clouds.

"It's beautiful," I say, but in my head I have so many questions. Who are these people up there? How long did it take to draw them? How was the painter positioned while drawing? Was he standing on a tall ladder or laid flat on some sort of construction?

"These are the Habsburgs," Iraklis says and points to the ceiling, "They were the monarchs who had this palace as their summer residence. Queen Maria Theresa was a great fan of the Gods. She had this whole place designed with us in mind." He looks at me and chuckles.

"Did you meet her?" I ask.

"Yeah, I did. I liked to party, and the best parties were at the royal court." He shuffles from one foot to another, looking around. "Anyway, I don't like to talk about it. Come, let's find our seats." He heads forward as I stare at him, trying to guess what type of partying he did within these walls.

A long table covered with white linen stretches from one end of the room to the other. Golden chairs match the gold plates, candle centerpieces flicker, reflecting in the shiny surfaces. We stroll slowly, Iraklis looking for the placement cards with our names while I look around. I hear Poseidon laughing, talking loudly, surrounded by beautiful women who giggle, touch their hair, and send him longing stares. He seems to relish the attention. While my eyes move across the faces of all the guests I feel like I am being watched. An unpleasant sensation sends shivers down my spine. I concentrate and spot Clio standing next to a tall man dressed in a tuxedo, she is speaking to him, but she is looking at me. Her face is stern and her mouth moves fast. She is frowning, taking quick sips from her champagne glass. When our eyes meet, she turns her back to me, the tall man bends down closer to her, and a few moments later he walks out of the room. Something about that woman tells me that I have to be careful with her. I decide against telling Iraklis about my suspicions. I don't know how strong those family ties are after all, instead I will just keep an eye on her.

When all the guests are finally seated, I find that Poseidon is to the right of me and Iraklis is to the left. Poseidon leans in and chinks his glass with mine.

"You're breathtaking today."

"Thank you," I reply. In the corner of my eye I notice Iraklis turn his face away from me. His hands grip the fork and the knife so tight that his knuckles turn white. I place my napkin over my lap, and my hand slides over his thigh giving it a light squeeze. He turns to me, his eyes are a stormy blue sea, brows pressed close together. He glares at Poseidon who is now cheerfully talking to a beautiful brunette across the table from him.

"When I like someone, I don't go after all the other shine and sparkle," I lean in and whisper to Iraklis. When he looks at me, his eyes soften.

"I'm sorry." He shakes his head apologetically.

I smile at this giant of a man who proves to be more emotional than he wants to admit.

Clio sits in the middle of the long table on the opposite side from me. I catch her staring at me in between the elaborate meal courses. When she gives her welcoming speech, thanking the guests for their generous donations to her arts and history foundation, she looks nervous, she stutters, and takes breaks, sipping water out of her glass. To most people she appears nervous from the public speaking, but to me she looks like she is afraid of something else. She laughs between the forced jokes, her hands shake, she speaks fast, and she looks relieved when she is done with her speech. When everyone stops paying attention, I keep my eyes on her as she excuses herself and leaves the table, walking briskly toward the exit.

Iraklis and Poseidon are both preoccupied talking to their neighbors at the table. When I leave, they don't get suspicious. I follow Clio, the double doors lead me out to the white and gold room where we had our hors d'oeuvres earlier. I stand and listen, trying to figure out where she has gone. There are a few guests strolling around and admiring the room and several are out on the terrace. My eyes drift to the outside across the garden and past the Poseidon fountain; right there at the top of the hill sits a Gloriette. A structure with many arches supported by columns and crowned by an eagle, it glows white in the evening light. For some reason I am drawn to it and decide to follow my instinct.

Outside, the evening is cool with gusts of wind threatening a downpour at any moment. I take in my surroundings, listening to the sound of any stirring. I catch a shadow of a figure moving to the right of me, I recognize Clio right away. She walks fast up the hill along the dark side of the path.

I take the path to the left and move slowly so as not to attract any attention. I wonder why Clio is going to the top, which for now appears to be empty. The climb proves to be steeper than I expected. I'm getting hot, my back is wet, quickly cooled by the gusts of wind, making me chilly. Clio must be tired, after all she is older than me and heavier. I am not that far behind her. When she reaches the top, she pauses before coming out of the shadows. When she does, I can tell she looks tense, although I can't make out her face clearly. I see she hesitates before making each step, she twists her hands in front of her, turning her head quickly, looking around. I stay hidden, watching her, my heart is beating fast, my chest burns from the walk. I am panting. I cover my mouth, fearing that my breathing is too loud and she will hear me, but she doesn't. She keeps looking and a few minutes later, when nothing happens, she turns and starts walking back the way she came. I hear a sound that makes her freeze. It is faint, but I recognize it at once. It is the sound of flapping wings. I glance at Clio, she stops short and stands still looking up at the dark sky. I follow the direction of her gaze, but I see nothing, it is too dark, the sound of flapping wings is getting louder. Soon I make out a bird, it glides gracefully toward Clio, its wings move slowly, taking advantage of the wind. I know that bird, I saw it before, it is a falcon. I hold my breath and move deeper into the darkness of the shadows.

When the bird lands right in front of Clio, it takes another shape, a human form, it's Enzio. Clio rushes up to him, throwing her hands around him, laying her head on his chest. Enzio places his hands around Clio's waist. They talk, but I'm too far away to hear their conversation. Enzio's body doesn't give out any emotions, but Clio, she is easy to read. She gesticulates toward Schonbrunn, shaking her head. She then listens to Enzio intently, her whole demeanor gives away that she is taken by the man in front of her. He is taller than her, she looks up at him, her face doesn't move. Clio clasps her hands over her chest. Enzio places his hands on her arms, his face moves close to Clio's, he looks threatening, but Clio doesn't run, instead she nods her head fast in agreement. Enzio then embraces her, when he lets go, her whole body is leaning toward him. Her chin is up, she looks like she is longing for a kiss, but Enzio doesn't show her any tenderness. There is no kiss, not even a hug, instead he turns around, takes the shape of the falcon and flies off. Soon Clio is standing alone as the flapping of the wings grows more and more distant but she keeps looking into the distance, even after the bird has disappeared from her view. She touches her face, it looks like she is wiping a tear. What is going on between these two? Does Enzio have something on Clio? Does she have feelings for him? Is she not a friend to my father? Has he made a mistake entrusting Clio with a secret that was meant for me? I watch this woman slowly start her descent and I move down with a spring in my step, rushing to tell Iraklis that we can't rely on Clio to help us.

CHAPTER 26

AURORA

I linger behind in the dark so Clio goes inside first. I take a deep breath, straighten out my posture and walk inside slowly. In the periphery of my vision, I see Clio rushing across the gallery, ignoring friendly greetings from her guests. She grabs her purse, stops in the corner and dials her cell phone. She must be planning an escape, but where is she going? Did she already give Enzio the helmet? I search the room for Iraklis and spot him moving through the crowd. He is at least a head taller than everybody else and stands out like a lighthouse among the rocks. He moves slowly, but his pressed brows and stiff jaw tell me that he is concerned. When he sees me, his face relaxes for a moment, and he smiles, but the smile soon disappears as I can't hide my concern. His slow pace increases as he starts pushing aside everyone who is in his way. When he gets closer, I tell him everything. He nods without saying a word and places both his arms on mine and gently moves me aside.

"Clio!" his voice rumbles, and I jump from the unexpected turn of events. I thought we would just follow the woman and see where she would go, but as Iraklis said, he is more of the straightforward kind of man.

I feel everyone turn and look at us. Those who were still eating have their forks frozen midair to their mouths, their eyes dart from Iraklis and I and back to Clio. Those who were dancing stand still as the band continues to play for a few minutes at first but then stops as the sound of the instruments die down and there is complete silence, only interrupted by the sudden drop of a utensil.

Iraklis draws a deep breath of air through his nose and then slowly breathes it out. His eyes darken, his brows are in a tight knot. He lets go of my arms and his hands clench into tight fists. The room suddenly feels small and stuffy, the golden glow of candles darken. I turn around and find Clio across the gallery. She is no longer talking on the phone. Her eyes dash nervously across everyone's face, her chest rising fast, but after a few moments she steps forward. The sound of her heels echo in the silent room, her chin is lifted in protest, she marches toward us ready to attack. Iraklis and I remain where we are, waiting for her to come closer, she needs to cross the whole ballroom before she reaches us. She starts to speak before she is near us, her right arm extended and pointing at Iraklis with her index finger as if it were a spear.

"You cannot change the course of history, Iraklis!" she shouts. "What is meant to be needs to happen," she starts. I feel hundreds of eyes watching us, waiting, holding their breath until there is a definitive side to take.

"And who decides what is meant to be? Huh? You? Enzio?" Iraklis says.

"I've watched this world be destroyed by people long enough. They don't learn their lessons. They need structure, they need guidance." Clio finally comes closer, just within arm's reach. Her cheeks are flushed, her nostrils flare, her eyes sparkle with agitation and passion for what she believes.

"These are Enzio's words, not yours, sister."

"Don't call me sister. I've despised Zeus for a long time, but I will not do so silently anymore. I will no longer be the scribe of what is happening. There is a lesson that I've learned by being the keeper of history." She wags her finger at us, "Sometimes you have to wipe the slate clean and start over, because the do-overs and corrections just dirty the page even more. Everyone will hear me and know me as a great muse who turned the flow of history into its correct channel."

"But my father trusted you," I yell in desperation.

"Your father was a calculating man. He thought that I was the same Clio who was a passive observer of the events. The man had changed, but he didn't realize that others could have changed too. When he asked me to keep the helmet, I saw the opportunity that would decide our future. I'm glad he trusted me. It's fate that made him miscalculate," she speaks fast, her face and neck getting blotchy red.

"So you're willing to plunge this world into darkness. You want Enzio and the Titans to massacre millions. This is madness!" Iraklis says.

"No Iraklis, you are looking at it the wrong way. Remember all the human mass deaths…? What followed, huh? Prosperity, intellectual growth, it was glorious." She opens her arms wide and looks up with gratification as the faces in the crowd smile and nod.

"My father wouldn't want that!" I tell her, anger rising inside of me. Why did he trust her? He was always so careful about trusting people. It seems that I didn't really know my father at all.

"Your father had become too soft, he started to care about what's right, that humans should decide their own fate. But he didn't always have such high morals. He used to decide the fate of others. He locked up Gods without trial. All he cared about was his own well-being." Her eyes dart to Iraklis and he takes a step back. A wave of whispers rolls through the room as the crowd tightens a circle around us.

"He preferred everyone to have the freedom of choice, you sick, self-righteous bitch." I raise my arm and swing it at her, but Iraklis catches it midair. I jerk away from him, "Are you protecting her? She has a hand in my father's killing. She is conspiring with Enzio to destroy the world, and you," I press my finger into his chest, "you are trying to stop me."

"Awe! Isn't it precious, a lovers' quarrel," Clio hisses with a sweet pretense.

The air escapes my lungs. How could she have known? I look up at Iraklis, but his face is an unbreachable wall that doesn't give away his emotions.

"Did Iraklis tell you that he has commitment issues?" Clio continues with a devilish smirk in her eyes. "He never stays with any of his women. Many have tried, and he leaves all of them." Her pupils are large, small drops of sweat glisten by her hairline.

"Enough," Iraklis cuts her off, and I feel that the crowd is getting closer and closer to us, tables and chairs are pushed against the wall, and the dance floor is now empty. They are no ordinary people, they are not afraid. They are like vultures, looking to see who will fall and become their meal. We are encircled by the crowd, they are all waiting for the culmination of their entertainment.

"Why, Iraklis? You don't want to hurt your lover's feelings? If you are for the freedom of choice, why don't you let her know who you really are and what you did to your wife and chil—"

"I already know," I cut her off. She steps back, her mouth quivers. She is seemingly unsure whether to form a smile or to press her lips tight.

"Well, well…I see you are not bothered by a wife and children killer then." She waves her hand in a dismissive gesture of disgust toward Iraklis.

"Enough." A loud thunder of a voice rumbles through the room as the wind picks up, even though the windows are closed. Lightning strikes, everyone gasps and moves against the walls, yet not fleeing. When my eyes finally adjust after the bright flash of light, I look at the spot where the lightning has struck and where a cloud of smoke rises from the blackened floor. When the smoke dissipates, there stands a man. He is a mountain, that is the only word that comes to my mind. Just as tall as Iraklis, although his face bears more lines and his hair is dusted with greys, yet he is muscular. He is dressed plainly, in a pair of jeans and a checkered shirt. Small lightning flashes sparkle around his clenched fists, and he slowly moves his gaze from person to person while everyone is avoiding his.

"Son." He nods when he looks up at Iraklis.

"Father." Iraklis returns the nod.

"Zeus," I whisper.

"Keymaker." He smiles. "Greetings, vultures. I could smell your stink thousands of miles from here. You ugly beasts circling for an opportunistic meal." He raises his index finger, pointing at every person while slowly turning. He stops when he sees Clio, "My daughter, you've disappointed me."

"Don't call me that. You abandoned me. You've lost your right to call me your daughter." She points her finger at Zeus. His eyes soften for a split second, he takes a deep breath, and I see his jaw tightening as he swallows.

200

"I have abandoned the old ways. They are no longer needed. I'm no longer interested in that life. I want a simpler existence. You talk about humans as if they are unable to exist in prosperity without being ruled, but look at you…" He spreads his arms to the sides and makes a slow turn. "You, the Gods and the divine beings, you squabble, lie, and cheat. You look for ways to bring back the past even though history has told you you're no longer needed, life goes on without you. You, the great beings, are like mice who are scared of life as if it is a big hungry cat that will eat you alive. Haven't you realized that it's not humans who need us, but we…" he hits himself in the chest, "…we who need them. What happened, Clio? You miss the old times? You miss the sacrifices? The wars? Deaths? Illnesses? What is it you want? You need people to bow to you, to your knowledge? Speak now. Is that what you want?" Zeus' voice grows louder and louder. "The greatest power is in knowing that you can destroy it all yet having the compassion for life to let it figure itself out while you stand and watch as an uninvolved observer. I've done my part. I've locked away the Titans. You want to free them. You want to make Enzio God. He has shown little regard for the precious gift of life. He will eliminate you all, one by one because he will see you all a threat to his rule."

"That's not true. He, he loves me," Clio says.

Zeus slowly turns on his heels toward her, arching one brow high and rubbing his bearded chin.

"The Oracle, come forth," he says with a smirk and snaps his fingers. A flash of lightning forms next to Zeus. Out of it steps our ill-suited friend as if ready for a corporate interview, pushing his spectacles back onto the bridge of his nose. He digs in his pocket, swings his arm, and throws a sparkling fistful of dust in the air. Small particles glitter as they slowly fall toward the ground. Zeus opens his right hand and sends small electrical impulses toward the dust. It comes alive, the electricity magnetizes the dust and it moves to form a screen. I look intently into the golden, translucent screen and soon I see fires, scorched earth, and collapsed cities. Dark clouds are obscuring the sun and there is a mountain that rises from the black smoke. I look closer and realize that the mountain is made of dead bodies. I recognize my father and my aunts among the dead. Zeus' battered body is at the very top, even Hades has succumbed to death. Iraklis is there too, his body is covered in wounds and bruises and there in his embrace, I gasp, it's me, motionless and grey. At the very top, with a helmet under his right arm, and my medallion dangling in his grip is Enzio. He looks like a proud hunter who has killed the most valuable game. His right foot is on top of a dead Clio. Behind him there are more mountains of men, women, and children. The room fills up with gasps and murmurs. The dust screen sparks and falls to the ground.

"You fools, I thought I could leave it all behind and let you all just be but I was wrong. Your thirst for former glory brought the apocalypse to our door," says Zeus and the lightning sparks in his fists. "I should end you all, right here. At least I'll be merciful enough to make it quick. When Enzio comes to power he will make you suffer. You will writhe in pain like maggots in dead flesh and, he, he will enjoy your torment. Is that what you want? Answer me." His voice grows louder as he turns about the room. "Answer me you damn fools!"

"Brother," Poseidon comes forward with his hands up defensively. "Please, be merciful, all is not yet determined. Without your guidance certain Gods have lost the righteous path. We were not made perfect, we make mistakes. I think the Oracle's prediction opened everyone's eyes to what awaits us if we keep on aiding Enzio, am I right Clio?" When her name escapes Poseidon's lips all of the room's attention turns to her. She steps back nervously, "I, I…" her voice trembles and her eyes fill up with tears, "I didn't know. I couldn't have. He told me he loved me, he promised me it'll be better."

"Did you give him Hades' helmet?" I ask.

"No, no." She shakes her head. "I promised I'd give it to him today when I would steer the two of you in the wrong direction." She twists her fingers, her gaze is lowered to the floor.

"You have to give us the helmet now sister," Iraklis says and Clio nods as her head hangs low. He then looks at Zeus and gives him a quick nod. Zeus lifts his arms above his head and a ball of lightning forms between his palms.

"I am Zeus, the defender of all those who cannot protect themselves, the supreme of all that is divine. My time has come to pass on the burden to the one who shall continue being the beacon for Gods and humans. He shall defend those who are weak, guiding us into the future." He lowers his hands with the ball of lightning floating in between, its energy buzzing loudly. Zeus steps toward Iraklis and looks him in the eye.

"I pass on my power to Iraklis, my son, who has proven himself to be the best of us, yet vulnerable enough to see his imperfections and work on them." His voice is thunderous, it penetrates deep into my chest, reflecting within me, charging my pulsations with an energy I haven't felt before.

"Father, no," Iraklis says in a low voice. "I cannot accept your gift."

"This gift is not mine to give, it's fate itself who has shown me, that it's time. I'm ready and I know you are too. Take it and be the leader of Gods and humans," Zeus replies, his voice is low and deep. Iraklis glances at me, then back at his father, his Adam's apple moves in his throat. He takes a deep breath and gives a nod. Zeus smiles.

Iraklis lifts his hands and places them under the lightning ball. Zeus closes his eyes and starts a chant in a language I don't know. Small bursts of lightning erupt from the ball, the buzzing of it is getting louder, the air inside the room fills up with electricity. Zeus lets the ball of lightning float above Iraklis' hands and places his own hands above. With the last words of his chant, he slaps his hands over the ball. The electric sphere collapses over Iraklis' palms, sending sparks all around them, blowing out the windows and throwing everyone including me to the ground. When I open my eyes, I see lightning moving up Iraklis' arms, his body is tense as he looks upon the power that is overtaking him. The energy reaches his shoulders, it dives into his chest, and lifts him off the ground. He throws his head back, rips his tuxedo open revealing a glowing within his chest. He shrieks. I rush to him but I am thrown back by an invisible force when I get too close. I feel my body tingle as if millions of tiny needles prick the surface of my skin until it's numb. My mind races to decide what I should do. How can I help Iraklis? Is he in pain? Did he realize the agony of the process before he agreed to it? I look around to see if I can ask anyone else for help but everyone seems to be in a trance. Their eyes are either closed or transfixed on the light that is emitting from Iraklis. Their lips are moving, saying something that I can't comprehend.

I get up even though my body aches and make another attempt to get closer to Iraklis. Just as I take a step, another forceful flash of lightning erupts but now from Iraklis himself. I shield my eyes and look away from the bright light and when I look again, Iraklis is gone. Guests are cheering on and hugging each other. Clio collapses onto her knees in front of Zeus.

CHAPTER 27

AURORA

"I'm sorry father. I…I," Clio mumbles, avoiding looking up at Zeus.

"I know, Clio, it's not your fault." He offers his hand to her, which she takes, and he pulls her up to stand.

"Your feelings for Enzio are not your own. I sense there is an enchantment around you. Go make a call to Aphrodite and see what she can do about it. Go, go now." He pats her arm lovingly, she nods and walks off, dialing her cell phone.

I grunt from the aches in my body and pick myself up off the floor. No one comes to me to explain what has just happened. I'm overwhelmed by all the questions that are forming with the speed of light inside my brain. I decide to go to Zeus to seek my answers. "Er, Hi!" I extend my hand for a shake.

Zeus smiles big and grasps my hand. His large hand covers mine completely. He squeezes it and I almost wince from the firmness of his grasp.

"Well, well. I am honored to meet our new keymaker. I'm Zeus."

"Ah, yes, it's a pleasure. Can you please tell me what just happened and where did Iraklis go and when is he coming back?"

"I know you have a lot of questions about our ways. I wish Portus had prepared you better," he says and starts walking toward the patio outside, guiding me by my elbow to follow him. The crowd recoils, whispering as if a snake that retreats back, letting us through, they watch our every step in silence as we walk out.

I'm about to say that my father and I had a falling out and he didn't prepare me because he was trying to protect me, when Zeus cuts me off, "But he was a better father than he was a God. He loved you and cared for you more than his divine duties. I guess he felt he was protecting you by keeping you out of our world. Yet, here you are, fulfilling your destiny."

We make it outside and he makes a turn, leading us toward the green hedges. He stays silent and I don't want to be the first to talk. I feel he is taking me somewhere purposefully; it is not a stroll where our surroundings don't matter. I decide to be patient and wait for him to reveal what he has in store for me. We soon come upon a white structure with a rounded roof, supported by an arched entryway as if it was transported from the rising stone shore of Santorini. I vaguely remember the place from a trip to Greece with my mother and my father. I must have been seven or eight. I recollect the balcony of our white walled villa with a bright blue dome. Warm sun was rising from the sea, the glow of sunshine and the heat of its rays was pleasant and soft. All around me were traditional white houses, the color reflected the sunlight, keeping the inside cool even on the hottest days. I imagined that the sun must be happy to see the shores of Santorini every morning. They must look like shining stars to her. I would close my eyes and imagine myself a star that the sun was looking upon. I smile at the memory. A sound of cascading water reaches my ears as we get near a little white house. Zeus opens the iron gate for me and lets me inside.

The walls of the building are decorated with the carvings of large leaves and reeds peeking in between the tall stems. They rise all the way to the flower garland cut into stone that sits right at the top. Right across from us is the statue of a nude woman sitting with a vase under her right arm that lays on its side with water spilling out of it into a basin below. I gasp, instantly recognizing where I am. This is where my father wanted me to go. He wrote me a message, a puzzle that pointed to this place.

"Aurora, you have questions and Egeria is here to answer them," Zeus says, his voice is soft and kind.

"Yes," I whisper.

"Egeria was a nymph, the smartest of counselors. Many sought her guidance. Schonbrunn means "a beautiful spring," many royals used this water to satisfy their thirst, but this spring has much more to offer for those who seek it. Come." He pulls me closer to the statue. He touches the water with his finger and contrary to the laws of physics the rings of water start to form at the edge of the basin and move toward Zeus' finger. Small droplets of water separate and start to levitate above the surface as if they were soap bubbles rising, ready to float away. The water that was flowing from the vase now starts to flow back inside it. I feel the ground underneath me vibrate. Zeus closes his eyes and his lips move in an inaudible whisper. I grasp his hand when I start to feel unsteady, his face doesn't change, he continues his chant. I feel the strength of vibrations get stronger and when I look down I realize we are a levitating a few inches above the ground. I don't feel scared, instead of panic, I feel fascination. We float just for a few moments and when we touch the ground, Zeus opens his eyes, they are the color of steel, "Drink," he orders me.

I cup my hands and fill them with the flowing backwards water that doesn't seem to empty out of the basin. The water is cool and doesn't feel any different to regular water. I bring it to my lips and take a sip. When it enters my mouth, I feel every molecule of it permeate deep into my gut and into my bloodstream. It rushes to my head, attaching to my brain and there it shows me everything: the early times of Gods and humans and the most recent history. It gifts me the knowledge of languages. I see words and sentences, understanding all of them. It shows me my father hunched over the table, he is working on something. I am about to see it, but a voice in my head, it whispers, first weakly, but then growing stronger, louder into the chorus of thousands, yelling, "Keymaker's key, keymaker's key, keymaker's key." I turn around and when I look back my father is no longer there, instead I see fire and lava all around me. The heat is burning me, hot air enters my lungs singeing the skin inside my nose. Iraklis appears in front of me, he is doubled over on his knees. I can't see his face. When I run to him and try to lift him up, I shudder at the site of a dagger in his ribs, blood streaming from the wound, it has formed a red puddle that is reflecting the flickering of the fires all around us. I whisper the spell to stop his bleeding but the blood keeps flowing. Iraklis' skin turns grey and his lips purple. Despite us being surrounded by fire, his skin feels cool. Snowflakes appear from nowhere and swirl around us. They quickly cover the ground with a white blanket. The anger burns high in my chest. A stream of hot tears rolls down my eyes, a deep sense of loss fills me as I let out a scream, and Iraklis draws his last breath. Then a force pulls me away from him. Now I am a little girl, my mother and I are lying in tall grass. I am on my back, staring into the sky, trying to figure out what animals and objects the clouds look like. My mother lies on her stomach propping her head up with her arm. She looks at me with her dark brown eyes. They are so kind, with little crinkles in the corners because she is smiling. She doesn't say anything, but I know she is thinking about me. She is so young. Her fingers touch my cheek and then she places a quick kiss on me before rolling on her back and staring into the sky with me. "I love you Aurora, remember to follow your heart, the heart is the key," she continues to talk, but I'm torn away from her and thrown onto a rocky surface. In front of me are lush green trees as far as I can see, the sky is blue, the shrill of birds fills the air. I call out, "Hey!" and wait, but no one answers. I repeat my call, and still no one returns it. Am I the only person here? Where am I? But soon the sky turns dark, the wind picks up. I put out my palm to catch the white snowflakes that start falling, but I soon realize that those are not snowflakes, but ash. I turn around and there is a mountain of bodies among the rubble of buildings. I close my eyes and let out a scream. When I open them back up, I stand in front of Zeus. The water is flowing as it is supposed to into the basin from the vase, but I still feel the smell of burned bodies. I feel hot and I tremble as tears fall down my cheeks.

"What you saw is only for you to decipher. This is not what will be, nor it is what can be prevented. Fate shows you the possibilities of the future, the influences of our past. What you do with it is your destiny."

Zeus pulls his hand, closed in a tight fist, out of his pocket, and places it into my hand. "I finally earned your father's trust."

I look up at him quizzically only to find him smiling warmly at me. He opens his palm and I feel a small, cool object in the center of my hand. Zeus winks at me, closing my fingers over the small thing that he has given me. "I now place my trust in you to save us all." I slowly open my fingers, cautious and at the same time curious at what it is I now own. I gasp as soon as I see the metal ring that matches my mother's.

"My father sent you his ring?" I ask.

"He did. I received it yesterday." Zeus nods.

"Did he write to you? Did he give any explanation?"

"For once he was brief and his writing was clear. Here, you can read it." He passes me a white folded piece of paper.

I trust you will do the right thing.

I turn the paper over, looking to see if there is more, but it's completely blank. I return my father's note to Zeus, feeling disappointed yet again. I have all three parts of the lock, but I still don't know how it works.

"Don't wish for what you were not given. Don't regret what has become. You have it all right here. It's up to you what to make of it," says Zeus. I nod slightly and force a smile. I recognize the deep meaning of his words, but they do not make me feel better.

"Iraklis, where is he?" I ask as my voice shakes.

"Iraklis has been given a gift. Now he is being tested to see if he's strong enough to live with it or if he prefers the life that he lost a long time ago," Zeus replies as his eyes drift somewhere into the distance behind me.

"What do I do now?" I ask. "Iraklis and I, we had a plan, but it all came crashing down with Clio's betrayal. I have to come up with a new plan. The time of the alignment is coming."

"You know what you have to do." Zeus gives me a side look. There is no smile, no warmth in his voice. I swallow hard and make a decision to go back to Schonbrunn and find Clio.

###

Clio stands alone saying her goodbyes to the last few guests. She smiles to their faces, but that smile quickly disappears once no one is looking, she is twisting her fingers, biting her lip.

"Clio," I say as I march toward her. It seems that I have startled her, she takes a step back and looks around as if to summon someone to help her face me. When she finds no one, she hangs her head low and takes a deep breath.

"I need the helmet. Give it to me," I say. She nods quickly and when she looks up her eyes are full of tears.

"I am sorry," Clio sobs as her body shakes. "I made a mistake. I shouldn't have trusted Enzio, but…but it's been a long time since…" She looks up and lets out a forced laugh and then takes another breath before speaking again, "…since anyone said they loved me. It's lonely for us in this world. I spoke to Aphrodite, it seems that Enzio used a love spell on me but I suppose I was an easy target, all too willing to love someone."

I feel sorry for this woman. With all her powers of knowledge and history she failed to protect her heart.

"Are all the troubles resolved?" I turn around and find Poseidon walking toward us. I nod.

"I'll take Aurora to the helmet," Clio says.

"I'll come with you then," Poseidon says firmly and Clio doesn't object.

She has a car waiting for us outside. Poseidon takes the front passenger seat, Clio and I take the back. Vienna is already overtaken by the evening darkness. The drive is a quick fifteen minutes through mostly tight streets lined with parked small cars. The city looks clean and orderly. Nothing is out of place, nothing is flashy or loud. It seems so comfortably quiet. No one speaks until we park. Clio tells us to follow her when we get out. We clear the buildings after walking briskly and come onto a large square. In the center of it is a beautifully terrifying church. My mouth opens in awe as I look up at the black peaks of roofs, they look like tall, sharp, ragged edged knives piercing the sky.

"Ah! St. Stephen's. I remember the Danube River carrying the stench in its waters for months." Poseidon bunches up his nose in disgust.

"The stench?" I ask.

"There are crypts under the church. When the plague hit Vienna, bodies were stored in them. The corpses rotted until the smell made it impossible to be in or near the church. Then some poor souls were sent down to clean the flesh off the bones and stack them to make room for more dead," Clio says as we move closer. The church gets more massive and dark. The triangular roof is tiled, forming a detailed picture of a double headed black eagle with a crown over its heads.

"Oh," I say. "That's some dark history."

"It also has thirteen bells. Ooooooooh." Poseidon makes a pretend terrified face by lifting up his hands, shaking them, his eyes are big, but that quickly changes into laughter when Clio gives him a stern look.

When we finally make it inside, I am breathless as I suddenly feel small under the overwhelming beauty of the church. Even though there are few lights, their glow dances, reflecting in the golden statues, frames, and light walls that form sharp arches above us. It seems that the whole church is gilded. Dark wood pews line two sides, drawing the eye to the centered pipe organ and the crucifix. Each step echoes throughout. Groups of tourists walk around, speaking in hushed voices.

"Wow," I whisper, looking up and taking in the beauty of this church.

"Follow me." Clio takes the lead without looking around. Just midway through the church we come upon a staircase that can easily be missed among all the statues, decorative architecture, and the massive size of the building. Clio motions for someone and her driver walks up to her from behind us. I hadn't realized he had been following us all this time. She whispers something to him and he stands guard in front of the stairs as we begin our descent. The wide staircase soon turns into a winding narrow path, the temperature drops and the ceilings get lower. There are no adornments on the walls, just smooth brown stone that is cool and rough to the touch. Once we reach the bottom, the air feels thick, goosebumps erupt on my skin, thinking of all the dead that lay here. We pass small rooms on both sides of the corridor containing coffins. Small jars are locked up behind bars within carved out cavities in the walls. It's eerie and we all stay quiet. There are rooms with small barred windows, I peak into one and quickly step back, terrified of the skulls and bones neatly stacked up to the ceiling. I back into the wall. When I look behind me there is another small barred window, and behind it another room where the bones are piled into a messy mountain.

I gasp and Poseidon and Clio look back at me. "I wasn't prepared for the creepiness."

"Come here, it's this one." Clio stops in front of another door. She gets the keys out of her bag, the door lets out a loud screeching sound and she steps inside. Poseidon motions for me to follow before him. I take a quick glimpse of my surroundings, close my eyes and slowly breathe out. The room is full of bones. They are neatly arranged into a pattern, a row of skulls, then a row of long bones, followed by another row of skulls and then a few rows of bones, alternating in such arrangement all the way to the ceiling, forming a wall on all three sides. Clio takes a few skulls out and reaches into the opening, pulling out a smooth, shiny helmet and passes it to me.

"Here."

"This is it? This is the helmet?" I am surprised by its unimpressive appearance. The metal is smooth without any engravings, the front has the strategic curves of the metal that would protect the face, leaving only the eyes exposed.

Clio shrugs her shoulders.

"The Helm of Darkness," Poseidon says and takes the helmet out of my hands, examining it.

"You've never seen it before?" I ask.

"There are few who have possessed the helmet," Clio says. "The helmet to Hades is like the trident to Poseidon or the lightning bolt to Zeus. Come we have to get out of here."

"What do I do with the helmet?" I ask. "I'm sure Enzio will try to come for it now that it's not hidden."

"The sooner Hades is in possession of it the better." Poseidon passes the helmet back to me. "I'll give him a call." He runs ahead to get a signal on his cell.

"But what about now, how do I protect it so no one takes it away?" I ask Clio.

"You're the keymaker, you know how to keep things locked away," Clio replies.

I swallow hard, thinking of all the things that I don't yet know. But I remind myself that I drank from the fountain, I've been given the knowledge, and I have my powers. I hold my hands over the helmet and say the words that come to me from somewhere beyond my existence, yet I feel I've known them forever.

214

"I'm the keymaker. The wizard of locks. I lock this object to me until the true owner makes claim and I release it to thee." Just as I finish the words a soft light appears from my palms. It surrounds the helmet, elevating it and, as seconds go by, the helmet slowly fades away until it vanishes as if it never existed. The light dims slowly and when it's gone completely I dust my hands, look up at Clio, and shrug my shoulders, "You're right. I know how to do it."

She presses her lips tight, nods, and heads up the steps.

We leave the church and decide that it's best to return to the hotel.

I take a shower, change and go downstairs to eat and have a much needed drink. The hotel's restaurant is busy and there is a small crowd waiting for a table. The hostess offers me a spot at the bar which I accept. I order a martini and play with a napkin while waiting.

"He'll be back soon. He'll struggle, but he'll make the right decision." I turn around and see Zeus sitting a seat away for me, with a pint of dark beer in front of him.

"Where is he? Why won't you tell me?" I ask.

"Everyone is sent on a different quest to prove their worth. I have no idea where he is." He takes a large gulp of his beer, looking ahead, his eyes squinting mischievously.

"How come I wasn't sent on a quest?"

He stares at me for a long time without saying a word, then takes another big gulp of beer and says, "You will have your quest."

CHAPTER 28

IRAKLIS

I've accepted the transfer of power from my father. Where did it take me? Do I want to know? I stare into the darkness. Although the ground underneath me is firm, I feel slightly dizzy from the inability to see my surroundings. My ears perk up at distant sounds of men and women screaming and moaning in pain. The air is thick with heat and humidity, it stinks of rot and burned flesh. I don't need my eyes to tell me where I am. I've been here before. It's hell, the underworld, Tartarus. It's the place where wicked souls are abolished for endless torment.

I felt I was ready, but now I am not so sure. I know I will be faced with a challenge before the transfer is complete. I will be judged by the higher power if I am fit to face life with the new abilities that my father has given me. My mind then trails off to Aurora. I left her surrounded by strangers, possibly enemies. She is unprepared, she is defenseless. I need to figure out what I am doing here so I can return to her. We still need to stop Enzio.

Just then I notice a stirring a few feet away from me. My eyes begin to adjust to the darkness, but I can't yet make out what I am seeing. Is it an animal or a person? The stirring object shifts, it is small, dressed in grey rags. It whimpers and comes out of the shadow. It is a woman.

"Who are you?" I speak loudly and the woman shivers into an even smaller shape than before. "Don't be afraid," I speak softer and slowly step forward and then bend on one knee in front of her. "I am Iraklis."

The woman cries, the sound is barely audible, but it grows stronger, louder, angrier, her nails scratch the floor, she growls, raising her head. "I know who you are, bastard."

I bolt from the small woman. I know instantly who she is. That mad laughter has been the sound of my nightmares.

"You!" I gasp.

She rises up. The Queen of Gods, the wife of Zeus, Hera, my nemesis, the woman who hated me for simply existing. The one who stopped at nothing to end me, she couldn't kill me, so she went after my wife and children, worse yet she made me their murderer. I hate her for that. I loathed her existence. Yet death would be too simple of a punishment for her. My father could no longer look at Hera after what she'd done. He left Greece, but only after he asked for my forgiveness. He lingered in front of me, his lips ready to ask for mercy for the woman that was his wife. At the end he had no strength to say it out loud, and I knew I would find no mercy in my soul. He never asked about her fate. I orchestrated her banishment to Tartarus. I wanted her to pay for what she had done. I wanted her to be tortured endlessly, forever.

She stands before me, a shadow of the woman she once was. Her face is gaunt and her once luminous skin is grey, covered in deep wrinkles and sores. Her arms are bony extensions with twisted hand joints. Her hair is a grey, stringy mop and not the long, dark, thick braids that used to sit like a crown on her head. She makes a step forward with an out-stretched hand toward me, but moans in pain and collapses to her knees. Her dirty fingers digging deep into the ground as her arms shake. Her skin is covered in old scars and fresh wounds.

"Help me," she says in a trembling voice, "Help me," she repeats.

I shake my head and move away from her.

"Pleeeaaase, before it starts again." She lifts up her head and looks at me. Her eyes are red and swollen, tears roll down her face. She crawls toward me slowly, her face grimaces in pain with every move. She extends her arm to me again. "Pleaaase."

"No." I shake my head, get to my feet and turn to walk away. I don't want to know what she is terrified of. I asked fate itself to choose the punishment. I don't want to know what it is. I am able to take just a few steps into the thickness of the dark when a deafening scream pierces me to the bone.

I turn around to find Hera still on the floor, but her arm is bleeding as she sobs, staring at it. I come up closer and see that a chunk of flesh is missing from her left forearm. A pulsating stream of blood gushes from the severed blood vessels. I tear off a sleeve from my shirt and throw it to her to wrap around the wound. I hate the woman and this is as much as I want to do for her. I want to leave her, I don't want to know what tortures her. What she did to me and my family is unforgivable, she deserves what she got.

She flinches, but takes the piece of the shirt and begins to blots her wound. I turn around and walk away, but I hit an invisible wall that doesn't let me go any further. I push, punch and kick all around, but I can only make ten steps in every direction and no more. I sit down on the floor, breathless, my sweaty back is against the dark wall that doesn't let me leave this dreadful woman. I close my eyes and sigh, then another bone chilling shriek comes from Hera and when I look at her, a piece of her cheek is missing as she tries to cover it with her hands. She shakes, crying, blood streaming through her fingers.

"You deserve it all," I say through my teeth.

"I...I...all I did was love your father." She manages to say between her sobs. She moves her hand away from her wound and the flesh on her arm has already healed and is starting to heal on her face. She looks up at me with tears in her eyes. "Do you know what it's like to love a man who doesn't love you back? Huh, Iraklis? Your father took any woman that he wanted, while he expected me to stand by his side and be a devout wife."

"That's not my problem," I say, closing my eyes again.

"All I wanted is for him to look at me like I was the only woman in his life, that my children and I were his world, but no." Her voice is a low whisper, "He bedded women, he made children and then he recognized them as his own and I, Hera, was to turn a blind eye."

"I still don't care," I grunt.

"When you came into the world," she continues, "I had never seen your father that happy. He bounced with joy. He saw something in you that he'd never seen in his children with me. He was hopeful, he looked ahead into the future, not fearing it, but wanting to create a better world for you. I was foretold when you had children of your own that you would bring on a change to the world, that you would have Zeus' powers, that the way of the Gods would be forgotten. I just wanted to protect everyone," she gasps, crying out.

"You murdered my family so you could preserve your…your lifestyle…you…you vile woman," I spit, feeling my body heat up as anger rises in me.

"I didn't want to do that…I didn't, believe me." She crawls to me fast and touches my arm from which I jerk away. "I asked Poseidon for help and he gave me a potion. He said if I gave it to you, you would step off the path of your destiny, that you would not even want to be a God yourself. I…I would never want to kill a child. I didn't want to murder your wife." She is screaming the last words, she is breathless, she stares at me without blinking.

"You've gone mad in here. Now you blame Poseidon for your devious act?" I say through my teeth, pressing my fists into my eyes.

"You have to believe me. Poseidon is the one who did this," she screeches.

"I don't have to believe anything you say," I groan. Hera shrills in an animalistic high pitched voice and when I look at her, a gashing wound has formed on her chest.

"What is happening? Why are you getting these wounds?" I finally succumb to my curiosity.

"This is my punishment." Her eyes dart at me. She looks pitiful, her hands pressing against the torn off flesh. "These wounds appear and then heal, but the pain, the pain is always there. It burns like fire, piercing, it throbs through my sleep. When I wake up it stabs me, taking my breath away. Pain is the only sensation that I've known for all these centuries." She fixes her rags, covering her wound as if she has revealed something too intimate to me. There is something that starts to tug at my heart, weighing it down. I realize that I am starting to feel bad for Hera. I'm starting to doubt my choice of punishment for her.

"You took away something so precious from me. I wanted you to know my pain," I tell her, there is no anger in my voice, I am relaxed as I stare at her.

"You called for fate to decide my punishment and I accept what I've been given, but why are you here?" she whispers and crawls away from me, her head trembles, her eyes are full of fear.

"I'm not here to hurt you Hera." I calm her. "Zeus stepped down and I have been given his powers. Fate has sent me here on my initiation quest."

"Zeus has given his power freely?" she asks.

"Yes."

"Then the prophecy was true, only…only I thought it would mean something else, something terrible."

"A lot of things have changed for the Gods. We are no longer the beings that people look up to. There are no sacrifices, and temples are filled with tourists. We hide our powers, we do not rule, we are not supreme."

"Oh," she says. "And you and others agree with this?"

"I thought we did…but the alignment of the planets is coming and some are looking to release the Titans," I tell her. For some reason I feel at ease talking to her. I don't feel threatened. I don't perceive her as a mortal enemy. She is a woman scorned and she has been punished for centuries. Will I ever feel satisfied that she was hurt enough? Probably not. But maybe there is another way of thinking about it. Maybe I should consider if she's had enough?

"Who is seeking a change?" Hera asks.

"Enzio," I reply.

"Enzio? The messenger?" She frowns and bites her lip. I nod affirmatively. "No, no, it can't be, it can't be right."

"He killed the keymaker," I tell her.

"There must be another who is hiding behind him. It has to be Poseidon. It has to be." She curls her hands into fists and presses them into the ground.

"Don't you dare speak ill of him. We have his support against Enzio. He is a trusted friend Hera," I snap at her.

"No, no, he is wicked. He is just waiting for a chance, for a moment to strike when you least expect it. Believe me," she pleads.

"Enough of your madness," I growl and she moves away, curling up into a small ball, shaking.

Another scream escapes her and she lunges forward, writhing on the ground, contorting her body. There is another gash on her upper back, one she can't reach. I go to her and help her get up. I tear off another sleeve, apply pressure to the wound, and whisper the words taught by Artemis herself to ease the pain of injuries. Hera's breathing steadies and her body relaxes.

"Thank you," she says softly.

"I know I will never get my family back. I know I'll never forgive myself but I have to forgive you. My pain made me blind. But your torture will not return my wife and children to me. I promise I'll no longer be the judge and executioner. I release you Hera," I say. She doesn't look at me. Her body begins to tremble and I realize she is crying. She collapses to the ground, pressing her arms into it, lifts up her fists full of earth, and raises them up.

"With this earth that has been soaked with my blood, I, Hera, relinquish my powers. My soul is unburdened by the guilt. I've paid for my sins. I wish to be the light. I want to guide those who are led astray and give them a shimmer of hope when all is lost." She looks back at me, her face is calm, tears flow down her cheeks, but she is smiling. The darkness above us parts. A ray of sunshine pierces through up above, it moves like a searchlight until it finds Hera. It covers her in its glow and she stretches her arms up. Her grey skin turns a healthy color, her wounds and scars disappear, long dark hair flows down her back, and her rags turn into a golden tunic. She keeps crying, her lips are moving, but I am not able to make out the words. The golden dust within the light lands on her and she herself begins to transform into a golden shimmer that travels up with the light. Just before she disappears completely, she looks at me, and her gaze is full of worry. "Don't trust Poseidon, Iraklis and don't forget the light that you carry in your heart, it will shine on the right path for you." She is gone after she utters the last word. The beam of light grows bigger, filling the space that dissipates like black smoke. I am all of a sudden on a field of dark green, tall grass, just like the one I used to have in front of my house, many, many centuries ago.

And just like then, the smell of fresh bread enters my nose and I hear children's laughter, the laughter of my boys. I hear my wife calling them for dinner. I turn around and it is like I've never left. My house, the one I built with my bare hands, sits in the midst of the green. My sons race across the field toward their mother who is waving to them. They do not see me. I want to call out to them, but my throat constricts as tears pool in my eyes and I laugh with the joy of seeing them.

"They are happy." A familiar voice says behind me and I feel a hand rub my back. "Stop blaming yourself, friend. There is much joy that awaits you among the living. Unburden the dead and your soul will be light and be free."

I turn around to face my friend, Iris, who I've missed more than I was willing to admit to myself.

"Iris, am I glad to see you." I pull her into a hug as she laughs. I savor the embrace, burying my face in her shoulder. I take a deep breath, but stutter as the sob tries to escape my chest. I close my eyes tight and cough to hide my emotions and when I pull away and look at her, I smile. I squeeze her arms, she feels real, warm, and soft.

"Now, now. Don't you get all soft with me." She pats my chest. "Come, I want you to see." She takes my hand and leads me toward the house. I pull away, hesitant. "They won't see us, but you need to see their happiness." She pulls me and this time I follow her. The sun shines warmly as it is getting lower on the horizon, the smell of wild flowers fills the air. As we get closer to the house, I recognize the smell of lamb stew, my favorite that my wife used to have ready for me as I would come home. My boys' voices are loud and happy, they play with their wooden swords in front of the house, and my wife claps, cheering them on.

"Don't they miss me?" I ask Iris without taking my eyes off my family.

"You left your wife's warm bed this morning with a promise of coming back. You kissed your boys as they lay asleep, exhausted from the day before when you chased them across the field, teaching them to throw a spear. You went hunting and they know that you are coming back tonight. They are filled with hope that tonight will be just like any other evening, happy, and tomorrow their day will play out the same again. And they will never be bored or get dull, or question any of it, because for them days like this one are the happiest, this is what fate gifted them in the afterlife."

"This is what happiness is?" I ask.

"It is for them," she replies, smiling, looking at my family.

"What will mine be when I die?" I ask Iris.

"You'll decide and fate will deliver." She glances at me with a mysterious side eye.

"If I come up to them and touch them, will they feel nothing?" I take a careful step forward.

"It will be a pleasant warm breeze that will carry your scent and they will know that you're returning to them soon, but no more."

I look at my family that I've lost and then back at Iris. She must sense my hesitation because she smiles warmly at me and gives me a reassuring nod. My next step is a confident one, then the next one comes faster, and the next thing I know I am running to them, my chest is quivering and tears run down my cheeks. I gasp for air and I smile as I get closer. I can make out the details of their faces: my youngest son's freckles over his nose, my older son's scar over his brow which he got when he fell and split his skin, my wife's beauty mark over her shoulder that I loved to kiss and she would giggle with joy. They smell of bread, fresh air, and salty sea. I fall in front of them to my knees and shudder in tears, asking for their forgiveness, telling them how much I've missed them. I lay my head on my wife's lap as my boys sit by her side, looking to the horizon, waiting for me and I just keep saying to them, "I am here, I am here, I am here." But soon the sun disappears and they decide to go inside, "Come kids," my wife says, "let's eat and lay down to rest. Your father will be home at midnight."

I rise up and follow them inside. I sit at the table as they eat. I listen to their stories and the adventures of the day that has passed. I walk with my sons as they bring water into the house and I kiss my wife's beauty mark as she cleans the table. I am there to tuck my sons into bed and kiss their foreheads.

When my wife lays her head on the pillow, I blow out her candle, and kiss her gently on her lips. She touches them and smiles. I wonder if she is thinking of me when she closes her eyes. In the moonlight streaming through the window she lays peaceful, beautiful, real and I wonder what our life would have been like if I didn't do what I did. I lie down next to her, breathe in the scent of her hair, and squeeze her tight, saying again, "I'm sorry." I wonder if I will ever feel that I've said it enough times. The moon rises higher and the room grows darker. I don't want to leave them. I cherish this gift that fate has given me, but as I look up I see Iris floating right above me, surrounded by a soft glow.

"It's time," she whispers. I nod and give my wife a last embrace, get up, and kiss my boys before I walk out without looking back.

I look up at the sky, close my eyes and take a deep breath of air.

"What now?" I ask.

"You know the task ahead, fate will deliver you to where you have to be, but there is no more looking back, only the road ahead matters and what you do along the way. The future of the Gods is in your hands, help those who need it, guide those who are lost onto the right path. Ask for help. The burden you are asked to carry will be easier if it is shared. There are people who will happily share it with you."

"Aurora?" I look at my friend.

"She needs your help the most, for she is the key to saving us all right now, and she is your salvation to start anew. You must not be afraid to let her into your heart."

"Iris, I have much doubt in my ability to save anyone, yet I have accepted the power and now I must persevere, but I'm afraid that for Aurora to be safe, we'll have to keep our

226

distance from each other. She will never be safe by my side," I say grimly.

"You can't push people away to protect them. Love makes you strong, it gives hope and it will—"

"It will always make someone jealous, someone will always want to take it away," I cut her off.

"No, no." She shakes her head vigorously and puts her hands on my cheeks. "Don't let your enemies poison your future. You have to have the courage to let yourself be happy again. This is how you win," she says with firm conviction. "It's time. You have to go. You will come out a different man."

"And you?" I ask.

"I'm living a dream." She laughs softly and looks up at the sky. "I can shine the light on my friends from here when they need it most, and I can put a spotlight on the enemies when they least expect it. I will look after you, my friend. Go!" She pulls me toward her and kisses me on the forehead. I close my eyes, taking in her words, trying to remember her just as she is right now, hopeful, strong, and full of light, my friend.

"I'll miss you," I murmur and when I open my eyes she is gone, only a cloud of fireflies floats above the tall grass but soon all disappears out of view. Something traps my legs and suddenly I am pulled down into the depths of Tartarus. I'm dragged with force and I'm unable to move my arms or legs, unable to fight off my invisible captor. I can't make out my surroundings. There is no light in the pitch black, it's just getting hotter, and harder to breathe as the air burns my lungs. Finally, I am slammed onto the ground. I get up and swing my arms, trying to punch what has brought me there, but my fists move freely through thick and humid air, unable to deliver any punches because there is nobody there. I am in the depth of Tartarus.

CHAPTER 29

AURORA

One Day before the alignment

"Here." I hand over the helmet to Hades. He extends his trembling, bony hands to me, his eyes are those of an excited child who is receiving a gift he was hoping for.

"Thank you," he breathes out.

"I hope it will forever be in your possession?" I tease him. He glances at me and nods, smiling, he mumbles something indistinguishable and the helmet disappears into black smoke.

"You will always be a welcomed guest in my kingdom. Here, if you ever need to cross the river Styx." He takes my hand and places something into it, pushing my hand closed tight. I look at him puzzled, but he just looks at me with a mysterious smile. When I open my fist there is a heavy, gold coin in my palm. I look up at Hades for an explanation.

"You'll need to pay Charon, the ferryman to cross the river, he'll accept this as payment. And this…" He places a thick, heavy bracelet on my right wrist. "This will shine bright in my kingdom and blind Cerberus, my guardian dog so you can pass to the world of the dead and complete your mission. Just raise it high above your head when you need its light."

I stare at the intricate and delicate craftsmanship of the bracelet. At the center of it, there is an engraved star with its long rays extending out, wrapping the curve of the bracelet, with smaller jewels of stars glistening in the exquisite piece. "I'll make sure you're not bothered by the dead and the demons on your descent. I wish you well on your quest and hope you'll succeed against Enzio. I feel for him, but even I concede that the time of Gods is no more. We must forget our pride and glory and let the humans craft their own fate."

"Why can't you take me to the underworld?" I ask him.

"You need to take a leap, that's the only way for you to enter."

"What do you mean?" I grow impatient with how elusive he is of direct answers.

"You have to travel to Greece, to the ancient town of Tenarus. There you will find a hidden entrance to my kingdom. You must leap into it and only then will you arrive in the underworld," Hades speaks, walking circles around me and as soon as he says the last words he disappears into smoke.

"Well that's great. What does he mean leap? Just jump into it? Trust Hades, he just told me how to kill myself so he will have one more soul, and look at me I will go and do it," I say to myself, wishing Iraklis was here with me so he could calm me down, and I could lean on him for support.

###

I see Poseidon and tell him of my traveling plans, he offers me his jet without hesitation, and I feel better when he tells me that he will go with me.

A few hours later we are up in the sky. Poseidon stays in the cockpit and I take him up on the offer of taking the bedroom and getting some much needed sleep. When my eyes shut, I dream of a dark, cold place, water splashing against the cave, echoing throughout. I am rocked in a long boat on an underground river. A tall figure paddles a large oar, his back is toward me. He doesn't say anything and I am fearful to ask. I listen to the water and put my hand down to touch it. It speaks to me in whisper, "Sleep, forget, let it go." It lulls me and my fingertips almost touch the surface giving in to the powers that I don't control.

But suddenly I am jerked back down, the bony hand of a ferryman is on my shoulder, his face is concealed by a large hood but in the depths of it his eyes glow icy blue. "Don't listen to the river. The river Styx carries the water of Lethe, the river of forgetfulness. Drink from it and you will forget about everything."

I nod to him and sit back down, now looking ahead. I think of my mother and father and wonder if that's the same journey they took when they passed away. Were they scared? Did they know that they were no longer coming back to the world of the living? Were they thinking of me? All these questions weigh down on me, pressing onto my chest. I gasp for air, and my eyes fill up with tears.

"Who are you?" I ask the ferryman.

"I am Charon. I carry the souls of the dead to the shores of the underworld," he replies without turning to me.

"I am—"

"—Keymaker," he interrupts me.

"How do you know?"

"My queen of the underworld, Persephone has told me. I care not for the troubles of the living but I would never refuse my queen's request." He continues to paddle. "Acheron river flows into the river Styx as well and bathes everyone in its misery." Charon turns around, piercing me with his icy gaze. "Great sorrow must be known to appreciate great happiness. Weep, Aurora, share your tears with the water, and they will mix with the tears of those before you, feeding this river," he says in his sad, raspy voice.

"What about you Charon? Don't you feel woe?"

"No," he answers without hesitation. "I'm the child of the Nyx, the night and of the Erebus, the darkness. The Gods so ancient, they knew Earth when it was molten lava. I bathe in the waters of Lethe. I have no care for the world of the dead or the living, only my duty. If I fail, the balance will crumble. I am the gatekeeper, child." We get to the stony shore and he gives me his hand to help me out of the boat.

"Thank you," I say.

"You are a kind soul Aurora. May the waters of the Styx bring you fortune. Test those who swear falsely to you when you are in need of a friend. They will forget all their lies and will be compelled to be truthful. Safe travels keymaker." He waves his bony hand and then throws me a small object. I catch it and find it to be a dark green, glass vial, filled with luminous fluid.

I wake up and find myself still on the plane, the steady humming of engines is all that I can hear. I rub my face and ponder the dream that felt so real. Today is the day of the alignment. Today the fate of Gods and people will be decided.

When I untangle myself from the blankets, something shimmers as an object tumbles away. I catch it, bring it closer to me, and I realize it is the same small see through container with luminous fluid inside that I was given in my dream.

"What the…" I mumble as a knock on the door startles me and Poseidon peaks into the room.

"Ah, you're up. Good. We are landing soon, best to take a seat and buckle up."

"OK." I nod and force a smile.

"You're alright?"

"Yeah, yeah." I clasp the bottle firmly in my palm. "Just woke up, must still be dreaming." He gives me thumbs up and closes the door. I get dressed, check my bag, where I put Charon's gift and where I have been keeping the dagger given to me by Iraklis. I don't know what lies ahead, if I am in danger this dagger is the only protection I have. The plane lands smoothly about half an hour later. Bright sunshine streams through the windows and my skin erupts in goosebumps in the air-conditioned plane from the heat of the rays on my skin. I smile and rub the spot where the warm ray landed on my lap. "Hi, Iris!" I say softly. For a second I think the ray blinked in return to my greeting, and somehow it makes me feel better that I have a good friend looking after me.

We disembark in a small airport that seems abandoned. There are no other people except for the two who assist with taxiing and bringing the stairs to the door. Poseidon and I have only our carry-ons. I hesitate at the top of the stairs, police lights in the distance alarm me, as Poseidon confidently takes the lead.

"What?" He looks back, realizing that I am not coming down.

"The police." I nod in the direction of the two police cars ahead. I am technically a fugitive, suspected of murdering my own father. What if I get caught? What if they put me in prison? Then our quest will fail and everything and everyone will be in danger once Enzio releases the Titans.

Poseidon looks to where I am pointing and chuckles. "That's our security and escort. I am quite known here, a celebrity. Believe me they won't pay much attention to you and your documents are as real as they can be. No one will suspect anything."

One of the Policemen gets out of the car and waves to Poseidon, who does the same in return.

"Oh," I breathe out with relief.

"We'll take a car into town and from there we'll go by boat." He starts walking ahead as a black Mercedes pulls up, a driver gets out, takes our bags, and then opens the door for us to get in.

"I think you'll like this place, it's unlike anywhere else in Greece," Poseidon speaks excitedly.

"Where are we exactly?" I ask.

"We are on Peloponnese, the southernmost Peninsula of Greece," he says.

We quickly arrive in a small town. It blends completely into the surrounding gray and brown stony terrain with its houses built of stone. This town has stayed the same throughout the centuries. Scarce tourists with their sunglasses and phones look completely out of place, as if they have been transported back in time to when technology didn't exist and people believed Gods resided on Olympus. The car moves slowly down the narrow twisty streets until we finally arrive at the seaside. We get out and salty air caresses my face, my lungs expand, taking it in. I close my eyes and enjoy the bright sun on my skin, the sound of splashing waves against the rocky shore, seagulls squawking as they glide above.

"Ah!" I breathe out. "So peaceful."

"It's Poseidon."

"Huh?" I ask.

"This." He makes a sweeping motion with his arm. "This was called Poseidon. This was where I was worshiped," his voice booms. "Come, I'll show you something very special to me." Poseidon leads me first to the stony promenade then down to the wooden docks where small boats bob on the waves. He walks up to a small motorboat and helps me inside. He unties the rope, jumps in, and starts the motor. We are soon racing across the sea, curving around the shore. When I look at the coast from our speeding boat, I realize that Poseidon is right. This part of Greece is nothing like the one I visited with my parents a long time ago. There are no bright white houses with blue roofs like Santorini, or the beautiful white villas nestled in between the sparse green of Mykonos. It is all brown rocks. They start at the depths of the sea where the water is clear, many feet down and rise all the way to the sharp wall of the Peninsula.

Poseidon is grinning from ear to ear as he drives the boat. I catch him glancing at me when he thinks I am not looking and something in that stare feels strange, unpleasant, it puts me on alert.

We make a wide bend around the edge of the shore and Poseidon lets the boat coast with the motor off toward the pebbled beach. When it scrapes the shore, Poseidon jumps into the water, lifts me out, and brings me to the dry surface. He pulls the boat onto the shore with ease and takes the lead, hiking the rocky path. "Do you need help with that backpack?" he points to my backpack that has the dagger and the magic water from the river Styx. "No, I got it." I squeeze the straps of it tight. He turns and heads up the beach. When we reach the top it offers nothing but the same view of bare, rocky terrain.

"Over there." Poseidon points to a small mound of rocks. "It was a temple of Poseidon." He runs up with seeming ease across the rocks which want to catch your foot and twist your ankle. I hop carefully, avoiding large cracks and it takes me several minutes to reach him. When I catch up to him I follow his gaze to the ground. Under the yellow dust, among the rocks there are the remains of a white mosaic floor. It's a miracle it has made it through the centuries. But nature is slowly working on taking over what was man made and claiming it with small patches of grass growing through the mosaic, soon all but erasing it. Poseidon kneels down and wipes away the dust gently, staring at the ornately laid out small white pieces in the ground and I hear him sigh.

"This was once a beautiful place. Peaceful. People came to pray to me." He slaps his chest, "I felt I had a purpose. I felt that I was needed." He swallows hard and looks up at the sky, squinting his eyes, his forehead is glistening with small beads of sweat. "I should have been the supreme God, not my brother Zeus." He frowns. I shrug my shoulders, holding my tongue. I have a feeling that he is hiding something from me, that he is not the friend he is pretending to be. While he speaks I decide to put a few drops of the luminous water from the river Styx in the water bottle I have in my back pack. I have to make sure that Poseidon is my friend.

"Thirsty?" I pass him the bottle of water. He nods and takes it, finishing it all but the last drop which he spills on the mosaic "Aaaaah!" he breathes out. "Water is divine. It gives life and sustains it. Yet I, the God of the Oceans and the Seas was never as revered as my brother Zeus." He looks into the distance and before I can reply he starts walking away rather quickly from me. "Let's go Aurora, time is running out," he yells without looking at me. There is a coldness in his voice that I haven't heard before. I have no choice but to follow him, he is my guide to the underworld. I might need help on my way to the Titans' prison and for now I have no one else I can rely on other than Poseidon.

I run after him reaching him in a few moments when he stops suddenly, and stares into the ground. He has stopped before a dark, gaping opening in the ground. If I kept running I would have fallen into it.

"This is it?" I ask. I was expecting a large cave within the mountain and not an unremarkable whole in the ground. Poseidon nods. I look into the darkness of the pit and hear the distant splashing of the waves, but I can't see the bottom. I kick a small stone with my foot into it and count one, two, three, four, five, six, seven, eight until I hear the echoing sound of the rock hitting the bottom.

"It's deep," I mumble, putting my backpack down on the ground, thinking that we will take a little break before we climb down into this cave. Poseidon turns to me and smiles with a wicked gleam in his eyes. I take a step back away from him, feeling uneasy. "So how do we actually go down?" I ask cautiously. Poseidon steps toward me, silent. I freeze in fear, like prey that is about to get murdered. I start to back away slowly, but Poseidon gains on me quickly and hugs me tight, over my arms, he lifts me, and carries me toward the pit. "You trust your soul to the unguarded fall," he whispers into my ear and jumps into the darkness, holding me and now I am left defenseless because my backpack is left lying on the surface above with the dagger inside. I look up and scream. My voice echoes in the darkness and turns into a chorus, yelling out in desperation. I squeeze my eyes shut, bury my face in Poseidon's chest and count one, two, three, four, five, six, seven, eight. We should have hit the ground already. I open my right eye and see that instead of a fast, uncontrollable fall, we are floating. I open my left eye and just then my feet touch the ground softly. Poseidon releases me and I step away from him.

"Why did you do that?" I yell at him.

"You wouldn't jump on your own free will." He shrugs his shoulders.

"No, no, you don't make those decisions for me. You should have told me, you should have explained." I point my finger at him.

"What's done is done. We're here." He ignores my attacks and stays calm. It's dark all around us. I raise my head to the circle of the pit entryway, which shines bright like it's the sun above our heads, but there is no warmth from it. I look around the large cavern, illuminated by a narrow beam of sunlight, as my eyes get used to the darkness. I make out the unremarkable surroundings of a dome like roof of wet rock above our heads and small brown pebbles under our feet. It's too dark to see the walls of the cavern and I get an uneasy feeling staring into the pitch black, there is something there, watching me, waiting for me, a shiver runs down my back and I clasp my necklace to calm myself. I listen, there is no sound of life, just the slow drip of water down the walls of the rock, and in the distance the slow whoosh of waves hitting the shore. I walk toward the sound, at first, Poseidon trails behind, but soon confidently walks ahead. He doesn't look around, his steps are firm. I conclude he is not a stranger, but a frequent visitor to this place.

"Do you know where to go?" I ask.

"This way, we have to cross the river." He motions with his head and I continue to follow him.

We reach a wall of steep smooth rock. There is a narrow, low opening within it, Poseidon ducks and disappears into it. I hesitate to enter.

"C'mon," Poseidon calls out from the darkness and I follow into the dark entry. There is nothing but pitch black for a few moments as I slowly shuffle forward, feeling my surroundings with my hand and finding only wet, hard rock, but soon the narrow pathway opens up into another large cavern, the luminous water of a river flows gently as the light of the water reflects all around, creating a pleasant glow. Large stalactite icicles hang from the ceiling. Drops of water drip with unchanged rhythm, tick tock, tick tock, like an eternal clock. I wonder what it is counting.

"The ferryman, Charon, he'll come soon," Poseidon says confidently, looking into the fog that begins to spread over the water. I hear rhythmic splashing, it gets closer, the long nose of a boat appears first, then a long oar, and soon the owner of the boat himself emerges through the thick white blanket. I've seen this before, the hooded tall figure, the bony fingers grasping the oar tight, the sound of the dripping water tick tocking. This was a dream, but I put my hand into my pocket, and there I have the small glass vial that is very much real. The boat scrapes the rocky surface and Charon doesn't say a word to us, only outstretches his hand to me.

"We need to cross, Charon. Let's not play these games. It's me, Poseidon. I brought the keymaker to make sure the Titans stay locked up." But the hooded giant just shakes his head no and keeps his hand outstretched.

"What do you want? I have money, credit cards, rings." He takes a wallet out of his pocket and throws the contents of it into the boat, then he takes off his ring and holds it up for Charon to take, but he shakes his head no. "You listen to me, we have to cross. I am the God of the Seas. I am Poseidon. I command you to take us across." But Charon still shakes his head no.

Poseidon clenches his jaw, his hands tighten into fists.

"I am the ruler of all that is water," Poseidon's voice booms, echoing. "These waters will listen and obey me and shall carry me to the other side." He raises his arms and the calm waves of the river stop their lazy roll. It's as if a storm has started, the water begins to swell, and the waves become larger, beating against the shore. Charon's boat rocks and many would have already fallen down, but he stands still, seemingly unaffected by the violent rocking of his boat. Poseidon comes closer to the water and is about to make a step onto the wave that foams, waiting for him. Charon lifts his oar and with a loud thud, hits it on the bottom of his boat. The water recedes instantly and the calm waves return, gently splashing against the rocks.

"I am Charon. This is my river. You pay or you stay on the shore," he whispers.

"I have a payment! I have a payment!" I yell and show the large gold coin to Charon that I have kept in my pocket. He nods and puts his oar into the water.

"Wait, wait! You can't leave me here. I have to go with her. Aurora, you won't be able to do this by yourself," Poseidon growls. I get into the boat and when Charon pushes off I ask, "Tell me Poseidon, do you seek to unleash the Titans?"

He presses his lips tight, covers his mouth with his hands, but despite those efforts the word escapes his lips, "Yes." His eyes dart back and forth, he steps back, pressing his lips in. His face changes, he gets red as blood vessels pop on his forehead, he begins to shake and finally yells, "Your father should've given me the helmet and the key a long time ago. I tried to persuade him. I tried to show him that the world of humans is existing on borrowed time. I will not let you destroy what will bring on the new world order." He points his finger at me as the boat slowly moves away from the shore. He then starts pacing the shore like a lion that lost his prey, angry and brooding, but soon disappearing from my view in the fog.

I swallow hard to compose myself before I say loudly in a steady voice that carries over the water, "My father might have lived as an ordinary man, but he lost his life protecting everyone else's and that makes him exceptional, you worthless mermaid."

Charon moves his oar slowly from one side to the other, moving the boat smoothly across. He delivers me to the other shore in silence. As soon as both of my feet are firm on the ground he pulls away, and only the distant splashing of his oar tells me about his eternal presence on this river.

CHAPTER 30

AURORA

No one told me where the actual prison of the Titans is. I have no map. I look around, there is no clear path, just rocks and boulders, there is nothing but black abyss above me, a white fog floats like a blanket high up to my waist. I can see shadows move and float in the distance, hiding behind the rocks, but no one comes forward. I make small careful steps forward away from the river. Soon I can make out a rocky wall in front of me, hoping to find a path within it. I nearly twist my ankle several times, but push on forward slowly, my feet ache, my legs burn from cuts and scrapes from the sharp rocks.

I reach the wall and feel the hard, slippery and cold surface with my hands up and down. I shuffle parallel to the wall, hoping to find an opening for me to continue on. I trip and fall on the rocks that are hiding under the fog, my elbows are scraped and bleeding. A feeling of desperation rises, tightening its lasso on my throat, whipping hope into retreat, kicking my heart with its spurs to race faster.

I don't know where to go next. I have no friends. I am completely alone in this quest. The sudden sound of heavy breathing reaches me and then a growl echoes loudly, reverberating deep within me. I stare into the darkness, trying to make out the beast that is getting closer, but I see nothing. I know I am being watched and then I remember the gift that Hades gave me. I raise my right wrist high up in the air and the jeweled star on the bracelet shines bright with a white glow. I can finally see the monster. A giant dog with three heads, the eyes are black holes, large mouths filled with sharp teeth, the hot, rotten stench of its breath filling the air. It could stomp me with one of its paws, but it shrieks as the light touches it. He backs away, its head thrashing, trying to hide from the glow, "Back away into your dark abyss and let me pass," I yell, pushing my chest forward. The monster squeals, does just that, and soon I am alone again with the darkness pressing all around me and the only light coming from my bracelet.

My eyes flood with tears, making everything blurry, when I wipe them I see a glowing female figure in the distance but I can't make out her face. She lifts her slender arm of white alabaster skin and with her skinny finger motions for me to follow her. I climb the rocks, toward her, she leads me into a cave tunnel that is tall enough to fit me in, but so narrow I have to turn sideways to squeeze through its tight opening. I scrape my shoulders, my fingers hurt as I glide them along the rough surface of the cave for guidance, but I keep moving. I can't stop. There is little time left.

"Hello. Hi. Who are you?" I ask her, but she says nothing and disappears into the darkness, far enough that the light of my bracelet barely reaches her. I continue to follow the figure. Maybe if I catch up to her, then she can tell me where to go, and what to do. I run after her, but she is always far ahead, just enough for me to make out her shape in the darkness. She is like a lighthouse that points the way. I feel that if I follow her light I will be safe, and I know that I am on the right path. She is leading me somewhere deep down. The chill of the cave has disappeared and now it is getting hotter as the path twists down deeper. The clothes on my back are wet with my sweat, my hair is sticking to my neck, and face, and it's getting harder to take in deep breaths of air. The woman keeps moving forward, she is slender, ethereal, her figure seems to be almost see-through. The race reminds me of the games my mother and I used to play in the backyard of our summer house. We would chase each other, she would pretend to struggle to catch me as I ran, zig zagging, shrilling, breathless. Finally, she would catch up to me, we would both fall to the ground, and she would tickle me. We would both laugh, get up, and then I'd chase her. She was beautiful, blonde long hair just like mine streamed down to her waist and her white alabaster skin glowed in the sunlight. I try to remember her face, but it has been obscured by time. I run after the woman in front of me, trying to catch her to look into the face I will know, but she keeps moving too fast. The cave has opened up. The smell of sulfur is heavy in the air. There is a winding narrow rocky path and a river of lava on both sides of it. One misstep and I fall to my death. The smolder of the fiery, thick liquid makes everything around me glow red. The lava sizzles, splatters and bubbles, climbing to the edge of the rocky pathway, trying to erode it. Black smoke rises up high from the lava and ash floats in the air as if snowflakes, it burns when it lands on my skin. Hot air burns my nose and stings my lungs with every breath. Shadows move and dance in the crevices of the rocks. I begin to think that they are beings, they move fast, following me, but never get close, never reveal themselves. There is a distant howl that's coming from somewhere ahead, it grows louder as I keep running. The howl becomes a chorus of many voices crying in pain, they yelp, and shriek, but I don't see anyone. My legs begin to burn and there is a stabbing pain in my ribs from running. Tears stream down my cheeks, I reach out my hand, but the woman moves away from me. There is nothing else above or below, just lifeless rock and fire, and the twisting path that keeps moving ahead, deep down. A steady growl rises from the depths of Earth itself, a distant pounding that makes the surface beneath me shake, sharp icicle shaped rocks collapse, and fall all around me. The time is here. I need to get to the Titans before the alignment is complete. I take as deep a breath of air as I can, pull my head down, and force my legs to keep running despite the numbing burn of my muscles. The path twists through the rocks, curves, spiraling down deep, with the river of lava getting wider, encroaching on the narrow rocky ledge that is getting thinner. I feel like I am walking a tightrope, balancing between two fiery rivers and the sharp edged rocks. My pace slows and the woman disappears out of my view. My feet burn from the heat of the ground and the soles of my shoes feel soft and sticky, melting on the hot ground.

I come down a bend, I have to wave my arms frantically to keep my balance because the thin path ends abruptly. I hold my breath, one wrong move and I will fall into the nothing that is in front of me. The river of lava flows like waterfall off the edge of the cliff, ahead of me and below is nothing but pitch black. Just as I think my balance will falter the female figure floats up in front of me and I recognize my mother instantly. She puts her arms up, flies toward me, and then right through me. I feel a breath of fresh air penetrate me, a warm sunlight, the smell of my mother's perfume, the sound of her laughter, a kiss of her lips on my forehead, and I regain my balance in that minute. She is all but gone, all that is left is the image of her smiling face that is fresh in my mind. I feel something pulling on the back of my pants. When I turn around it's Iraklis, holding me from falling forward. I throw my arms around him and he nuzzles into my neck, squeezing me tight in an embrace.

"You're here. I felt so alone. I…I…"

"Shhh. You're not alone. I'm here." Iraklis pulls away, and holds my face, staring directly into my eyes. "I'm here."

I nod, smiling, putting my hand over his, pressing it into my cheek. "Where have you been? What happened?"

"I found forgiveness," he replies and a relaxed smile appears on his face. His blue eyes are as clear as a perfect summer sky. I place a soft kiss on his lips and press my body into his. I've missed him.

A twister forms from the depth below us and grows larger, rising above our heads. The pounding beneath our feet is growing more and more terrifying. I take off the rings and my medallion and place them in the center of my palm. "Two keys one lock," I murmur and look at Iraklis who nods reassuringly. I trace the design on the rings with my finger, under my touch the circumferential Greek key design on the rings rotates, expands and becomes larger than the diameter of the rings themselves. The sharp, linear, up and down steps of the design shine and my medallion gleams. I put my father's ring into the grooves of the medallion. The grooves of my mother's Greek key design are the perfect fit to the reverse side of my medallion.

"This is the key. We got it!" I laugh with joy, but our celebration is interrupted when we hear Poseidon.

"Give me the key, Aurora," he demands, walking down the path with a falcon flying behind him. It lands and transforms into Enzio. He walks behind Poseidon with a scowl.

"We have to destroy it Poseidon or it will destroy the world!" I yell as the wind picks up and I have to cover my eyes from the dust and hot air.

"And then we will rebuild," Poseidon's voice booms, Iraklis pushes me gently to stay behind him. He is a wall of muscle and I have to peak under his arm to see what is going on. He clenches his hands into large fists, small lightning bolts start to erupt, and go down his arms.

"There are two of us against you Iraklis," Poseidon snarls. "Give us the key. Let us recreate a new world, where people have enough food and shelter, where we can avoid wars…"

"You're delusional Poseidon. Wars were waged when humanity was still in its infancy, people went hungry when food was plentiful on our tables. You just want glory, you want the bend of the knees, the sacrifice, the adoration, the fear."

"I'm not the only one who wants that." Poseidon shrugs his shoulders and glances at Enzio.

"How did you get here?" Iraklis asks and I wonder what Poseidon did to let Charon get him to the other side.

"You forget that Hades is my brother and now he possesses the invisibility helmet, Charon wouldn't even know that he carried me in his boat and Enzio, he flies, he doesn't need to be carried across the Styx," Poseidon says and Hades appears right beside him, taking off the helmet that was making him invisible.

"You lied to us after all," I say from behind Iraklis.

"I just couldn't resist the opportunity. What can I say?" Hades shrugs his shoulders, smiling wickedly and bows to me, "All the souls that I will get if the Titans are released…" he closes his eyes and takes a long breath in through his nose, "It's, it's invigorating."

"Hey, little keymaker," Poseidon salutes me with his two fingers at the forehead. "Why don't you give us the key so we can help the Titans come out. Looks like the time of the alignment is here."

We all look up above us to the roof of the massive cave that seems to have no visible boundaries as the eye of the tornado has become wider. It churns black smoke, twisting and rising up. Iraklis moves away from the edge and I shuffle behind him, careful with my steps on the steaming hot surface. I squeeze my hand tight around the rings and the medallion and hide behind Iraklis' back. I have to think, think fast about what to do, how to keep the Titans locked up.

"Don't make it harder than what it should be Iraklis. We don't want to hurt Aurora, we just want the key," Hades says with false sweetness.

"Go to hell," Iraklis replies. Just then, Enzio turns into the falcon, rises fast into the air, and Hades rushes toward Iraklis. When he gets close enough, Iraklis swings his arm and lightning erupts as it meets Hades' jaw, sending him flying into the lava below us. His helmet flies off his head and bounces on the stony path. The flames engulf him instantly. He shrieks and thrashes, but it is useless, he is soon overtaken by the lava and disappears underneath it. Just then Enzio the falcon dives from above but instead of Iraklis he goes straight for me. I get low to the ground, clenching the key in my hand. I put the other one up in defense and wait for the claws and beak to tear into me, but they never reach me. When I look up I see that Iraklis has shot a lightning bolt above me, protecting me from the falcon. The bird tries to fly up, but is too slow. Iraklis grabs the falcon by its legs, swings it several times around, and then lets go, throwing Enzio so far that he disappears out of view into the black smoke.

"Stay there," Iraklis yells to me, staring down Poseidon who spreads his arms wide. Drops of water appear in between them, moving quickly toward each other until they make a shape that is his trident which he points at Iraklis. He twirls his weapon around above his head and charges at Iraklis who ducks, and tries to take Poseidon down, but misses. Poseidon jumps, using his trident as a pole and lands behind Iraklis, kicking him in the back. Iraklis loses his balance and almost falls down the slope into the river of lava, but quickly recovers as Poseidon aims for Iraklis' back. I gasp and rush toward him to stop the trident piercing the back of the man that has become so dear to me. But with the other end of his trident Poseidon hits me in the middle of my abdomen. The power of the punch takes the breath out of my lungs. I stumble and fall to my knees, gasping for air, squeezing the spot where I was hit, only then realizing that the medallion has fallen out of my hands and is now laying at the edge of the cliff. Fighting the pain and while Iraklis wrestles with Poseidon, I crawl toward the medallion. Just as my fingers are about to touch it, a shadow falls on it. I look up as the ear-piercing scream of the bird above my head deafens me. The bird races through the air with its claws out to grab what is mine and to hurt me. In a split second I reach and put the necklace on my neck. Just as the falcon is about to tear into me, I instinctively clasp my hands over my chest, stretch them out in front of me, shutting my eyes tight, and turn my head away. I wait for the pain to come as the bird's beak and claws reach me to rip my flesh off. But that never happens. I open my eyes when I hear the bird scream in pain. In front of me is a wall of light, streaming from my own hands. The falcon hits it hard. He lies on the ground, his neck twisted unnaturally, and only one of his wings flapping while the other stays motionless. I created my own shield. I can lock myself away behind my power for my own protection. I can defend myself. I am the lock and the key all in one. I can lock anything away and I can release what my heart desires.

I run and grab Hades' helmet and whisper a chant that wraps the helmet in my light. It disappears for me to keep safe and for no one else to have it. I don't know if Hades is dead but he will not be able to do anything without his helmet. One more enemy is left. Just then the wind picks up even more. It pulls me toward the abyss, but I push forward, toward Iraklis. He is bloody and bruised, and still fighting Poseidon. The lightning from Iraklis' fists meets its match in swift defense from Poseidon's trident. Poseidon's face is swollen from the punches, but yet he shows no signs of being tired. He will fight to his death to get what he wants. I have nearly reached them when one of the rocks from above comes crashing down between us. I fall back and when the dust settles, to my horror I see that Poseidon has his trident blades on Iraklis' neck, his foot on his chest while Iraklis' leg is crushed under the rock.

"No!" I plead.

"The medallion," Poseidon barks, extending his free arm to me but not taking his eyes off Iraklis who lies motionless. I grasp my medallion and squeeze tight, pressing it to my chest, crawling backwards.

"Now," he growls and presses on the trident. I hear Iraklis moan in pain. I tug on the necklace and it becomes undone. I keep squeezing it, the metal digging into the skin of my palm. I am on the edge of the impossible. I either save the world, but condemn Iraklis to death or I save him and let the world as I know it be destroyed.

We are right in the middle of the eye of the tornado. The wind is no longer blowing and there is complete silence. The rocky ceiling above us collapses, admitting into the underworld the view of the dark night sky. It feels so close as if I am in thrust into the depths of cosmos to view the alignment in its proximity. I look at its black, glorious expanse with stars shining brightly. Among randomly scattered distant planets there is an almost perfect alignment of Jupiter, Mars, Saturn, Venus, and Mercury. The deciding moment is now.

"Here." I throw the medallion to Poseidon. He takes his eyes off Iraklis to catch it, in that moment I lunge at him, and press my palms together. I feel my power surge from within me, charging through my veins and through each fiber of my muscles. I open my arms wide, a green wave of light erupts from within me. I can't tell where I find the words as I speak them.

"I am the keymaker. I make the lock and the key to keep away my enemies and their dark desires. No man or God shall break my locks. I condemn you, Poseidon to be locked away with the Titans until such time comes that you have repented," I chant and Poseidon stays frozen, his eyes grow large from the shock of witnessing my rage, my power. He lifts his trident from Iraklis' neck and the next thing I feel is a sharp pain, tearing, burning, as the blades pierce the soft flesh of my stomach. I fall to my knees, the metal taste of blood fills my mouth. I feel a strange tingling in my arms and legs. My head feels light, dizzy, I glance toward Iraklis, he struggles to get up, and can only lift himself up onto his elbow. I smile at him and tears fill up my eyes. I can't make out the details of his face.

"No." A bare whisper escapes Poseidon's lips. "No, no." His voice is trembling, growing louder as my green light creeps up his feet, up his trident, and from his fingers up his arms, consuming him as he begins to scream. "You have condemned all of humanity and all of us, divine beings to death. Humans will destroy it all. I could have saved so many. I could have built a better future. Can't you see my vision, my sacrifice. What have you done, Aurora?"

"It's no sacrifice, you planned the murder of millions. There will be no prosperity built on the death of the innocent." I strain to speak through my pain. The trident evaporates, the sharp blades no longer impale me, but bright red blood streams from under my fingers when I press the palm of my hand against my wounds.

Poseidon's face changes from rage to recognizing his failure and defeat, he tries to speak, but his mouth is taken over by my light. The green glow creeps up my enemy like a smoldering fire slowly burning away a piece of paper. He can't move, he can't shake off the slow, burning flame. I look into his eyes and I see no regret, he will not be asking for redemption in his last moment, and I don't feel any guilt for his demise. Soon, only an airy ash is all but left, and is carried away by the wind.

My medallion falls right next to me. I pick it up and raise it up above my head just as the planets align and a stream of light shines on me from the cosmos.

"I am the keymaker. I have locked away my enemies and I shall keep them locked away. I am the lock and I am the key and this lock will stay locked for eternity." The beam of light from the cosmic alignment spreads over me as my own glow forms a protective shield. I stagger to my feet, holding the medallion up high with one arm, while the other keeps pressing against my belly, where my flesh is warm from the blood that keeps flowing. The screams of the Titans are loud, their pounding is like earthquakes, but they can't break my lock and soon the alignment passes and the light disappears. I fall back to the blood-soaked narrow path knowing that I did it. I saved everyone from the coming of the Titans. I know that there will be no carnage that would have killed so many. I crawl to Iraklis, my arms and legs shaking. I can see he is smiling, a small smile, careful, unknowing, and I smile back.

"I did it," I whisper when I reach him and fall into his embrace. He feels warm and strong. I giggle, show him my bloody hand, and then begin to shiver. Iraklis rubs my arms, kissing my shoulder, my neck.

"I know, I know. You did it. You saved us. You saved me." His voice cracks.

"I feel like I'm floating," I whisper.

"No, no, no. Stay with me. Listen to my voice, stay with me," he pleads, but my eyelids grow heavy and all I can feel is my pain and his warmth. The sound of his voice begins to fade, growing distant until I can no longer hear it and there is nothing but darkness and silence.

CHAPTER 31

IRAKLIS

"No, no, no." I keep repeating, pressing my face to Aurora's still warm cheek, wet with her tears. My legs are crushed under rock, my ribs are sore and every breath is excruciating pain, but none of it compares to the terror that tears my heart as it seizes at the loss of this woman. I free my legs and pull Aurora closer to me. A gentle touch on my shoulder makes me turn around, "Iris," I'm able to breathe out.

"What's this? Iraklis, my friend, weeping as the world gets to see another day," she says in her kind, ever understanding voice. She is the friend who has always been there, without me asking her, without me knowing that I needed her support. She is here again, even her spirit sensed my need for her friendship. She always found the right words to comfort me, to make me see hope in the most bleak and desperate situations.

"The world does, but she doesn't." I brush away tangled hair from Aurora's face, kissing her while rocking.

"She turned out to be the key after all." She kneels beside me. I don't reply. I don't care what she is. All that matters is that she is taken away from me and I couldn't protect her.

"It's a strange thing forgiveness." Iris continues to speak in her low, serene voice. "It is a gift that lightens the heart, frees the mind, gives hope or an opportunity." She looks at me with a twinkle in her eye. She raises her arm up high, from somewhere up above small specks of light appear, and begin a slow descent toward us. "I draw the light from the universe and give it back," she says as the sparks of light land on Iris' hand and she smiles, bringing her hand filled with divine glow over Aurora. She releases the light and it falls like gentle snowfall over the still laying girl that holds my heart. It touches her skin, melting into it and the wound in her stomach heals before our eyes. The color returns to her cheeks, new tears begin to flow from under her long blonde eyelashes as her eyelids flutter, and I begin to kiss her face. When she opens her beautiful eyes, they are green, just like the wave of light that she released to save us all. She stares at me, not saying a word and all I can do is lift my head up toward the dark sky above us to hide the tears that burn my eyes. I look back at Iris and mouth, "Thank you." But she just smiles.

I compose myself and sit Aurora up. My bones are crushed, the skin has turned a deep purple blue, and the swelling is getting worse with every second. In Tartarus nothing gets better, this is where people come to die or be tortured for the mistakes they've done during their lifetime. I have no chance. I will not be able to get back to Charon. But it seems that fate feels gracious today as I see Artemis and Pia running to us. I have no words, my throat is dry and all I can do is laugh, loudly, exhausted, happy to see them. Artemis' stride is wide and confident. She runs as if she is storming into a battle with her bow behind her back. Pia scurries behind, her small steps are light and gentle. She falls behind, carefully stepping over rocks on the narrow path that have fallen during the alignment of the planets, and swaying trying to balance and not to fall down into the molten lava.

When they reach us, they collapse on either side of us. Artemis quickly looks over my wounds and shakes her head.

"It looks bad." I tell her and she nods.

"Here, let me fix it." Pia takes out a small bottle of liquid from her pocket. "The water of the Styx shall heal you," she says, pouring the luminous liquid over my legs. Artemis closes her eyes and I know she is saying one of her healing prayers. The swelling and bruising on my legs begins to disappear and soon I am able to move. I know that my bones have fused when I can bend my legs. Aurora still says nothing, she seems to not care that Artemis and Pia have come to our aid. Her stare is blank. Even though her body is present here with us, her mind seems to be far, far away and it scares me, because I don't yet know if she will come back to me.

"Is she hurt?" Artemis asks me after taking a quick look at Aurora's arms and legs and not finding any visible wounds.

"I, I don't know," I reply. "I think she is in shock, she is drained. I've never seen anything like what she did here. The surge of power was, it was..."

"Miraculous," Pia says.

"Give her the water." I reach for the bottle, but Pia pulls away.

"She can't eat or drink anything in the underworld or she will be bound to stay here," she warns.

"We need to get her out of here. She needs to be in the light. She needs fresh air. She needs to be among the living," Artemis urges.

I nod, get up on my feet first, and then gently pick Aurora up. She doesn't object, in fact she shows no emotion. Her body is limp. Her gaze doesn't concentrate on anything.

"What about Hades and Enzio?" I ask. Neither has been seen since I've thrown one into the molten lava and the other one is lying on the ground with his bones broken.

"Go ahead, cross the river. Pia and I will take care of them," Artemis says.

I nod and quickly pick up the pace, looking back once in a while to check on Iris who runs by my side toward Charon.

He stands tall like a beacon, emotionless. He doesn't move when I come close. I have no payment for him to cross the river and I hope I don't have to have another fight. When I make an unsure step onto the ferry, he doesn't object, nor does he try to push me off, instead when I get seated, he puts his oar in the water and starts a slow paddle to the other shore. I look back to check on Iris only to realize she never got on the ferry. She is standing on the shore, smiling as she waves to me. I carefully lay down Aurora and get up to wave to my friend, moving to the very edge of the ferry so I can see her for a bit longer.

"Don't let the Styx take you," Charon says in his low raspy voice.

"My friend, Iris, she is—"

"Dead," he cuts me off.

I raise my arm higher as the fog begins to obscure the shore of Tartarus and the details of my friend's face who keeps waving to me.

"Thank you, my friend," I say under my breath.

"Don't close your heart to the light." I hear the voice of Iris travel across the splashing of the waves. I put my hand over my heart when she disappears out of view completely. The thought of her will forever bring light to me.

We soon reach the other shore, I scoop up Aurora, and step off the ferry.

"Thank you," I say to Charon. He bids a small bow and pushes off, disappearing into the white fog.

I climb up a narrow path, soon I am in a large cave with translucent blue waters, and a circle of sunlight above our heads. I know we are out of Tartarus because the air is filled with sounds of life, the screeching of seagulls, the flapping of the wings in the wind, the beating of waves against the rocky shore. The air is light, the soft breeze is refreshing, bringing the smell of the salty sea. I step into the bright circle of the sunlight and squint my eyes. Right at the edge up above me, I see the heads of people moving, but I can't make out who they are, the sun is blinding. I glance at Aurora and although she is warm she looks as if her spirit is gone.

Soon a rope is dropped, I wrap my arm around it and throw Aurora over my shoulder. We are then slowly pulled up to the surface where Doti and C are waiting by a helicopter. I lay Aurora on the ground and drop the rope that is attached to the helicopter pulley system back into the cave for when Artemis and Pia need it.

"She is completely drained," Doti gasps.

"What does she need? Magic, medicine? Tell me!" I demand.

"She needs rest," Doti replies softly and smiles, touching my arm, giving me a reassuring rub. I nod.

"We found this." C shows me Aurora's backpack. "I think it belongs to you." He passes me the dagger.

"Thanks." I put it into the backpack and throw it over my shoulder.

The rope gets tugged and C turns on the pulley. Soon, Artemis and Pia are pulled out. Artemis has Pia over her shoulder, while she holds onto the rope with just one hand. Her face is stern, jaw tight, I think I see Pia wipe away a tear when Artemis puts her down.

"We didn't find Hades. He might be using his helmet," Artemis says, marching toward us. I shake my head no and explain that Aurora has hidden it with her powers and I threw Hades into lava during our fight.

"Without his helmet he will not be able to cause much trouble. Hades will not be able to leave the underworld without it. Enzio is hurt, his arms and legs are broken. Charon will not let him out of Tartarus on my orders," says Pia.

"Let's go," Artemis commands and we all head to the helicopter with Aurora slumped in my arms.

Artemis pilots to the small airport about ten minutes away where a private plane awaits us. We take our seats after I lay Aurora to bed in the small bedroom in the back. Her eyes have been open all this time, the color of green soft moss. I kiss her cheek gently and sit by her side, holding her hand in mine, giving it a light squeeze but not getting anything in return.

"She needs to sleep," Pia says, standing in the doorway. I didn't realize she was there. I nod in agreement and cover Aurora with a blanket. Pia kneels at the side of the bed and holds her hand in front of Aurora's face, her own head bows low and she closes her eyes. Pia rocks ever so slightly and hums a pleasant tune, it sounds like a lullaby. Pia's fingers touch Aurora's eyes, they close and she looks peaceful in a deep sleep.

"You have a gift of sleep enchantment?" I ask and she nods.

"Hypnos once taught me a few tricks for my kindness toward his mother," she says of a God whose power is to be able to put anyone to sleep.

"Does he still live with his mother?" I ask. His mother is a dreadful, mean woman who could bring on the darkness as if the night came too early.

"She has passed on." Pia sighs. I made sure she was comfortable in the underworld, her son was grateful for that.

"Mm-hmm."

"There are so many of us that are no longer under the sun. It's sad, isn't it?" Pia says as she looks on lovingly at Aurora. "She has so much ahead of her, so much hope. It gives me strength. I'm happy she came into her own." She turns to me and smiles.

"How long is she going to be asleep?" I ask.

"As long as she needs to be," Pia replies and walks out of the bedroom.

I linger, standing over Aurora. I am still concerned over what awaits us when we land. I leave and head to the cockpit to find Artemis and to my surprise Doti as a co-pilot.

"You're flying planes now?" I tease her lightheartedly.

"Yes, yes I do." She punctuates each word. "I am a modern woman, I can do a lot of things."

"Well that's nice, but what is going to happen to Aurora when we are back in the states? She's still a suspect in her father's death. Are we going to get off this plane without customs arresting her?" I ask.

"Leave customs to me. I already arranged for paperwork for Aurora to be transported as a person in need of medical care. We will have cars waiting for us as soon as we get off the plane and customs will be under my spell. They will see nothing and think of nothing except for me." She turns and winks at me.

"You are a dangerous woman Doti," Artemis says without taking her eyes from what is in front of her.

"What can I say? I am filled with love and everyone loves love." I leave the two of them to guide us safely across the sky and take my seat across from Pia in the main cabin.

"You look tired."

"I'm alright," I reply, chuckling. I haven't slept a deep, restful sleep since I lost my family. I am tortured by the nightmares. I can bear a few short hours of sleep but today I will not fall asleep at all, too much needs to be worked out: what lays ahead, for me, for Aurora, for all of us who call themselves Gods.

"Sleep." Pia leans fast toward me and the last thing I remember is her hand in front of my face and the scent of lavender on her skin.

I open my eyes when Pia nudges my shoulder gently. "Wake up, sleepy head."

I rub my eyes, and look out the window where the darkness has set in, and a few bright lights shine on the buildings in the distance. We have landed.

"Where are we?" I ask.

"New York," she replies.

"Did you…"

"You needed to sleep." She cocks her head to the side and looks at me inquisitively.

"Thank you," I tell her. "Don't do it again."

She frowns.

"Next time, do it while I am in bed. I have a terrible neck pain from sitting in this chair for hours." I chuckle and she smiles.

"I tried to fix your head a few times, but it's so damn heavy, all my attempts were futile." She smacks me lightly on my arm. "Get Aurora, she's still asleep. I'll head out."

I nod and do just that. Aurora's breathing is deep and slow, she is warm when I scoop her out of bed into my arms. I bury my face in her neck. "Get all the rest you need, I'll be here." I press her tight against me and carry her out where three black SUVs are waiting with Artemis, Doti, Pia, and C already inside.

Our motorcade leaves the airport without any delays and takes us directly to Doti's apartment. I lay Aurora in a guest bedroom and all of us gather around watching her as if she were Snow White and we were grieving dwarves.

"She's lost a lot of strength," Pia says.

Doti sighs heavily and C just shakes his head.

"We can give her a bit of our own," Artemis tells us and looks at us, moving her gaze slowly, waiting for our replies.

"I am in," Pia replies right away.

"I didn't know that could be done, but I'll do anything for her," I add.

"We don't know what it will do to us," Doti says with a nervous tremble and C shuffles uncomfortably right beside her. "Our powers have dwindled to next to nothing, I don't know how much I have left for me to go on and if, if I have nothing…I'm not ready…I'm not ready to disappear." She starts to sob.

"This girl just saved us all. If it weren't for her you'd be gone already. There would be no place for love and beauty in the world ruled by the Titans," Artemis chides her.

"She is our goddaughter, we promised Portus we'd take care of her," Pia says gently and touches Doti's arm.

"Yes, yes, of course, you are right." She extends her shaking hand and we all put our hands over it.

"Ah what the hell, count me in." C puts his hand on top and I am the last one to finish off our clasp. We give Artemis a slight nod, she closes her eyes and begins, her voice booming and I feel electricity tingling throughout my body as it surges and travels, ready to charge our gift to Aurora.

"I am Artemis the protector of all that is female, the guardian of fertility. I am giving part of me willingly to restore Aurora."

"I am Persephone the Goddess of harvest, I am giving part of me to Aurora to bring her back to health and glory."

"I am Aphrodite, love itself, a goddess of beauty, I gift my love and beauty to Aurora for I am grateful for her sacrifice."

"I am Cupid, the God of desire and affection. I share my power with the one who saved us all, Aurora."

"I am Hercules and the God of lightning reborn, I give part of me willingly to Aurora." The electricity prickles the tips of my fingers, traveling from inside of me, encompassing our promise and our hands. It moves up each one of our arms, not punishing, but energizing, not aiming to singe, but instead warming. It surges through each of our bodies and exits the other arm. We all instinctively extend our arm to the person next to us, forming a circle. My lightning circulates through the molecules of our being, taking the DNA of our powers, splitting, and fusing it together into something new, something that will restore Aurora. When the electrical current has finished its task it beams down our clasped arms over Aurora and enters her as a flash of bright light without leaving any marks at the entry. She arches her back, her whole body down to the tips of her fingers tenses, and then quickly she goes limp again. We wait, holding our breath, the air around us is charged and heavy with the magic of what has happened and the sense of not knowing if it has worked.

Aurora stirs and takes a deep breath. She mumbles something, still deep in her dream. We all lean as one, closer to make out what she is saying.

"I am so tired," she says clearly, then turns onto her side and puts her hands under her cheek, pulling her knees closer to her. She looks like she is just asleep and not drained of everything that she is, just a shell of a body that is left over. We all breathe out a sigh of relief and look at each other, exchanging smiles. Pia hugs Doti, Artemis pats my back, I then turn around to C to give him a pat on the back as well, but he rushes in and embraces me in a tight hug. "This was beautiful," he says tearfully, his voice is muffled as his head is pressed tight against me.

"It was, it was," I hug him.

"Look, her hair," Pia says and we all turn around to watch how the red color drains from Aurora's hair, changing into shiny silver.

"Let her sleep," Artemis says and they all head out. I stay behind and pull a blanket over Aurora. I run my fingers through her new hair that makes her look so luminous. She is the light that I didn't seek, but she has brought warmth to me. I am happy, it seems that our magic has worked, but all will be more certain when she wakes up, when she looks at me, when she says her first words. For now I have to wait a bit longer.

CHAPTER 32

AURORA

First day after the alignment

I open my eyes and look around while keeping still. I recognize my aunt Doti's place right away. I listen, and hear the sounds of dishes in the kitchen and a steady male voice, unemotional, must be a TV. I try to remember what has happened to me, but my memory is blank from the moment I glanced into the pit on the edge of Greece. I stir, and grunt from pain. My whole body feels as if I were punched and kicked. I roll over slowly from my back to my side and then rise up, propping myself up with my arms. I feel lightheaded sitting up and decide to take a few breaths and sit still before I attempt to get up. As soon as my lightheadedness passes, I put one foot on the floor first and then another, tilt forward and slide down slowly until I am standing, although unsteady. I make a small step forward, lifting my arms up slightly for balance. A silky gown feels comfortingly cool against my skin. I've never owned a slip like this, it must be one of Aunt Doti's. I spot a matching robe on a chair which I put on and open the door to leave when something odd catches me in the reflection of the framed picture on the wall. I touch my hair, it's no longer red, neither it is blonde as my own natural color, instead it's pure silver grey, all of it. I run my fingers through it, it feels the same. I look myself over and otherwise everything else is just as it was. But there is something that has changed, something I can't yet figure out.

I walk slowly, holding onto the wall toward the sounds of someone in the kitchen. There is only one person in there, the one I want to see the most, the one I feel I have a longing for, the one that feels just right for me, Iraklis. He is sitting with his back to me, a glass of orange juice is in front of him and he is watching TV. An anchor is describing unusual aurora borealis sightings across the world. "Scientists describe this new type of northern lights as the dune."

Iraklis chuckles when the news commentator says it.

"What's so funny?" I ask and my own voice feels strange coming out of my dry throat.

He slams the glass on the table, the juice spilling from it, and turns to me. His eyes are big, they look me up and down, examining every inch of me, asking questions, full of tenderness. He rises slowly, his mouth is open. He takes a step forward, extending his arms to me. I let go of the wall and take an unsteady step toward him. I sway as I get dizzy again but Iraklis is quick to sweep me off my feet into his arms. We stare at each other, I wrap my arms around his neck and put my head on his chest where the sound of his heart is drumming a comforting beat. He sits down, putting me in his lap, hugs me tight, burying his face in my hair, his breath warming me up. "I was afraid, I thought I lost you."

"I don't remember anything, the last thing is me staring into the pit," I tell him as I caress his stubble covered cheeks.

He frowns, breathes out a long stream of air, and runs his hand through his hair, looking away, "We were cornered by Poseidon, Enzio and Hades. Turns out they were all in on it. I defeated Hades, Enzio is stuck in Tartarus with his injuries. Poseidon and I went at it for a while and before I could defeat him, he pierced you with his trident right here." He puts his hand on my stomach, his fingers flex lightly. "But something saved you, I can't say for sure, it was magic or fate or some divine light, but it healed you and it banished him. The force of your power locked away the Titans. Pia and Artemis found us and helped us to get out of Tartarus. We brought you here."

I stay quiet, processing all of the information that Iraklis has revealed. I look into the depths of my memory for any confirmation of what he is telling me, but it's just darkness. I shake my head. "I don't remember."

"When we brought you here, you were just a body, warm, breathing. Your heart was beating, but you were not there. We performed a ritual, we have each given you parts of us to restore you," Iraklis speaks slowly.

"You did?"

He nods, "Your power now is something that has never existed before, you have part of Doti and C, something from Pia and Artemis and…"

"You?" I cut him off, frowning. Iraklis nods again and interlocks the fingers of his hand with mine. "What does it mean?" I ask. Iraklis shrugs his shoulders and his gaze trails off.

"Time will tell. The powers will show themselves when you need them most."

I slide from his lap and sit in the chair opposite from him. I drop my head into my arms, digging my fingers into my scalp.

"I like your hair," Iraklis says and I giggle, but it's a nervous laughter, scared, because there is so much that is uncertain. The world has gotten so much more complicated in the last few days, so unpredictable, and fragile.

"I'm still a suspect in my father's murder. What am I going to do? Will I have to be a fugitive for the rest of my life?" I ask as my head feels heavier with a brewing headache that is pushing on my forehead. The knock on the door interrupts my brooding.

"Ah, just in time to give you some answers." Iraklis springs to his feet, smiling, and goes to answer the door. He returns back a few seconds later with Gabriel confidently walking behind him without his glasses.

"Hi, Aurora." He beams and points to his face. "I got contact lenses."

"Hi, Gabriel, you look great!" I tell him. He pulls up a chair and sits across from me, his head is bobbing cheerfully, yet he is not saying anything, torturing me with what's to come.

"C'mon Gabriel, I can't take it, what is it?" I urge him on.

"I've received a message from Tartarus. Enzio wants to make a deal."

"What does he want?" I sigh with exasperation.

"It seems the punishment the fate is doling out to him in the underworld is much too harsh. He is willing to confess to murdering your father in exchange for a transfer to a prison here." Gabriel rubs his hands together, seemingly satisfied with his message.

I glance at Iraklis, who is rubbing his chin, apparently in deep thought.

"I don't know." I shake my head. "I don't know if it's right. I don't know if it should be done."

"It has to be done." Iraklis slams his fist on the table. "Aurora, he has committed a crime here, he has to answer for it here. Sometimes fate is what we make it to be, not what is decided." He takes my hands into his and looks into my eyes.

"I'm afraid to make a wrong decision here. I'm afraid of him, what if he…what if it doesn't work?"

"It'll work, he will be delivered and his confession will be recorded before he is handed to the Police. He will not escape this," Iraklis says and Gabriel nods in agreement.

"I feel strange deciding his fate." I still hesitate.

"You are not deciding it. He made a choice when he killed your father and sided with Poseidon in his treacherous plans. He will be tried for what he has done. And you will be cleared," Iraklis presses.

I stay quiet, thinking, processing, remembering and in the end I give a nod. It's a slight one at first, barely visible, followed by another one more confident. "Yes…yes, I agree to that."

"I'll personally make sure that everything goes smoothly," says Gabriel and rises from the table. "I'll head out to send the message. I'll let you know once he is delivered to the police."

"Thank you, Gabriel."

"Keymaker." He gives me a barely there bow, smiling. "Iraklis, glad to see you in your new glory."

"See you later, Gabriel." Iraklis chuckles leaning back into his chair. My headache is getting worse, pressing on my eyes, drilling into my skull. I massage my temples and grunt.

"You need to get more rest, you're still weak." Iraklis puts the palm of his hand on my cheek and I lean into it, closing my eyes.

"I'll sleep better if you hug me," I tell him and when I look at him he is smiling. I take him by his hand and lead him to the bedroom. Once the door is closed behind us Iraklis leans close to me. I feel his warm breath on my neck, his fingers untie my robe and I let it fall to the floor. I grab his t-shirt and he raises his arm, letting me pull it off. I do it slowly, enjoying the view of his tight muscles over his flat stomach and wide chest. Just as the t-shirt reveals his lips, I stop and raise on my tippy toes, kissing his mouth gently, he smiles and takes off his t-shirt completely. I cock my head to the side and lick my lips, tantalized by his proximity. I hook my finger into the button of his jeans and undo them one by one as our eyes are locked in on each other. As soon as the last button is undone, I attempt to slip my hand inside his jeans, but he is too quick and grabs my wrist, shaking his head and smiling at the same time. He steps back and takes them off himself and as soon as he is down to his boxers he sweeps me into his arms, plunging us both into bed.

"Sleep now," he orders sweetly and I can't help but giggle. He pulls the covers over us as we lay together, my back against his chest, my feet playing with his. Iraklis hugs me tight and I feel him burying his face in my hair, releasing joyfully and relaxing, "Ah. This is heaven."

I smile, pleased that he is feeling at peace. My own thoughts are like a swarm of bodies climbing atop each other to reach the top. Will Enzio really go through with the deal? What do I do after? What happens to my father's company? What happens to all those who call themselves Gods? How many of us are out there with divine powers? Are there others who want to cause harm to humans and bring on their tyrannical rule so they can be bowed to and worshiped? Do we continue living in shadows, letting the events of the world pass us by without any input or do we show ourselves and let fate decide what wrath awaits us? My headache fills my head and I close my eyes, sinking my head into the pillow. Iraklis' embrace offers reassurance that I have a friend I can rely on and I decide for now to relish in the moment.

I awake headache free, my bed is empty and cold. Iraklis must have gotten up a while ago. Through a slit in the drawn curtains I can tell it's daylight. Distant sounds of cars reach me from the street and louder voices come from the kitchen. I raise pain free, and step onto the floor without any dizziness. I wash up and get dressed into jeans and a t-shirt laid out for me. When I get to the kitchen everyone turns to me and suddenly all conversation stops and everyone stands motionless.

"Hi!" I raise my arm and wave, overwhelmed by all the attention. "What day is it today and is it morning or afternoon? Seems to me I've turned into a sleeping beauty."

My little joke relaxes the atmosphere and everyone chuckles.

"You make a wonderful sleeping beauty," C chuckles, raising his glass of coffee, holding it with his pinky pointing out straight.

"A beauty to be reckoned with," Artemis adds. She comes up to me and puts her hands on my shoulders. I think I spot a quiver in her chin as if she is about to sob, but she pulls me in for a hug and I think it's so I can't see her true emotions. She releases me from the embrace quickly and goes to pour herself a cup of coffee, taking it to the window so no one can see her face.

"A stunning beauty."

"Thank you."

Pia and Doti come closer and each take my hand. They don't hide their tears, they don't perceive it as a weakness of character and no one would expect them to behave otherwise. We wrap our arms around each other, leaning our foreheads together and soon tears become laughter.

"Come, sit down. Eat and let's discuss what the future has in store for us," Pia says, gently pulling me toward the table, where someone puts a plate full of food for me and a cup of coffee with milk and no sugar, just as I like it.

"Enzio was delivered to the police. He has signed his confession and will be held until trial. As security, he was stripped of his shapeshifting gift forever," Iraklis says and sits down next to me. His hand slides under the table where it finds mine and gives it a squeeze. He then brings it to his lips and kisses it. I feel my cheeks burn at this open gesture of affection, but when I look at the people around me I see no judgement, they are smiling approvingly and joyfully.

"What of my father's company?" I ask, turning to Iraklis.

"Your father was a keymaker, now you, Aurora, are the keymaker. I can't think of anyone better to keep the secrets of the Gods secure. I know your father wanted to protect you when he pushed you away, but I also know that he would be happy for you to inherit what he has created. The company is expansive, there are secrets hidden within it that should never be revealed, and there is more in the world that will need to be secured and preserved. The company works with the Gods and other creatures who want their powers hidden to give them new identities when needed and to help them exist in the world of humans," Iraklis says. His pace is steady, his face is tense and he squeezes my hand tighter.

"The work ahead of you is massive, but you have us. I promise to be your adviser if you let me."

"And me."

"I will help."

"I'm here for you."

Everyone joins in and I feel tears pool in my eyes from the overwhelming love and support that I feel.

"This is yours." Iraklis shows me his closed fist. I look up at him quizzically and he opens it up to reveal my medallion. It is fused together with the rings of my mother and father. I take it into my hands, "Two keys, one lock, one true keymaker," I say to myself and smile, thinking of my parents.

"Thank you," I say and put the locket on my neck, pressing it tight against my chest. The weight of responsibility is enormous, failure will be disastrous, but I would never be able to live with indifference. I put my hands together, the rough scars on my palms are palpable, the power that surges within me is bountiful. I twist one hand clockwise and another counterclockwise. I open them just a bit and the interrupted bars of scars on palms merge into the light. It forms a circle of a Greek key, the sign of eternity, the twisted path that lays ahead of all of us. But the light is warm and promising hope. I raise my head high and look at the eyes that stare at me with expectation.

"I am Aurora, the keymaker, I am a key and I am a lock. I shall be the light that protects and secures those that need it."

The End